£6·60

# DEAD ON LINE

*Also by Malcolm Hamer*

FICTION
Sudden Death
A Deadly Lie
Death Trap
Shadows on the Green

NON-FICTION
The Ryder Cup – The Players
The Guiness Continental Europe Golf Course Guide
The Family Welcome Guide
(*with Jill Foster*)

# DEAD
# ON LINE

Malcolm Hamer

**HEADLINE**

First published in 1996
by HEADLINE BOOK PUBLISHING

10 9 8 7 6 5 4 3 2 1

British Library Cataloguing in Publication Data

Hamer, Malcolm, 1940-
    Dead on line. - (A Chris Ludlow golfing thriller)
    1. English fiction - 20th century
    I. Title
    823.9'14 [F]

ISBN 0-7472-1551-0

Typeset by
CBS, Felixstowe, Suffolk

Printed and bound in Great Britain by
Mackays of Chatham PLC, Chatham, Kent

HEADLINE BOOK PUBLISHING
A division of Hodder Headline PLC
338 Euston Road
London NW1 3BH

To Jill

I would like to thank Bob Gowland of Phillips Son
and Neale for giving me the benefit of his expertise and
Alison Finch for her invaluable help.

# Chapter 1

'I'd advise you to piss off and not waste my time. And don't bother to come back.'

The words issued flatly from the fleshy lips of David Reynolds, the senior partner of Reynolds, Jayne & Stacey, solicitors. Since he hadn't expressed himself in the measured cadences of drivel that lawyers normally affect in order to confuse laymen, I grasped his point without difficulty.

Reynolds picked up his telephone, punched a couple of numbers and said, 'Tania, Mr Ludlow is leaving. Would you show him out please.'

He stood up, his manner indicating even more emphatically than his words that our meeting was over. I knew there was no future in prolonging a discussion that had gone nowhere. Nevertheless, I stayed in my chair and looked steadily at Reynolds for a few moments. I wanted him to know that he couldn't intimidate me. He was a big man and his dark suit did nothing to disguise his bulk. The jacket was flashily cut, the shoulders padded and the waist tapered. His dark hair was swept away from his broad forehead and fell in waves nearly as far as his shoulders. He could have been a bouncer on the door of a South London night-spot or a showbiz accountant with a nice line in expensive off-shore tax evasion schemes.

Despite his Italian suit, I could see that the powerful, sloping shoulders were genuine. So was his height. I'm around six feet tall but he had at least a couple of inches over me and he probably weighed in at well over sixteen stones. There didn't seem to be much fat on him. He had only the suspicion of a second chin and there was no tell-tale straining of buttons at the front of his colourfully striped shirt. But it was his big square hands, with knuckles the size of golf balls, that really dictated that this was neither the time nor place for me to have a confrontation with David Reynolds.

I had tricked my way into an appointment by telling him that I planned to set up a company in the sports promotion business and needed his advice. When I'd given my real reason, that I was there to collect a debt incurred by one of his partners, his manner had changed from interested and courteous to abruptly dismissive. I didn't blame him but I wasn't there to worry about his sensibilities – I was there to help my friend and neighbour, Mrs Bradshaw.

I got carefully to my feet and, as Tania entered the room, said, 'I'm sorry you're not prepared to help, Mr Reynolds. I repeat that one of your partners owes my elderly neighbour nearly five thousand pounds. As the senior partner in a firm of solicitors, that sort of misconduct should trouble you. On second thoughts, since you've already tried to bully her, I don't suppose it does. Mrs Bradshaw is a widow. The flat that she rents out is her main source of income.'

'Don't make me cry,' Reynolds said, his voice as devoid of expression as were his dark eyes. 'Now, get lost.'

He turned his back on me, plucked a heavy tome from the shelf behind his desk and carried it over to one of the wide windows which looked out over the Strand.

I shrugged in the direction of Tania, who was studying the pattern on the carpet with interest. She was embarrassed and I was frustrated because I'd had as much effect on Reynolds as a gnat bite on an elephant.

Moments later I was walking down the Strand towards the underground, reflecting that I hadn't had a leg to stand on in my efforts to help my neighbour – and Reynolds knew it.

It was true that Paul Stacey, Reynolds's partner, had reneged on three months' rent and several bills, including a sizeable amount owed to British Telecom. But I had been economical with the truth when I'd said that rent from the flat made up the primary source of Mrs Bradshaw's income. Her late husband had been a senior official at the Home Office and had left her an excellent portfolio of investments. I knew because she occasionally asked my advice. Although it had been a couple of years since I had worked in the City, I had spent nearly five years in the employ of Norton Buccleuth, a firm of stockbrokers, and still kept up my contacts in the Square Mile.

The chief executive, Andrew Buccleuth, was fanatically devoted to golf and had given me a job as part-time salesman. I spent the rest of my time as a caddie on the professional golf tour and Andrew had revelled in his vicarious involvement with the top echelon of the game. But the dramatic collapse of the stock market on Black Monday, 20 October, 1987, and the subsequent severe trading conditions had eventually forced him to sell his firm to a Swiss Bank.

Several of my colleagues had been dismissed and Andrew had been unable to save me. In the eyes of his new Swiss masters I'd had no credibility. Though my salad days had been rudely terminated they'd been great fun while they lasted. At the same time Jack Mason, for whom I'd caddied for a couple of years, had traded me in for a young female caddie.

At least I was single, with little in the way of financial commitments beyond a mortgage on my flat. Some of the others who'd lost their jobs had overheads, eagerly embraced during the rose-petalled boom years of the mid-eighties, that would have daunted a medium-sized Third World country.

Occasionally I missed the camaraderie of City life but I had no great desire to return there and had drifted from one casual job to another. My caddying had been a financial lifeline and the occasional bonuses earned for a high finish in a tournament kept me afloat.

An introduction to a golf architect called Calvin Blair changed my life. Jack Mason had arranged it. He'd played on the European Circuit with Calvin, who'd needed a part-time assistant. At first I'd been attracted by the lure of helping to design golf courses but I'd ended up protecting Calvin and his family from a group of environmental extremists. My efforts on both fronts, however, brought their rewards because Calvin had kept me on the payroll. Now, while he was directing operations at a new course in France, I was overseeing the changes to a few holes at the Royal Dorset Golf Club. It had a magnificent location above the sea and mine was an interesting, if undemanding, task. For that reason I could spare time to try to help Mrs Bradshaw.

I lived in a flat on the ground floor of a Victorian building in south-west London. Mrs Bradshaw occupied a flat on the first floor and on the opposite side of the house. On the day I'd moved in, some years before, she had dispensed tea and sandwiches to me and the two friends who had helped me with my meagre assortment of furniture and belongings. She had continued to be a generous neighbour, who insisted on giving my flat 'a proper clean' every week. She stopped well short of being intrusive and treated me like an amusing, but potentially errant, nephew. In return I did odd jobs for her and kept an eye on her investments.

Mrs Bradshaw had inherited her other flat in Holland Park from an aunt and I had assumed that it was let on a long-term basis. A few weeks before my abortive visit to David Reynolds's office I learned more about it. I'd been having a drink with Mrs Bradshaw to mark her return from a visit of several months' duration to Australia. Her daughter lived there, as did several friends.

My neighbour gave me a rapid account of her holiday and then showed me photographs of her daughter's two children. She enjoyed her role as a proud grandmother and, no doubt, distance lent enchantment to her grandchildren. It was our tradition that I had to be bribed to make the right sort of noises when looking at pictures of the children and she'd brought some splendid wine for me to taste.

I flicked rapidly through the photos, making a few half-hearted 'mm's' and 'ah's' but, although she smiled when she noticed that I was admiring the last photograph upside down, she wasn't entering into the spirit of the occasion. She caught my eye and said hesitantly, 'Chris, I need your advice.'

I looked at her sharply. Her normal style was not hesitant. Forthright would have been my description – even brusque, on occasion. Awful possibilities raced through my mind – had she contracted an incurable illness? No, she looked very well, lightly tanned and elegant in one of her longish tweed skirts and a pale blue sweater. She'd walked and swum a lot in Australia and appeared younger and fitter than for some time. That was it! She'd fallen in love – with someone half her age.

'Fire away.' I prepared myself for the worst. 'What's the problem?'

'My tenant in Holland Park.' I heaved an inward sigh of

relief. 'He's left the flat and owes me three months' rent.'

'He's done a flit.' She nodded. 'I thought you had an agency managing the flat for you. What are they doing about it?'

'Very little, Chris. They say they're sorry. He paid his first quarter in advance and was late with his second quarter. They chased him and he asked for some repairs to the bathroom and refused to pay until they were done.'

It was probably a familiar story to anyone involved in renting out property. The tenant had spun out the rest of his lease without paying any more rent and had disappeared. His references had been impeccable and the man was a lawyer but the letting agency had been unable to help Mrs Bradshaw.

'Is there any point in going to the Small Claims Court?' I asked.

'Apparently not. He's abroad, according to his firm.'

Mrs Bradshaw leaned across the table and tipped some more semillon into my glass.

'It seems so unfair, Chris,' she said. 'The flat was in perfect order. You know I wouldn't dream of having it otherwise.'

'Why don't you write to the senior partner of his firm, explain the situation and ask him to intervene?'

'Yes, I suppose I could try that.'

It was predictable that no reply came from Paul Stacey's firm, despite several telephone calls from Mrs Bradshaw. Reynolds and the other partner simply refused to speak to her and she never got beyond the telephonist.

One evening I arrived home at just after six o'clock and, as I jumped out of my ageing Porsche, saw Mrs Bradshaw entering the drive.

She was wearing one of her smart suits – the dark blue one that she said made her look like a Tory councillor. But not today, I thought. Something was amiss. She looked stooped and tired.

When she spotted me, Mrs Bradshaw straightened up and waved in my direction. 'Don't dash away, Chris. I need a drink. Are you free to walk down to the pub?'

'You look as if you've had a long day,' I said. 'I'll drive you if you like.'

'No, no. Let's walk. I've had a frustrating time. I'll tell you why when I've got a drink in front of me.'

The pub was getting busy with the early evening rush. But we found a table and settled down with our drinks; a pint for me and a g-and-t for Mrs Bradshaw.

'So, what've you been up to? I asked. 'You look very businesslike.'

'I wasn't going to let those lawyers, Reynolds and company, ignore me, Chris. So, I put on my best bib and tucker and called on them. I decided that I'd sit in their office until someone deigned to see me.'

'And it took all day?'

'All day. I arrived there at just after ten o'clock this morning and Mr Reynolds finally gave me a few minutes of his precious time at half past four.'

'The miserable bugger,' I said. 'How come you didn't catch him on his way out to lunch?' I was surprised that my neighbour hadn't simply walked into Reynolds's office and demanded an audience and I told her so.

'The answer to your first question is simple. That ghastly creature Reynolds has his own entrance to and from the offices,' said Mrs Bradshaw. 'As for walking into his room unannounced, well, he'd have had every right to throw me out and, at my age, it's wise to maintain one's dignity. So I just kept asking the poor girl at the reception desk when he would be available. I felt sorry for her. She was rather sweet actually. She kept offering me cups of tea and gave me a sandwich at lunchtime.'

'So what did he say when you finally got to him?'

'He stonewalled. Mr Stacey's private affairs were nothing to do with him. He had the utmost confidence in him, a man of integrity, blah, blah. He suggested that if I had a problem, I should consult a lawyer.'

'Well, he would, wouldn't he? That's more grist to the lawyers' mill, isn't it? Your lawyer's letter, full of incomprehensible and ill-written legalese, has to be answered by another which is equally obscure. Before you know where you are you're up to your ears in solicitors' bills. Don't waste your money, Mrs Bradshaw. Come to think of it, does it really matter? So this fellow, Stacey, has done you out of some money but why not be philosophical about it? Don't waste any more time on him – or money.'

'First of all, there's the principle. Stacey owes me money and I'm not going to let him get away with it. He's a petty crook and he's arrogant with it.'

'Arrogant? I thought you'd never met him.'

'I haven't. The letting agents handled everything. But Reynolds gave me a message. Apparently Stacey wanted me to know that my flat wasn't worth the money and that he'd never had any intention of paying the second quarter's rent.'

Mrs Bradshaw waved across the room at a neighbour who'd just walked in and then said, 'David Reynolds is a nasty piece of work, by the way. He's a lout. At one stage I thought he was going to, well, start pushing me about. When I got up to leave, he came very close. And, Chris, he's a big chap. Even that late in the day his after-shave was enough to turn my stomach. But that's by the by. He tried to frighten me and he succeeded.'

I didn't really believe that anyone could put the frighteners on Mrs Bradshaw but I made sympathetic noises and she said, 'That's another reason why I'm not letting them walk away with my money.'

She seemed agitated by the affair and I heard myself promising, 'Look, I'll see what I can do. At the very least I'll go and talk to Reynolds. I may be able to persuade him to change his tune.'

Fat chance.

# Chapter 2

As I rattled down the M3 on the morning after my brief confrontation with Reynolds, I was still wondering how to find Paul Stacey. If he really was abroad on secondment (though I did not necessarily believe that), it would be supremely difficult. Maybe his bank would help, especially if Mrs Bradshaw gave them a real sob-story, but I doubted it. The bank would hide behind the principle of client confidentiality. What about one of the credit-card companies? No chance, unless I knew someone whom I could bribe to give me his address. It would be the same problem with his magazine subscriptions. He was sure to read the *Law Society Journal* or some such but I would have to buy the whole list of subscribers which would be expensive and impractical because I couldn't be sure which trade magazine he took. Anyway, Stacey sounded like the kind of man who'd borrow a copy. I wondered if the Law Society itself would help. I doubted it.

I thought about simply breaking into Reynolds's office and rifling the files for Stacey's current address. That might have to be a last resort. At least I had some elementary knowledge of breaking and entering, gleaned over the years from my brother, Max. Among his varied experiences had been a spell of two years in Northern Ireland with some shadowy arm of the security services. Even better would have been to get Max's help but he was somewhere in South America, a member of an expedition which was researching rare wildlife species.

I turned into the drive of the Royal Dorset Golf Club and approached the low-slung clubhouse with its huge bay windows. Arched walkways led off to other buildings such as the professional's shop and the changing rooms. The whole place had been rebuilt at great expense some years before and therein lay the cause of the ills which beset the golf course itself. So much money had been spent on the clubhouse that critical work on the course had been skimped. Slowly it had deteriorated until some of the members had realized that radical steps were essential in order to restore the course to its former glories. That was when Calvin Blair had been called upon for his advice.

On our first visit Calvin and I had played the course with two members of the club. The captain, Barry Trent, was the chief executive of an engineering company on the outskirts of Bournemouth. Full of nervous energy, he was clearly a man who 'got things done'. The other man, David Ingleby, was a local doctor and chairman of the greens committee in whose hands reposed the general care and maintenance of the course. His main preoccupation was to justify himself and his committee and he made it clear that he considered Calvin's presence to be a waste of time and money.

During the first few holes Trent could barely contain his impatience to hear Calvin's opinions, but my employer said little, despite the captain's promptings.

After the sixth hole, Trent could bear it no longer. 'What do you think of it so far?' he demanded.

'Not a lot but it's too early to tell. The greens have slowed up since I last played here. That must've been in the seventies, I think.'

12

Calvin had played on the professional golf tour in the seventies and early eighties and modestly categorized himself as a journeyman. It was a reasonable description because he didn't have that incandescent self-belief that the consistent winners and the champions possess – 'the ability to burn and burn and burn,' as an American player once described it. But Calvin Blair's charm and intelligence allowed him to develop his career in other areas of golf. He became an excellent after-dinner speaker, a commentator on the game and eventually discovered his true *métier* as a golf designer.

'This is a Harry Colt design, you know,' Ingleby said.

'No it isn't,' Calvin said sharply. 'The original course was sketched out and built around the turn of the century. Colt redesigned it, but not extensively, in the twenties. He wouldn't have countenanced all the blind shots you have here.'

Calvin knew when to assume the traditional bluntness of a northerner (he was born in Bury). I noticed that he'd cranked up his Lancashire accent to give his words more effect.

'It's a traditional course and we want to retain its character,' Trent said hastily.

'The next hole is a good example of that,' Ingleby stated. 'It's a superb design.'

Calvin grunted and hit a solid drive right of centre onto the elevated fairway. We watched as it bounced wildly to the right and disappeared.

'What's down there these days?' he asked.

'You may be lucky and be in a dip,' Trent replied, 'but there's a lot of heather there.'

We didn't find Calvin's ball because it had bounced down the hill and disappeared into one of the thick outcrops of heather and gorse.

'That's a bloody poor piece of design,' Calvin said. 'A drive hit where I hit mine should never be lost. OK, if it ends in the semi-rough, that's the rub of the green and you accept it. But not a lost ball. We ought to think about some re-contouring of the fairway and clearing some of that rubbish.'

'It's one of our most celebrated holes,' Ingleby protested.

'It's a bad hole,' Calvin said brusquely, as he dropped a ball on the fairway. Ingleby stamped away without another word.

Throughout the remainder of the round Ingleby was largely silent, although he cheered up when Calvin and I agreed that the seventeenth hole was one of the best we'd seen.

Afterwards we sat together at a table in one of the bay windows and ate sandwiches.

'First impressions, Calvin?' Barry Trent asked eagerly.

Calvin looked at me and I said, 'Very poor greens. They need a lot of treatment. Several bunkers are redundant and they can be taken out and grassed over. But many others need to be dug out and reconstructed. Lots of tree clearance is needed so that the air gets to the teeing areas. The course is scruffy.'

'A fair summary,' Calvin said. 'The whole course needs a face-lift. As Chris says, the greens are a bloody disgrace. You already know my views about blind shots. An occasional one, off the tee, that's fine. It adds to the fun for the average club hacker. But if you get your drive on the fairway you should be able to see the pin for your second shot.'

Calvin paused, swallowed some of his beef sandwich and chased it down with a draught of bitter. 'Chris is spot on about the look of the course. Scruffy is an understatement. Raddled, I'd call it. Whoever your head greenkeeper is, give him his cards. We'll find you someone who knows his job and takes a pride in doing it.'

There was silence for several seconds and then Trent smiled at Calvin. 'Thank you. You're very, er, straightforward and I for one appreciate that.' I don't think Ingleby did.

'Fine,' Calvin said, as he stood up. 'Chris and I will walk the course in a couple of days – on our own, please. You'll get my report a few days later with some recommendations and some costings. Then it's up to you.' I loved Calvin's style. He could have taught some of those long-winded City types a thing or two about running a meeting.

Once the report was delivered, the committee, no doubt cajoled by Barry Trent, had acted swiftly. Calvin Blair Associates had gone into action about six months previously, during the preceding autumn. It was our job to carry out the work we'd recommended and then keep an eye on the course to ensure that it was properly maintained. There was plenty of work left for me at Royal Dorset – at least another six months' worth.

'Morning, Chris.' As I climbed from my car I was greeted by the ebullient tones of the Club Secretary.

I waved and returned the greeting and we walked together towards the clubhouse. As I held the door open for Helen Raven, she gave me a vivid smile, full lips parted and dark eyes sparkling. She was a tall woman with wide shoulders and heavy breasts. I glanced with surprise at Helen's face, usually innocent of make-up. Today she'd given it the full treatment – lipstick, eye-shadow, the lot. Her brown hair, flecked with grey, was brushed neatly back from her face. Helen Raven was in her late forties and had recently retired from the police force with the rank of Chief Inspector. I could see her wielding a hockey stick or a tennis racket with vigour, like one of Betjeman's girls – Miss J Hunter Dunn perhaps.

Her appointment had been an unusual one for a club such as Royal Dorset, a seemingly impregnable citadel of male privilege and chauvinism – as are most golf clubs. I hadn't yet heard the full story but suspected that it had required some fancy footwork on the part of Barry Trent and his friends to defeat the innate conservatism of the other committee members.

At the end of the corridor we turned to go our separate ways and Helen said, 'We have an honoured guest today.'

'Who's that?'

'Sir Nicholas Welbeck. He's here to value some of our old clubs and paintings. It was Barry Trent's idea.' That explained the war-paint.

'He's the man, as they say.'

'Would you like to meet him?'

'Yes.'

'Come and have coffee with us, then, after lunch.'

Sir Nicholas Welbeck. A man well-known in golfing circles and an accomplished player in his earlier days. He had served on many committees and working parties connected with the game. I seemed to remember that he had been a selector for the Walker Cup, the biennial match between the amateurs of Britain and Ireland and those of America. He had a background in the art world and had become the acknowledged authority on golfing art, artefacts such as clubs and balls and memorabilia in general. It was a thriving market, driven by the demands of collectors in America and Japan.

The members' bar was on the route to my office which was a portable cabin at the back of the clubhouse, near the kitchen. I knew that there were reference books in the bar and *The Golfer's Handbook* might well have an entry for Welbeck.

Several members were drinking coffee and scanning the newspapers, preparatory to their morning rounds. One old boy was dozing quietly in an armchair by a window. I found the handbook, which was several years out of date, and turned to the Who's Who in Golf section.

Sir Nicholas Welbeck was born in Nairn in 1934 and his golf clubs were listed as the Royal and Ancient, the Honourable Company of Edinburgh Golfers and Royal St Georges: St Andrews, Muirfield and Sandwich, all of them venues for the Open. His victories as an amateur included the Antlers, the Hampshire Hog and the President's Putter. He was listed as having been a Walker Cup selector in 1979. So, Welbeck had an excellent pedigree in golf. I looked forward to meeting him.

Embroiled in a long discussion with the new head greenkeeper – the old one had been given his marching orders, as Calvin had recommended – I was late for my cup of coffee with Helen and her guest. They were sitting in a corner of the lounge at a large table littered with ancient hickory-shafted clubs, old balls, some mounted and some loose, books, and several letters which were preserved in folders. Welbeck stood up as Helen made the introductions. My immediate impression was of an elegant and urbane man who looked out of place in the humdrum surroundings of a provincial golf club, albeit a notable one like Royal Dorset. He should have been in a Bond Street gallery or swapping anecdotes with Willie Whitelaw in the Big Room at the Royal and Ancient.

A mane of silver hair crowned a long, thin face with a prominent nose. His dark-brown tweed suit was beautifully cut; the trousers had impossibly sharp creases and their turn-ups were impeccably positioned on ox-blood brogue shoes which shone like mirrors. To top it all off, he was wearing the tie of the Scots Guards.

'Ah, Mr Blair's assistant,' he said with a smile. I noticed that his teeth were so white and so regular that they looked unnatural. He'd spent some money with the orthodontists in his time. 'How is Calvin? Such an amusing speaker. A little coarse at times but very entertaining. He's not going to excise the charm from this lovely course, I hope?'

As I had expected, his voice was beautifully modulated and the diction precise, though overlaid with a slight drawl. He ended his question with a small lift of one eyebrow and a careful smile. He exuded effortless good breeding; he was so smooth that he probably made the average duke feel common.

'I hope we're adding to the charm of the course, Sir Nicholas,' I replied. 'It needed a lot of help. Nothing radical—'

'I'm glad to hear it,' he cut in. 'The club has great traditions and that extends to some of its possessions. Are you interested in antiques and memorabilia?'

I nodded and he continued. 'There are some fascinating pieces here. The club is lucky to have some beautiful pictures. The oil painting of your first Captain, for example, which is above the fireplace in the dining room. That was done by J H Lorimer, a notable artist from Edinburgh. It's rather valuable. So is the view of your seventeenth hole – and what a tester that hole is – by Thomas Hodge.'

'What about our watercolour by Harry Rountree?' Helen asked. 'That must be worth a fortune, surely.'

'I'm afraid not, Helen.' Welbeck said quietly. 'It's a copy, a good one, but a copy nevertheless. However, hidden in a dark corner by the coffee machine is the jewel in your crown. "The Winning Putt" is its title.'

'That pale little watercolour. It's so insipid.'

'Insipid or not, my dear, it depicts the great J H Taylor and was painted by Francis Powell Hopkins.'

'And it's valuable?'

'Extremely.'

'What about these golf balls?' I gestured at the ones on the table.

Welbeck picked up three of the old balls and said, 'A hundred pounds each, because these were probably made in the 1890s and are a mixture of gutta percha and rubber. Now this is more interesting.' He picked up a ball with a lattice pattern and pointed to its marking. 'As you see, made in Musselburgh. Probably around 1860 and worth at least five hundred pounds.'

Welbeck's patrician manner might have been unsettling to some people but his enthusiasm for his subject was obvious and he had no difficulty in communicating it.

I pointed at some of the other balls on the table. 'What about these gutties? Are they of any interest?'

'They are all of interest to the collector, Mr Ludlow, but they're not all gutties. Two of them are guttas. That is, they were made wholly from gutta percha in the middle years of the nineteenth century. The others are made from gutta percha and other materials and they are gutties. You might say that I'm splitting hairs but, to a collector, it's very important because guttas are much more valuable because so few of them survived.'

Welbeck smiled briefly, his eyebrow raised in what was obviously a characteristic manner. Carefully, he picked up one of the balls. 'Which brings me to this ball, a real find. It's a smooth gutta ball and therefore rare. But made even rarer because Allan Robertson's name is on it.'

Welbeck pointed at the name, 'Allan', on the ball.

'Why were the smooth guttas so rare?' Helen asked.

'They weren't made for very long, maybe only for half-a-dozen years, because the golfers discovered that marks or nicks in the balls improved their flight. Also they could be melted down and remoulded.'

'They were recycled in other words.'

'Exactly,' said Welbeck. 'Now, Allan Robertson was the pre-eminent maker of feathery balls. It was highly labour-intensive and the balls were very expensive. They cost between two and five shillings in, say, 1850. A present-day prices that's between seventy and one hundred and fifty pounds. Just imagine, you might have a mishit with an iron club on the first hole, the ball splits and there goes an awful lot of money. So you see, it was indubitably a game for the very wealthy.'

'So Robertson had a great business going, a vested interest in the use of featheries and along comes the gutta ball and ruins it,' I said.

'Yes,' Welbeck said. 'One of his craftsmen could, at his best, make four featheries in a day. It was hard work. He had to sew a hide cover together, leaving only a small aperture. Then he had to stuff a huge amount of wet boiled chicken feathers inside – traditionally enough to fill a top hat to the brim. Then the feathers dried out, as did the leather, and there was your golf ball.'

'And a gutta was cheap and easy to make in comparison, I suppose,' Helen said.

'Supremely easy and quick and it cost a few pence. Allan Robertson went so far as to buy up quantities of the gutta balls and destroy them but it was a futile gesture. Eventually he had to concede defeat and make guttas. But, by the time he began, the smooth version was already being overtaken by the hand-hammered or patterned version.'

'So we have something of great value here,' Helen said quietly. 'How much is it worth?'

'Heaven knows what you'd get at auction. Many, many thousands of pounds,' Welbeck said, pressing his fingers together judiciously.

'Good God. I had no idea,' Helen said. 'So what about the featheries we've got on display. They must be worth even more.'

'Yes. Usually featheries attract more interest. And I know

that you have a very good example of an Allan Robertson. It's valuable, of course.'

'Five figures?' I asked.

'Certainly, but don't quote me.'

'Sir Nicholas has told me to put some of these items under lock and key. Preferably in a bank.'

'You can always have copies made,' Welbeck added.

'The members wouldn't stand for it,' Helen replied.

'Well, don't tell them,' Welbeck said. 'The committee will see the sense of it. Tell the members you're having the pictures cleaned. And you should spirit some of your old clubs away, too. I know dealers who would kill to get their hands on that Hugh Philp driver you have. People call him the Stradivarius of club-making. And you have a couple of lofting irons, both from the middle of the nineteenth century, which may look ordinary to the layman,' Welbeck paused and smiled at both of us, 'but they are wonderful examples of the club-maker's art. It would be very easy to substitute copies of those clubs.'

Welbeck rose to his feet and said he must be on his way. 'I'm off to an exhibition of marine art at the Pall Mall Galleries. Another interesting area.'

He clasped Helen's hand in his own. 'I will send you an assessment of your many fine paintings and artefacts. Please heed my advice about security. You were once a high-ranking officer in the police force, so I'm sure you take my point.'

'I do indeed. But how can you tell what's real and what's fake?'

'Experience, Helen, and I have the eye.' He tapped one silver eyebrow and gave a thin smirk.

His omniscient manner was beginning to irritate me so I smirked back and said, 'Tom Keating fooled the experts for a while, didn't he? And I read somewhere that there are question marks over the Mona Lisa – it was nicked from the Louvre in nineteen hundred and something. Although it was found, some experts think the most famous painting in the world is a copy.'

'It was taken on August the twenty-first, nineteen hundred and eleven. And there is little doubt that the original painting was recovered.' His brief smile couldn't disguise the asperity in his voice. Clearly he was a man who resented any challenge to his authority.

He half turned his back on me as he said, 'Helen, it's been a great pleasure. Thank you so much for lunch.'

I was still smiling to myself when I sat down at my desk five minutes later. Patronizing old bugger.

# Chapter 3

A couple of days later Helen strolled into my office and waved a letter at me.

'Do you know Toby Greenslade from the *Daily News*?'

'I certainly do. He's a good friend of mine.'

Helen grunted. 'He wants to look around the clubhouse, at our antiques and paintings and so on. He says he's writing a book called *Famous Clubs and Clubhouses*.'

'Oh, it's true. And don't I know it. I'm suffering every creative step with him. I suggested he contact you about coming to Royal Dorset. I hope you don't mind – you don't sound too keen. Does that indicate a general distaste for the press or is it based on your experiences in the police force?'

'The latter. But if he's a friend of yours . . .'

'I hope you'll help him. He's making pretty slow progress as usual. By the way, did that old smoothie Welbeck write to you?'

'Sir Nicholas did write and it's a charming letter, I might add.'

'And what did he say about your bits and pieces?'

'It's confidential.'

'I won't tell anyone.'

Helen looked at me closely and I discerned some of the steeliness that had taken her up the ranks of the police force.

'You'd better not,' she said finally and then her manner relaxed. 'Those bits and pieces, as you call them, add up to well in excess of a hundred and fifty grand.'

'Bloody hell. Don't let the members get wind of it. They'll want you to sell the lot so they can have a subscription-free year.'

'I believe you. The British still think they should get their sport for nothing, don't they?'

The telephone rang as I nodded my agreement. It was extraordinary what the average golf-club member expected for his money: a course maintained to tournament standard, despite the lack of investment in modern green-keeping machinery; a well-staffed clubhouse with food and drink available at all hours of the day, at prices well below those of the local pubs; and a qualified professional in a shop packed with the latest equipment, despite the members' penchant for buying their clothing at chain stores, their clubs at discount centres and confining themselves to the purchase of a few tee pegs every other month. It was quite a bargain for about a tenner a week.

I picked up the receiver.

'Greenslade, man of letters, here.' His voice had that familiar gravelly timbre that indicated he had emptied one bottle too many on the previous evening.

'Yes, you've sent one to Helen Raven and she's in my office, wondering whether to let a hack like you into her hallowed clubhouse. I told her not even to consider it.'

'Very funny. Perhaps you'd care to put the lady on and I can make my arrangements.'

I passed the telephone to Helen and, after a brief conversation, she said, 'Next Friday then at ten o'clock. And you'll have a photographer with you. Here's Chris.'

'She sounds efficient,' Toby said. 'Now, I should be through

24

in a couple of hours next Friday, so why don't we have lunch afterwards? I take it there's a suitable hostelry somewhere in darkest Dorset. Lead me to it and I will find the wherewithal to pay the bill.'

'You mean your publisher will pay.'

'Publishers don't pay for anything, my boy, and certainly not for their authors' lunches. I'll finesse it on to a *Daily News* expenses sheet. See you on Friday.'

Toby had promised to pop into my office before his meeting with Helen Raven. At twenty minutes after the appointed hour, I decided to see if he had yet arrived in the car park. His notion of time was eccentric and I knew that he would receive a frosty reception from Helen if he was too many minutes adrift.

As I rounded the corner of the clubhouse I saw a white sports car reversing efficiently into a parking space. Toby drove a rather battered Volvo estate, so it wasn't him; or so I thought until I saw his portly figure, clad in a blue corduroy suit, levering itself out of the front passenger seat. He always complained bitterly about the cramped seats in my Porsche, so he had probably whinged terribly about the discomfort of this little Japanese model.

I was about to shout a greeting when I was distracted by the sight of a young woman jumping out of the driving seat, pushing it forward and reaching into the space behind. I am as susceptible to the charms of the female form as any other man but I try hard not to ogle. However, on this occasion, I was definitely ogling, the focus of my attention being the woman's long legs and her shapely bottom tightly hugged by her black jeans. Like one of Kingsley Amis's memorable characters, in a perverse way I was hoping that the rest of her would be a disappointment. As she backed away from the car, an aluminium case cradled in one arm and several cameras swinging from the other, I saw that this was not so. Far from it. She shoved the car door shut with one foot. Even though she was encumbered with photographic paraphernalia, her innate grace could not be disguised. So this was Toby's photographer. No wonder he hadn't mentioned her before.

'Hello, Toby,' I said, moving closer. 'Can I give you a helping hand?' I asked his companion.

'That's Laura,' he said, across the car's bonnet. 'Laura Stocker, meet Chris Ludlow. Ex-caddie, ex-stockbroker, used to have a half-decent golf swing, now masquerading as a golf-course designer.'

'Oh, hi,' she said. 'Can you hold the case for a sec while I sort out these cameras.' Her voice had a quality which can only an expensive education could have engendered.

Laura darted a smile in my direction, her deep grey eyes bright and friendly. Short fair hair was shaped around her tanned face and emphasized her finely boned features. Her neatly chiselled nose had a gold stud through one nostril. I wondered what Toby thought about that.

We all walked towards the entrance to the club and I fell back slightly to talk to Toby. That wasn't my only motive because I also wanted to observe Laura Stocker and she was worth observing from that angle. Eyebrow raised, Toby gave me an admonitory look and I grinned at him, then looked again at Laura as she strolled ahead of us.

'Is Laura joining us for lunch?' I inquired.

'I fear not,' Toby replied. 'She wants to get back to her studio and process the pictures. At least I'll be spared another crippling journey in that mobile handbag she calls a car. Don't the Japanese know that we're built on a more generous scale in Europe? Not that your car is that much more comfortable.'

'But you're prepared to overlook the discomfort if I gave you a lift back to London?'

Toby grunted. 'I'll pick you up in your office when we've finished,' he said.

The pub to which I took Toby was a few miles away on roads which were narrow enough to need indented passing places at regular intervals. It was worth the effort to find because it was a classic English inn, half-timbered and built in the time of the Tudors. Its garden lay in the shadow of a magnificent church with a soaring spire. Once again John Betjeman came into my mind. He would have drooled with pleasure at the scene: the sun striking the mellow stone of the church, the shadows cast on the garden by the trees, the murmur of insects and the call of birds. We sat on the terrace and supped at our pints of Ringwood bitter.

'How was your holiday?' I asked tentatively.

'A week of unmitigated misery,' Toby said gruffly. 'Except that it wasn't a week because the flight was over-booked and we were sent to Newcastle-upon-Tyne, overnight, on a coach to get a seven o'clock flight the next morning.'

Toby took a long and reflective pull at his beer. 'I haven't been on a coach, dear boy, since I was a junior reporter on a provincial paper.'

'I can't imagine you as a junior anything.'

'No, quite. It was OK when we got there. Minorca's a lovely island but I'm afraid that Isobel's darling son got on my tits. A week by the beach with a ten-year-old and his doting mother isn't quite my scene.'

'So what's the situation with Isobel?'

'All bets are off. We'll meet after a decent interval and see what happens.'

27

Isobel Watson worked for a television production company and was the latest in a line of women who had tried to take Toby under their wing. He had been married and divorced twice and blamed his marital failures on the demands of his job. I had a different theory; namely, that he was incapable of a stable relationship with a woman – not if there was a bottle of wine to be drunk first. I wondered why any woman bothered with him at all. As he rarely failed to point out, it had to be something to do with his brand of irascible charm.

'So what about Laura Stocker?' I asked.

'What about her? She's young and she has talent, if you can have talent at a minor skill like photography . . .'

'A picture's worth a thousand words.'

'What rubbish. Anyway, she comes from what was once called a good family. Her father's one of those Foreign Office mandarins and her mother's a Hoare.'

'A whore?' I said incredulously.

'The banking family, you imbecile. And she has a steady boyfriend, a nice young man in the City, so don't get any ideas, Chris. You couldn't keep your eyes off her. The way you were staring at her bottom, well, I was embarrassed.'

I happily visualized Laura's beautiful swaying behind for a moment and then asked Toby, 'How did you get on with Helen? Was she helpful?'

'Helpful, yes, but also reserved. She's a nice lady. Attractive, I thought.'

'Well, she is in your age range, Toby, and I know you like them large on top.'

Toby gave a pained frown at my vulgarity. 'I was talking about her personality.'

'Yeah, yeah.'

'Do you know the tale of how she got the job, Chris?'

I shook my head and Toby leaned conspiratorially towards me. 'I got the story from a hack on the *Telegraph*.'

'So it must be true.'

'Sarcasm doesn't become you,' Toby said sonorously. 'Anyway, the club had the usual bunch of applications. A couple of members fancied their chances and several retired military men applied, as normal. The selection committee weeded them out and came up with a shortlist of three. Barry Trent, the captain, wanted Helen on the list but he was outvoted.'

'That's no surprise, is it? Helen doesn't have a moustache, an evil-smelling pipe and an even more evil-smelling spaniel, does she?'

'No, the thought of a lady Secretary nearly gave the old farts heart attacks. Anyway, this is when Trent got busy. He had some support on the committee and there were one or two waverers. The interesting thing was that the opposition were all Freemasons, as Trent knew.'

'A little cabal.'

'I can think of a nastier description. But this is when Trent had a stroke of luck because he found out that there was a big function coming up for the boys with the funny handshakes. So he chose that very evening to schedule the final meeting to interview the candidates and to decide who should be offered the job of Secretary. And he put Helen Raven on the shortlist. The clever thing was that he called the meeting with only twenty-four hours' notice.'

'So, Trent's mates turned up . . .'

'But the opposition were busy rolling up their trouser legs elsewhere and Helen Raven's appointment was a foregone conclusion.'

'Trent must have *The Prince* as his bedtime reading.'

'Yes. No wonder he's a successful entrepreneur.'

'What a story,' I said. 'Helen's good at her job and most of the members like her. But what about the club's pictures, Toby. What did you think of them?'

'Marvellous. Though I was puzzled by that Harry Rountree painting. Helen tells me that Welbeck said it was a copy but it looks authentic enough to me.'

'Sir Nicholas is the authority on golfing art.'

'So they say,' Toby said sourly.

'It's ready, gents,' the landlord called cheerfully to us and we went into the dining room. The original stone walls were still in place and part of the room was open to the rafters. A plaque on the wall told us that it had once been a toll house on the wool routes which passed through the village.

A young waitress directed us to a table under a window, through which we had a clear view of the church. Our first courses were laid out: a herring-and-potato salad for me and for Toby – a dedicated carnivore – a rabbit terrine.

'How's the book coming along?' I asked dutifully.

'The first deadline is in a month.'

'A deadline is a deadline, isn't it?'

'Not in publishing circles it isn't, not when they're dealing with fragile talents like mine.'

'I thought you needed the money.'

'I did, but my agent, God bless him, has sold the book to an American publisher. Their advance on signature should take care of my tax bill.'

With a smack of his lips, Toby cleared a great part of a glass of Beaujolais and I asked him why he so obviously disliked Welbeck.

'Pompous ass,' Toby replied.

'Agreed, but there are plenty of those in your life and you laugh at them.'

30

'Yes, but Welbeck's so unremittingly grand. He was born with a set of silver spoons in his mouth. No wonder he talks through his arse most of the time.'

I laughed. 'Maybe, but he's made a niche for himself and he's an enthusiast.'

'He's convinced everyone that he's the leading expert on golfing art and artefacts but he's bloody mean with his advice.'

'Ah, I see. You've asked for his help?'

'With my book, yes. He was very sniffy about it. I think he wanted a fee. I knew him years ago, too, when he was just another art-dealer.'

'Who did he work for?'

'One of the big auction houses. Could've been Sotheby's. He worked in London and then went to New York for a while.'

'So, he's got a good background in the business?'

'Sure. But he's so arrogant. I wrote to him to invite him to lunch so that I could tell him about my book. OK, so it's obvious I wanted to pick his brains. He didn't even send me a personal reply. It came from his assistant who told me that Sir Nicholas was "preparing his own authoritative study of golfing art" and therefore "could not become involved with any superficial surveys for the uninitiated". He's so bloody precious. A confirmed bachelor, of course,' Toby concluded with spite.

'You mean he goes to Barbra Streisand concerts?'

'Probably prefers Shirley Bassey.'

The main courses were on the table and Toby, with a mixed grill in front of him, perused the wine list carefully before asking for a half-bottle of Côte Rotie. I was still toying with my second glass of Beaujolais.

'Anyway, sod Welbeck,' Toby said, as he cut into a piece of fillet steak. 'I've got Harry Goodison to help me.'

'Harry Goodison?'

31

'A great bloke. He runs the best golf auctions. There's always one just before the Open Championship and usually one or two more during the year. In fact, I'm playing golf with him and his partner next week. And you're making up the four, Chris.'

'When?'

'Thursday.'

'Well . . .' I hesitated.

'Come on, Harry's a fine player. He's still off a handicap of five, I think. I need your expert assistance. My game's a bit dodgy at the moment.'

That sounded ominous. If Toby admitted that his game was a bit dodgy, it meant that he was hitting the ball sideways.

'What about his partner?' I asked.

'Jonathan Wright. Don't know about his golf but he has many affinities with Welbeck.'

'A touch supercilious?'

'Takes lessons.'

'OK, I'll be there, Toby. But let's keep the side-bets under control.'

# Chapter 4

The piercing siren obliterated the *Today* programme on my car radio. I registered the blazing lights and gaudy livery of a police car as it overtook me at high speed no more than a hundred yards from a blind bend. It cut in sharply enough to force me to hit the brakes hard. Thank God I wasn't coming in the other direction with my foot down. There were four men in the car.

A few minutes later and just before eight o'clock I drove into the Royal Dorset car park and saw the car by the front entrance. It was occupying the space reserved for the Captain; he would not be pleased if he turned up for an early morning game. Alongside there was an ambulance, reversed as close as possible to the main entrance, its rear doors open.

My earlier resolve to make a brisk attack on the work which awaited me in my office was forgotten and I headed for the front door. What the hell had happened?

As I walked into the entrance hall, a man wearing black jeans and a jacket of an indeterminate brown colour intercepted me. He was about my height, slightly younger than me and already had an incipient beer belly. His hair, long and greasy, looked as if it hadn't been combed for a month and he had an unlit cigarette between his lips. He withdrew it with his left hand and tucked it into the top pocket of his jacket.

'Are you a member, sir?'

'Were you the driver of the police car?'

'What's that to you?' He fumbled in his pocket and flashed a card at me. 'Detective Constable Gimblett. Sir.' The sir was an afterthought.

'Whoever was driving could've caused an accident. I'd always supposed the police were trained to prevent accidents.' I looked at him in the eyes and waited.

'It was an emergency,' Gimblett said. 'Are you a member, sir?'

'No, I work here. What's the emergency?'

'You'll have to talk to the Inspector about that.'

I walked straight past Gimblett and he knew enough not to stop me – even though he wanted to do so. As I headed quickly across the lounge bar, three paramedics came through the doors which led to the dining room. Two of them were pushing a stretcher while the third was bent over the person lying on it. An oxygen mask and some dressing obscured what little I could see of the injured person's face.

Surely it wasn't Helen? As the paramedics rushed past me, to my great relief I heard her voice from the dining room. It sounded subdued, lower-pitched than usual. I went through the doors and the bare rectangles of pristine wall told me what had happened. Lorimer's oil painting of the club's first Captain had gone, along with all the other paintings. Robbery – with violence.

Helen was talking to a tall man in a weary-looking grey suit. He had sandy hair which was on the point of disappearing altogether, a few strands straggling sadly across his scalp. She stopped in mid-sentence when she saw me.

'What's happened?' I asked.

'It was Mike, the steward,' Helen said.

'He looked in a bad way.'

34

'Beaten up by the thieves. He must have heard something, come down from his flat and disturbed them. His wife found him this morning. She slept through it all.'

'Just as well she did sleep through it,' the man said severely. 'Mr Tilbury's got some broken ribs and very severe head injuries. He's lucky to be alive.'

Helen introduced him as Inspector Rattray. As I shook his hand I could smell the stale tobacco smoke on his clothes.

'We needed better security,' Helen said sadly. 'I'll never forgive myself if Mike . . .'

I touched her arm in sympathy. 'So do hundreds of other golf clubs,' I said. 'You can't blame yourself. Blame the people who came before you.'

'We need to know what's missing,' said the practical Inspector Rattray. 'Apart from the paintings.'

'I'm going to make a complete list,' Helen replied, 'but, at a cursory glance, everything of value. All the old clubs, including the Philp driver, the Allan Robertson feathery and the other balls. Even the bits of memorabilia in my office.'

'Like what?' Rattray chipped in.

'Some early editions of *The Golfer's Handbook*, Darwin's book on golf courses, a signed copy of Harry Vardon's autobiography. And there was a display case with thank you letters from Bobby Jones, Walter Hagen and Gene Sarazen. They played here together in the late twenties. The display also included a programme from the first Ryder Cup match signed by all the players.'

'Bloody hell,' I muttered. 'How did they get in?'

'Easily, sir,' Rattray replied. 'Professionals who bypassed the alarm system. But, then, a schoolboy could've done that.'

'Don't rub it in, Inspector,' said Helen.

'I'm a bit puzzled,' I said. 'This sort of golfing art and

memorabilia will be difficult for the thieves to sell, won't it? It's a specialized market. You're not going to get rid of an Allan Robertson feathery down at the pub, are you? As for the paintings, how will they get good money for those?'

'Stolen to order, Chris,' Helen said, 'just like many of the art thefts in the past. Some unscrupulous bugger wants them for his private collection.'

'That's right, Mrs Raven.' Rattray broke off as a mobile telephone in his pocket began to buzz. He moved away from us to a corner of the room. He said little beyond grunting an occasional acknowledgement of what his caller was telling him.

When he returned, I said, 'If you need photos of what's been stolen, a friend of mine can help.'

'Who's that, sir?' Rattray said, suddenly intent.

I told him about Toby's visit to the club in connection with the book he was writing. Little did I know what I was letting Toby in for.

It was the middle of the morning when I telephoned Toby. He was a late riser and any conversations with him before eleven o'clock tended to be unproductive.

At least he was at his desk when I called. 'Greenslade, scribe,' he said gruffly.

'Have you heard about the burglary?' I asked.

'Burglaries plural,' Toby replied sharply. 'There were two more last night. Winterbourne Golf Club near Salisbury got turned over and so did Harewood Forest near Andover. All their treasures were taken, just as they were from Royal Dorset. It's a hell of a story, Chris, and it'll add a lot of spice to my book.'

'And we don't need a genius to tell us that the same people did all three.'

'Quite. They must have been very busy fellows and very

efficient. There's nearly three-quarters of a million quids' worth of gear missing.'

'Stolen to order, according to Helen,' I said.

'And probably on its way to foreign climes already,' Toby added.

'Where? Japan? Hong Kong? America?'

'Who knows? But Harry Goodison will have a good idea. I'm about to ring him. Don't forget our game tomorrow. Two o'clock start at Hinton Lakes. One o'clock meet in the bar for beer and sandwiches. Don't be late.'

I *was* late – because of a long conversation with Calvin Blair who talked with great excitement about the course he was building near St Nazaire in Brittany; it was all ready for seeding. I didn't want to cut short his fervent account of the merits of his latest creation. I was looking forward to visiting it in the autumn.

The bar at the Hinton Lakes club was brimming with noisy groups of golfers when I finally arrived. There was a particularly vociferous bunch taking up most of the bar; their ties, patterned with a violent red, green and yellow stripe, told me that they were members of the same golf society. I edged past them and spotted Toby's solid figure at the other end of the bar. He was wearing a dark green blazer which looked smart and expensive. He was not noted for his sartorial sense and I guessed that it was a gift from his girlfriend, Isobel. Despite the crush around the bar, Toby had assumed his usual proprietorial position: one elbow on the counter and one leg crossed over the other. He looked at ease and also, I thought, a shade slimmer, but perhaps the excellent cut of his jacket was disguising his formidable belly.

'You look as if you've lost a bit of weight,' I said, as I arrived at his elbow. 'Not a touch of *angst* over Isobel, is it?'

'Don't be ridiculous, dear boy. When you reach my age—'

'You get fewer and fewer chances,' I finished for him.

'How cruel young people can be. What I was going to say was that one gets philosophical.'

'Nice blazer,' I said. 'A present from Isobel?'

'As a matter of fact, yes. Now, do you require a beer?'

I nodded and Toby said, 'Come and meet Harry. He's over there. There're plenty of sandwiches left, by the way.'

Harry Goodison was a bear of a man. He was wearing a thick yellow sweater over a check shirt, and dark brown corduroy trousers. His head was bald, except for a ring of unruly grey hair above his ears. He had a florid face and a wide smile, both of which betokened a man who fully enjoyed life's pleasures. As he greeted me, my hand disappeared into his much larger one.

'Where's your partner?' I asked.

'Oh, he was running late,' replied Goodison. 'He'll see us on the first tee.'

'I was asking Harry about those robberies,' Toby said.

'It's a tragedy for the clubs,' the auctioneer said. 'They've lost some fine pieces and they'll probably never be seen again.'

'For instance?' I asked.

'Winterbourne owned a wonderful painting by Sir Francis Grant. It was worth an absolute fortune. If I can draw a comparison, one of his portraits sold for nearly three hundred thousand dollars a few years ago. It's not the first of his paintings to go missing, that's the odd thing. One went adrift in the early sixties. It portrayed the first meeting of the North Berwick Golf Club and was last seen, in public so to speak, at the Scottish National Portrait Gallery.'

'Thank God I've already been to Winterbourne and taken

all the photographs I need,' Toby said.

'I expect the police will want copies, I said. 'It might help their investigation.'

'Harewood Forest had a superb collection of early nineteenth century long-nosed woods and irons made by the likes of Robert White, Willie Park and Robert Forgan. They had some lovely Doulton ceramics, too, and Winterbourne had one of the finest displays of antique silver I've seen in one place. Spoons, cups and other trophies, medals, buttons, tankards, cigarette cases, all kinds of things.'

Goodison shook his head sadly, drained his Guinness and glanced at his watch. 'We'd better get our togs on, eh. I'm looking forward to this. It's a long time since I've seen you swing a golf club, Toby.'

'Well, don't blink or you'll miss it,' Toby said. 'Better watch Chris, he can still make a decent pass at the ball.'

# Chapter 5

Jonathan Wright was waiting by the first tee, swinging his driver lazily up and down. At first sight he appeared to be slightly built because he was tall and slim-waisted, but a second look told me that his shoulders were wide and his arms were compact and sinewy. He probably did some weight training. He was wearing pale blue trousers and a pink shirt with the Gleneagles logo. A white cap, similar in style to that which Ben Hogan used to wear, sat low over his eyes. Curly blond hair, neatly trimmed, showed underneath the cap. As Goodison introduced us, he touched hands briefly with Toby and me, and then resumed his practice swings.

'What are the stakes, Harry?' he asked.

'Friendly,' Toby said quickly. 'Five, five and ten pounds. OK?'

He meant a fiver waged on the first nine holes, the same on the second nine, and ten pounds on the result of the match.

'We all take our shots from Chris,' Goodison said. 'He's off two. It'll be nice to have some shots for a change.'

In matchplay the player with the lowest handicap 'gives' shots to the others. This is calculated at three-quarters of the difference and I had to give two shots to Goodison, whose handicap was five, nine to Wright (playing off fourteen) and thirteen to Toby (playing off a highly optimistic handicap of nineteen).

Wright shot me a quick look when told of my handicap but his face remained expressionless and he said nothing.

To say that Toby's swing was eccentric that afternoon would have been a gross understatement. He had to play the course from its extremities on the right-hand side and was either in deep rough, of which there was an abundance, or even deeper water, of which there was even more. Walter Hagen, a genius who was the first man to make professional golf into a lucrative business, described his own swing as beginning with a sway and ending with a lunge. God knows how he would have described Toby's.

As I expected, Goodison was a very powerful player with the added merit of a sure touch on and around the greens. I would have had a tough time beating him, even though I was playing consistently as a result of my spending half an hour a day on the practice ground at Royal Dorset. But his partner did the real damage. Wright had a neat and unhurried swing which imparted great accuracy to his shots. When we lost the match on the sixteenth green I calculated that he had only dropped five strokes. Up to that point that probably equalled the number of words he had addressed to me or Toby. He gave a strong impression of a man who would rather have been elsewhere.

The seventeenth fairway wasn't clear when we reached the tee and, while we waited, Toby turned to Goodison and said, 'Harry, I don't understand these robberies from the golf clubs. The whole business seems perverse because there can't be a readily available market for antique golf clubs and certainly not for paintings like the Francis Grant or the Thomas Hodge stolen from Royal Dorset. Are we to assume they've been pinched to order?'

'That's a reasonable deduction,' Goodison replied. 'I would guess that the loot is already out of the country.'

'On its way to where?' I asked.

'Probably Japan or somewhere else in the Far East. Maybe to America.'

'I disagree,' Wright said sharply, as he teed his ball up and looked down the fairway. 'These theories that there are megalomaniac collectors around the world, building up private hoards of art and artefacts, are pure journalistic nonsense. The reality is probably that a bunch of crooks saw those golf clubs as easy targets. They'll melt the silver down and the ceramics will appear at car boot sales in Essex. It's as simple as that.'

'Why did they bother with the paintings?' I asked.

'Oh, they might try to sell them back to the clubs through some anonymous intermediary. More probably, the canvases have been cut out of their frames and burnt. And the frames have been sold to some dealer or other for a few pounds.'

Wright hit a drive down the right centre of the fairway. 'Don't you think that's a more likely scenario, Harry?'

'You may be right, Jonathan,' he replied.

Although the match had been lost and won, Toby played the eighteenth well by his standards. His drive ended in the light rough and he hit a mid-iron just short of the green. As we walked up the fairway I noticed two men leave the clubhouse and walk towards the green. They looked familiar and, as we got closer, I was able to identify Inspector Rattray and his sidekick, Detective Constable Gimblett, the Michael Schumacher of the Dorset roads. While I wondered why they were there, Toby enjoyed one of his rare moments of golfing excellence. He played a neat pitch-and-run shot to within six feet of the hole and nodded in a satisfied way, as if to imply that this was how he usually played the game and that all that

43

had gone before was merely an aberration.

My ball and that of Harry Goodison lay at the back of the green and I watched with surprise as Gimblett lumbered across the green, oblivious to the fact that his sizeable police-issue shoes were tramping on the line of my putt. Rattray, wearing the same grey suit as on the last occasion I'd met him, watched. The quiet breeze wafted his stale cigarette smell towards me.

Straightening up after marking his ball, Toby was confronted by Gimblett's bulky frame. The policeman reached into his pocket and flashed a warrant card in Toby's face. 'Mr Greenslade is it, sir? Mr Toby Greenslade?'

'Yes, it is, the one and only. Who the hell are you? And what are you doing trampling this well-designed green into submission? We're trying to finish a game of golf, so I suggest you get out of the way.'

'I'm Detective Constable Gimblett and that's my guv'nor over there. We need to talk to you,' he added doggedly.

I strolled over to Rattray and said, 'Your constable is in the way. Tell him to get off the green and let us finish.'

Rattray nodded and spoke sharply. 'Constable, get off the sodding green and let these gentlemen finish their game.'

Glowering in my direction, Gimblett stamped his way off the putting surface. Goodison shook his head in disbelief and putted up to within a foot or so of the hole. I followed suit over the depressions caused by Gimblett's size twelve shoes. Not surprisingly, Toby missed his putt and glared in the direction of the two policemen.

'What's all this about?' Goodison asked as we shook hands.

'I've no idea,' Toby replied. 'Let's find out.'

Wright shrugged and said, 'Harry, I must get back to London. I'm way behind with those valuations for Lady Ainsley. Thank you for the game,' he ended curtly and began to walk away towards the car park.

'Don't you want your winnings?' I called after him.

'Give the money to Harry,' he replied. 'Must rush.'

'I would normally say that we'd spend Jonathan's winnings on a couple of rounds of Pimm's,' Goodison said, 'but we'd better see these coppers off first, don't you think?'

Toby nodded and we walked towards the two policemen. Toby addressed Rattray, 'What's the problem, officer? Some overdue parking fines?'

'It's more serious than that, sir,' Rattray said. 'I'm Inspector Rattray and I wish to talk to you about the recent robberies at Winterbourne, Harewood Forest and Royal Dorset golf clubs.'

'Ah, yes. You'll want my photographs, won't you? Chris mentioned that. I'll have to prevail upon the lovely Laura to print you a set. If you'll give me your number I'll call you tomorrow.'

'Mr Greenslade,' Rattray said wearily, 'we wish to interview you, er, formally. You seem to have taken more than a passing interest in the various items of value at the clubs I mentioned.'

Toby's mouth gaped in surprise for a moment. He turned to me. 'I don't believe what I'm hearing,' he said. 'Somebody wake me up, I must be dreaming. Now look, Inspector, I am working on a book about the more celebrated golf clubs in these islands of ours and the many historical treasures which they contain. You can check that fact with my publishers. So, strangely enough, I've been going around looking at those treasures. I've been to Muirfield and Royal Dornoch and Lytham and Birkdale. Have they been burgled? No. So what connection have you deduced that I have with these robberies.'

'Calm down, sir. We merely wish to talk to you,' Rattray said.

'You can do that here, in front of my friends.'

'I'm afraid that's not possible. We require a formal statement from you.'

'Are you arresting me?'

'No, sir. We're asking you to help us with our inquiries.'

Several golfers had paused to watch this unusual scene.

Toby stood for a moment without speaking and then said, 'I take it you'll allow me to shower and change, Inspector.'

Rattray nodded. 'Constable Gimblett will have to stay with you, sir.'

'God almighty,' Toby said. 'Chris will you phone my editor and tell him what's going on. This will make a very good story for tomorrow.'

'Gimblett has two ts,' the constable said brightly but was quelled by a stare from Rattray's red-rimmed eyes.

Toby stamped off towards the changing room with Goodison in his wake, followed by Constable Gimblett. The episode struck me as being closer to farce than anything else: a heavy-handed confrontation by the police followed by Toby standing on his dignity and acting the role of fearless journalist. Nevertheless, I dutifully made a call to the sports editor of the *Daily News*, Neil McGrath. He was the living embodiment of tabloid journalism; if a story didn't involve bonking, royalty or showbiz, it wasn't a real story. If it involved all three he would move heaven and earth, and pay the latter, to get an exclusive.

After a delay of several minutes, I got through to him and caught the tail-end of another conversation. 'Is the bastard willing to say he took a bung or not? If not, tell him to forget the deal. Yeah, sorry, McGrath here.'

I told him briefly of Toby's predicament and that he'd be filing a story later that day.

'Well, well, so Toby's had his collar felt,' McGrath said with relish in his voice. 'You tell him I won't be holding the front page. We've already got a bloody good bonking story.' The sports editor began to laugh. 'Tell the old fart to make sure he gets beaten up because we can always run with a police-brutality story. Maybe they'll keep him inside for the night. It'll do the bugger good.'

'I'll pass on your good wishes.'

'Hey, Chris, you don't think old Toby's involved, do you? I mean, he's always short of money.'

'No chance.'

'I suppose not. What a pity. Tell him to keep tabs on the story. There might be a nice angle there somewhere. You know, golfing toffs sitting on millions of quids' worth of paintings and antiques and they don't even bother to lock their back doors at night.'

'I'll tell him.'

'Magic.' The line went dead.

The two policemen, one on either side of Toby, were escorting him across the hall when I left the telephone booth. Gimblett had Toby's holdall in his hand.

Toby stopped when he saw me and asked what McGrath had said.

'I cannot tell a lie, Toby,' I said. 'He was amused. But he told you to stick with it and all the resources of the *News* will be made available to you, if needed.' A white lie rarely does any real harm.

'Amused, was he?' Toby said grimly. 'Amused at this assault on the integrity of the Fourth Estate.'

'Come on, sir,' Rattray said. 'We're only going down to the local nick for a chat. This isn't the Bloody Assizes and I'm not Judge Jeffreys.'

'I'll give you a call later,' Toby said over his shoulder, as he was urged towards the exit.

'Drive carefully, Constable,' I said. Gimblett glared at me but said nothing.

# Chapter 6

I felt guilty about my inability to help Mrs Bradshaw in her quest to find Paul Stacey and recover the money he owed her. I had been stupid to go waltzing into Reynolds's office with the vain hope of solving the problem. My guilt feelings were exacerbated when my neighbour knocked on my door that evening to ask my advice about the wisdom of using a private detective to find Stacey.

'It can get expensive,' I said. 'You'll be throwing good money after bad.'

'I don't mind spending a bit if it means I can get that miserable little crook into court,' Mrs Bradshaw said emphatically.

She refused my offer of a glass of wine because she was playing bridge in less than an hour and wanted to keep her wits about her. I made us both a cup of tea instead. We talked about the problem in a desultory manner for a few minutes and I speculated again about trying to gain entry to Stacey's offices.

'I won't allow you to attempt anything illegal,' Mrs Bradshaw said. 'Not on my account. It would never do.'

'Do you remember Tania?' I asked.

'Yes. A sweet girl.'

'I wonder why she's working there. She seems too nice for the likes of Reynolds and Stacey, doesn't she?' Mrs Bradshaw nodded her agreement. 'Maybe if I could get her on her own, she might help. We just need a hint of where he is and we might be able to track him down. It's worth trying, don't you think?'

'Agreed, but how will you arrange it? She'll be wary of you.'

'I'll wait near the office and bump into her by chance.'

Mrs Bradshaw looked doubtful. 'She's not unintelligent. She'll smell a rat. I can also tell you that she needs that job and won't do anything to compromise herself.'

'Nevertheless, it's worth a try. If I can persuade her to have a drink and a chat . . .'

'Crank up the Ludlow charm.'

'One can but try because I don't have any other bright ideas. And, Mrs Bradshaw, you can help to set her up. Find out for me when she normally finishes work and I'll be outside on the pavement.'

'OK. Let's see, I'll pose as someone from a firm of couriers with a package to deliver. How's that?'

'Excellent.'

It wasn't long after Mrs Bradshaw had left for her bridge party that the telephone rang. I had just assembled the constituents for a pasta and salad meal: linguini, chopped spring onions, garlic and a few prawns and some shredded lettuce. I guessed it would be Toby and so it was.

'I'm out,' he said, with a gravity that suggested he'd survived fifteen years in a Chinese labour camp.

'My God, you survived a series of merciless beatings by teams of police thugs armed with rolled-up copies of the *Daily News*, did you?'

'That's not funny, Chris. It's a very unpleasant experience

to be under suspicion for robbery with violence.'

'Do they still think you're a criminal mastermind? The Moriarty of the golfing world perhaps?'

'I'd hoped you'd be glad to hear from me,' Toby said with a grave dignity. 'In the circumstances.'

'I am,' I said, stifling all traces of amusement in my voice.

'Good. I've just telephoned that suppurating globule of catsick—'

'Your editor?'

'Indeed. I wanted to write a diatribe about my wrongful arrest—'

'The inalienable freedom of the press . . .'

'But he told me to cool it. He wants me just to cover the robberies in a couple of paragraphs and then keep an eye on things. An "eye on things", for God's sake.'

'He obviously thinks there may be a good story there in due course,' I said, remembering my conversation with Neil McGrath.

'Of course there's a good story,' Toby snapped, 'and I'm going to write it. The first thing we're going to do is talk to Goodison again.'

'We?'

'Yes, I'll need your help.'

'I don't have the time and I'm not a journalist.'

'Nevertheless, you'll give an old friend a helping hand.'

'Well . . .'

'Good. I'll fix a time for us to see Harry.'


At a few minutes before half past five on the following evening I was standing outside a shop window about fifty yards away from the entrance to Reynolds's office. Pretending to be absorbed in a close study of the array of luggage in the window,

I felt conspicuous and rather foolish. I was hoping that my quarry would turn left out of the office towards Charing Cross and then I could walk casually towards her and ask her to have a drink with me. If she turned right or hopped on a passing bus, I would have to extemporize.

Luckily, Tania did as I'd hoped. I saw her slender figure come hurrying out of the office building towards me and I simply turned and walked straight at her. Head down, she was about to scurry past me when I hailed her cheerfully.

'Hello, there. It's Tania, isn't it?'

She hesitated, smiled weakly and said, 'Oh, you came to see Mr Reynolds, didn't you? But I can't quite recall . . .'

'Chris Ludlow.'

'Oh yes, your neighbour and some money owing. Mrs Bradshaw I remember.'

I gave her the big, charming Ludlow smile. 'Tania, I usually have a drink at this time of the day. Will you join me?'

'I ought to get back. My mother . . .'

'Just a quick drink. It would be nice to talk to you for a few minutes.'

She looked cautiously back towards her office. 'Fine. But it'll have to be quick.'

We walked across the road and up a side street to a wine bar on the fringes of Covent Garden. The square central bar was the focal point for a series of rooms which rambled outwards from it. Upended barrels were used as tables, with candles casually placed on china saucers; the walls were panelled in wood and there was sawdust on the floor. It was a proven formula for a successful wine bar and the place was crowded. However, I was able to grab a table from a pair of departing American tourists. I ordered two large glasses of Australian red from the catholic wine list.

I sat down opposite Tania, who was fiddling with a capacious handbag. Her clothes were dowdy; a dark blue shirt was covered by a grey cardigan. She wore no jewellery and only the merest hint of lipstick. But the swift smile she offered me as we clinked glasses transformed her face. She had blue eyes and frizzy fair hair. She was pretty, although it seemed that she was trying to hide her attractions rather than emphasize them.

'You mentioned your mother,' I said, to break the ice. 'You live with her?'

'Yes. She looks after Archie, while I'm at work.'

'Archie?'

'My son. He's three now.'

'I see.'

'I'm one of the army of single mothers. I'm the breadwinner and Mum is the babysitter.'

'Where's the father? I'm sorry, it's none of my business,' I added quickly, aware that it was a potentially awkward question.

'Over the hills and far away, I'm afraid. He's married. He was going to get a divorce. I expect you can guess the rest.'

There was only resignation in her voice, not bitterness and I grimaced at her in sympathy.

'Actually, I don't regret any of it,' Tania continued. 'For two years I lived and breathed for Andy. I wouldn't go anywhere at night or at weekends in case he phoned me. I used to wait at home for his call. Of course, the time we spent together was wonderful. We had weekends away sometimes and once we spent ten days together in France.'

I wondered why she was telling me all this and then realized that she probably had nobody in whom to confide. A full-time job and a half-time son wouldn't leave much time for close friendships.

'Mum's never forgiven me,' Tania said. 'Probably because

53

the same thing happened to her. She's elevated her variations on "I told you so" to an art form.'

I ordered two more glasses of wine, without any protest from her, and asked about her job and specifically how she got on with David Reynolds.

She shrugged. 'I get on with him because I have to. I need the job.'

'What about Paul Stacey?'

'I was wondering how long it would take you.'

My attempt to assume a look of injured innocence was a clear failure, so I smiled instead. 'Was it that obvious?'

'Yes, Chris, it was. You just happened to be passing as I left the office. Come off it, that's hardly subtle stuff, is it? And you don't happen to have a friend at a courier firm, do you?'

'Guilty.' I held up my hands in submission.

'The lady from the courier firm was Mrs Bradshaw, yes?'

'Yes.' It was obvious that Pinkerton's wouldn't be the right career move for me.

'I can't help you with Stacey. I'd lose my job and I don't fancy crossing Reynolds.'

'But you could help if you wanted to.'

'I didn't say that.'

Tania drained the rest of the wine from her glass and made ready to go.

'You're afraid of Reynolds?'

'Yes. I've heard him threaten people and it isn't pretty. He has a habit of getting his own way.'

'So does Stacey, it appears. At the expense of decent people like my neighbour.'

'I'm very sorry. Mrs Bradshaw is a charming woman. But Reynolds and Stacey don't give a damn about people like her – about anyone, I should say. They regard it as a game. They take advantage of people for the hell of it and then hide behind the law or just bully their way out of trouble.'

'Nice people.' Tania studied the surface of the table. 'Is Stacey really abroad?'

She grasped her handbag tightly and looked nervously at me. 'No. Reynolds has other offices, other interests. Property development, things like that. Stacey runs that side of things, but I really can't help you any more than that.' She was becoming agitated and finally she stood up and said, 'I'm going to be late. My mother will get worried and I like to spend as much time as I can with Archie. Thanks for the drink. I'm sorry I can't . . .'

With an apologetic smile and a quick flutter of her hand Tania headed swiftly for the door. So much for the Ludlow charm. All I'd learned was that Stacey was still in the country somewhere and that Tania was scared of Reynolds. Not that I blamed her for that. If I had to take him on at some future time, I'd want to be sure I had a clear advantage over him – ideally he'd be tied to a chair and I'd have a blunt instrument in my hand. I certainly didn't have the heart to hassle Tania any more about Stacey's whereabouts. Maybe I'd have to try one of the other women in Reynolds's office. I'd seen a stony-faced female in her middle years but I didn't fancy my chances with her. Maybe I should send Toby in to cast his spell on her.

I should have asked Tania for the name of the other companies owned by the two men but realized that there was an easy solution. I walked back to Reynolds's office block and went into the entrance hall. Many other firms occupied the building and I scanned a long list of names. There were several companies listed beneath that of Reynolds, Jayne & Stacey, Solicitors and Commissioners for Oaths. David Reynolds Enterprises, RJS Securities, DRS Promotions and finally RS

Developments. That seemed to be the most likely one. But if its registered office was in The Strand, London, how did I find out where the business was really based?

One place to look was Companies House, where the accounts of all firms are filed. The directors would be named, together with their private addresses. It was a job for my accountant friend, Tom Hector.

# Chapter 7

Mrs Bradshaw was philosophical about my failure to extract any useful information from Tania.

'But I have one or two ideas to try,' I concluded optimistically. 'You don't need to go wasting your money on some private eye who'll just go through the motions and then send you an inflated bill.'

'I'd go to a reputable firm,' Mrs Bradshaw said. 'Pinkerton's perhaps. It's such a nice name and one thinks of terribly correct men in post-war Hollywood gangster films.'

'They still handle security at the Masters in Augusta and the Oscar ceremony.'

'Well, there you are then,' said Mrs Bradshaw with a smile.

Tom Hector, the accountant, rang me the following morning. 'Nothing doing on your pal Stacey,' he said. 'All those companies you gave me have nominee shareholders. There's no sign of the bugger.'

'Any other ideas?'

'How much does he owe you?'

'He owes a friend five grand.'

'A private eye might do the business, if he's got the right contacts. It depends how much you want to gamble to get the money back.'

'OK, Tom, and thanks.'
'No problem. Let's have a game of golf soon, eh?'

Over the next few days I had little time to myself because
Calvin had asked me to look at the site for a new public golf
course in Wiltshire and talk to the developers. That took me
through to the following week when I was booked to do some
caddying work at the Catesby Classic at a comparatively new
course in Sussex. This was my first outing with Jake Bowden,
a golfer who had rung me out of the blue and asked if I'd look
after him at some of the more important tournaments during
the season. On other occasions he would use a local caddie or
ask his son to carry his bag.

I agreed immediately since it was just the arrangement I
needed, although I knew very little about my new boss. I
remembered that he'd been on the circuit years ago but had
retired sometime during the eighties. He had recently decided
to make a comeback and I was sure that I'd read somewhere
that he'd had financial problems. I looked him up in an old
edition of *The PGA European Tour Guide* and saw that his
best finish in the Order of Merit had been fourteenth, but his
career earnings showed that he'd made a decent living out of
golf.

My old boss, Jack Mason was the obvious source of
information on Jake. I knew that, in the week of the Moroccan
Open, he would probably be at home; he didn't travel far and
certainly not to North Africa.

Jack's delightful wife, Jenny, answered the telephone. We
swapped gossip for a while and she invited me to dinner. 'You
want Jack, I'm sure. You're in luck, he's just got back from the
gym.'

I was surprised because Jack's aversion to physical exercise was well-known. His favoured brand of exertion was drinking the strongest beers he could find in the many hostelries he patronized.

'What's up Jack?' I asked when he got to the telephone. 'Has your doctor told you to get fit now that middle age is upon you?'

'More or less,' he replied apologetically. 'I'm trying to get in trim for the new season. I still want to win tournaments, Chris.'

I asked him about Jake Bowden and he gave me a quick summary of the man. He was in his mid-forties, a strong player with no real weaknesses in his game and one exceptional strength. 'His short game,' Jack declared. 'If he's in trouble, or if he needs a really inventive stroke to get the ball near the hole, he's at his best. In fact, he's got a short game many pros would kill for.'

'Why did he retire so young?' I asked.

'Because he got seriously rich, that's why. I don't know the details except that it was some kind of betting coup. Ask Jake himself, he'll sure as hell make it an entertaining story.'

'And he's back on the tour because he's broke?'

'So they say. But that's typical of Jake. He's a wheeler-dealer. He's always got an offer available on something. Cheap airfares, cut-price televisions or stereos, cars, watches, you name it. He's a good lad. You'll enjoy working with him.'

Half an hour before our practice round for the Catesby Classic, I met Jake Bowden on the putting green. He was sinking putts of eight feet as if the hole was as big as a bucket. It was a promising start and I wondered if he could do the same thing under pressure. He was a stocky man with broad shoulders, but it was his face which caught my attention. Suntanned and crowned with a thick mop of greying hair, he had a massive jaw, long and square. It was augmented by a wide mouth, its corners turned up. It gave him a notably humorous look.

During the practice round our conversation didn't go much beyond the discussion of club selection and the tactics required. Despite having been designed by a renowned American golfer with seven or eight major championships to his name, the course was dull. It was particularly tedious in its reliance on artificial lakes and vast, bizarrely shaped bunkers.

'What a dog of a course,' Jake said at the end of his round. 'They should take it back to Florida where it belongs. We've earned a beer. Let's go to it.'

We settled on the clubhouse terrace, out of the wind, and I asked him who had recommended me as a caddie.

'Several people,' he said. 'But Calvin Blair told me that you were in the market for a few events and that suited me.'

'So why did you retire?' I asked bluntly and, even more bluntly, 'Why are you back on the circuit?'

'Money,' Jake said. 'I retired towards the end of nineteen-eighty-four when I suddenly became very rich.'

'How rich?'

'I didn't make a million, though the gossips said I did. People like to exaggerate these things, don't they?'

'How did you do it?'

Jake paused for a moment and then launched into his narrative. From his early days as a budding golf professional at a public course near Ilford in Essex, Jake had taken an interest in betting. It had never become an obsession but he learned to assess the odds and spot those rare occasions when they favoured the punter rather than the bookmaker. To his great satisfaction he cleaned up on several occasions, especially when backing player A to beat player B in a tournament, irrespective of where they finished. In this situation, Jake had unrivalled inside knowledge. I asked him whether he'd ever been tempted to take out some insurance.

'Insurance?' he queried, pretending not to understand.

'Yeah. Let's say that Smith and Jones are near the tail-end of the field on the final day. They know that, whatever happens, they'll only earn a few hundred pounds – this is back in the late seventies and early eighties, isn't it? So, you're on Smith and stand to win some money, a hundred quid . . .'

'And the rest,' Jake interrupted.

'OK, so maybe it would be a good idea to offer Jones a few quid not to try so hard, maybe miss the odd putt and so on.'

'Heaven forbid,' Jake said, with a theatrical wink, 'that would've been cheating.'

'Fine, so you're honest Joe. Now tell me how you made a killing.'

'I'm a bloody sight more honest than any bookie.'

'That's a truism.'

'If you say so, Chris.' He grinned at me. 'I was at some run-of-the-mill event in the Midlands. This was in eighty-three. There was a flash car, a BMW I think, on offer for a hole-in-one at the fourteenth. One of the big bookmaking firms were offering thirty-three to one against anyone doing it and the sponsors were smart enough to put three hundred quid on. I put fifty on. You probably remember the event.'

'Vaguely,' I said. 'I was at university. An unknown American holed out, I think.'

'Correct, old son. Joe Don Baker or some such. He did the business. The sponsors covered their investment in the car and got a lot of publicity. I walked off with over fifteen hundred quid, which was a bloody sight more than I earned on the course that week, and the bookies had egg on their faces.'

Jake drank his beer reflectively and told me how the episode planted the seed of an idea in his mind. Bookies were normally impregnable. They always made money in the long run and that was why they regarded all punters as mugs. But because there was so little betting on golf their knowledge of it was limited and, in particular, they had little idea of the statistics for holes-in-one at professional tournaments. To the uninitiated a hole-in-one is a minor miracle, thousands to one against. But Jake found out that they were much more frequent in professional events than anyone realized: almost one every week. He'd found a weak spot in the bookies' armour.

So Jake developed his idea and based his campaign on two principles. First, that holes-in-one were more likely at the more prestigious tournaments where the leading players were competing. He selected five events in the following year for his bets on holes-in-one: the PGA Championship at Wentworth, the British Masters at Woburn, the American Open at Oak Hills, the Open at Birkdale and the European Open at Sunningdale.

'What was the other principle?' I asked.

'I knew I had to avoid the big bookmakers. Apart from the lousy odds they offer, they'd wise up within hours to a lot of bets on holes-in-one and tell me to piss off. So, I went for the independent bookies and the small chains of two or three shops. I combed the Yellow Pages and made lists for every part of the country. I got street maps and marked the locations. I planned it like a military operation. Field Marshal Montgomery couldn't have done it better.'

'But how on earth did you manage it? The logistics, I mean,' I asked.

'I gave myself a couple of months. March, April and a bit of May. I had a war chest of thirty big ones and off I went. I got Maggie, the missus, to do some of the leg-work and I lined up a few mates, people I could trust. I paid them expenses, plus a commission. But only when they delivered the winnings.'

'If any.'

'Oh, I knew it would work.'

I asked Jake why the bookies hadn't rumbled him; presumably they talked to each other, if only to lay off bets. But Jake told me that they couldn't wait to snatch his money from his hand. He and his helpers acted innocent and had their story ready: they liked golf, went to a few tournaments and wanted to have a little extra interest in the way of a bet. Perhaps a bet on a hole-in-one at the PGA Championship would be a bit of fun.

'What odds did you get?'

'From a hundred to one down as far as two to one.'

'What were the real odds, did you think, at the time?'

'Evens, mostly.' I whistled and Jake smiled. 'When I got a real goer, and you know how flash some of these local bookies are, especially if their mates are listening, I dived in with doubles and trebles. I even got accumulators on all five events at some places. Only small stakes at lowish odds but you can imagine how it all stacked up.'

'So how many bookies did you hit in the end?' I was getting more and more intrigued by Jake's brilliant idea.

'Just over a hundred. We had to be reasonably selective and a lot of them did smell something wrong about the bet and threw us out.'

'And there was a hole-in-one at all five events?'

'Thank God, yes. The odd thing was that I got one of them myself. On the opening day at the British Masters. It turned out to be irrelevant because Langer got one in the third round, but it was a nice feeling.'

'Did the bookies pay up when the days of reckoning came?'

'Early on, yes. There was no trouble with the single bets. But then the doubles and trebles came home to roost and they started to squeal. And there was some publicity. We got into bother here and there and we had to use some arbitration. But most of them paid up in the end.'

'How much did you take them for, if I'm not being rude?'

'Not at all, Chris. Just short of a half a million.'

'So why are you back on the tour? I was told you bought into a Mercedes dealership and acquired a nice hotel in Brighton.'

'All true.' Jake looked at his watch. 'I've got to see a guy. About a Mercedes, funnily enough. I'll give another instalment of my memoirs on the way round tomorrow. How's that? See you at ten o'clock.'

# Chapter 8

It was Jake's ill luck to begin his first round in the Catesby Classic in driving rain. Although it was near the end of May the weather, in perverse British fashion, had reverted to its winter temper. Rollneck sweaters and rainwear were *de rigueur*. It is difficult for a golfer to keep his rhythm going and his determination intact in such conditions, and always a temptation to get downcast and blame the lousy conditions for the mistakes. I wondered if Jake was susceptible in that way. The hunch of his shoulders and the occasional resigned smile told me that he wanted to be somewhere else – somewhere warm and dry. But he stuck to his task over the first nine holes and only dropped one shot against par. His remarkable dexterity with his short irons saved him on several occasions and I saw, with relief, that his putting stroke stayed smooth under pressure.

During the second half of the round, the rain eased to become a mere drizzle and then it stopped altogether. Jake retrieved his dropped shot and then got to one under par when he chipped in from off the green at the twelfth hole. This encouraged him; he squared up his shoulders and clearly began to view the day with more optimism.

He scrutinized a scoreboard on the thirteenth tee. 'We're not doing so bad, old son,' he said. 'It's a matter of hanging on for the last few holes. Maybe the rain'll come back this afternoon and make it difficult for the rest of them.'

There was a long delay on the tee while one of the players waited for a referee to turn up and give a ruling on whether or not he was allowed to free drop. While his group waited, they called upon the group immediately behind them to play through. This all took time and we had to be patient.

'You were going to tell me what you did with all that money,' I said quietly to Jake. 'But maybe this isn't the moment to talk about things like that.'

Jake shrugged. 'No problem, Chris. We'll be here for some time by the look of it. It's better to try and relax or this game will blow your fuses. The answer is that I went great guns financially for a couple of years. Remember, we're talking about the mid-eighties. They were boom years, as you know, and I knew some guys on the Stock Exchange. They were wide boys but they looked after me and I must've doubled my money.'

'And you lost most of it on Black Monday?'

'No, I got lucky because I diversified.' Jake grinned at me. 'Just before the market went belly up. I bought a hotel in Brighton and put a manager in charge.'

'What sort of hotel?'

'A dozen bedrooms. Then I added a few more and extended the restaurant.' Jake looked down the fairway and saw that it was time to play. He wafted his ball down the left centre. When his two companions had played I shouldered his bag and off we went.

'I'd still got a few hundred big ones in the market,' Jake continued, 'and when the crash came the boys told me to sit tight until things sorted themselves out. I had some dodgy secondary shares but mostly it was decent stuff and of course, after a year or two, I was OK. I don't know why I'm explaining this to you of all people, Chris, because you were in the market, weren't you?'

I nodded. 'But I started a couple of years after Black Monday.' We had reached Jake's ball and I looked at the next shot he faced, a carry of just over 180 yards to a plateau green. 'Six iron?' I asked.

'No, I'll cut a five iron in. It'll stop quicker.' We had to wait for the group in front to finish the hole and Jake went on with his story. 'That episode worried me, even though I'd done all right. More by luck than judgement, though. I was just bloody glad I'd hedged my bets and bought the hotel. So, when one of those financial consultants approached me to look after my investments, I was in the right mood to listen.'

Jake took a practice swing with his five iron and opened his stance so that he could fade the ball in from left to right. I couldn't see much wrong with his action but he overdid the fade and his ball hit the right edge of the green and toppled into a bunker. 'Rollocks,' he said succinctly, handed me the offending club and strode on.

But Jake floated the ball out to within a foot of the hole and secured his par.

'Charles Freeman, he was called,' Jake said as we waited on the next tee. 'A smooth bastard. Tall, fair-haired, immaculate suits, always had a good-looking chick in tow when we met for a drink. An office in Kensington, the white BMW, the whole works really.'

'Gaiters and no breakfast,' I murmured.

'Eh? Oh, yeah. He seemed to know his stuff, though. I had a financial statement every other month and I was doing well out of it. I recommended him to one or two friends. I was happy as Larry. I kept a close eye on the hotel and I played quite a bit of golf – for fun. And that was a nice change.'

Jake flighted a mid-iron into the heart of the next green. 'Two or three years ago I signed a power of attorney in Charles's favour. It made sense, he said. He could deal with all the everyday stuff without bothering me for signatures and so on. I know what you're going to say, Chris, but I trusted him. He persuaded me to take out a mortgage on the hotel. There were tax advantages, so he told me, and he had a sure-fire property deal that was big and couldn't miss.'

'But it did?'

'Oh yeah, if it ever existed. Freeman's firm went bust for nearly twenty million quid and all the money went with him.'

'And the hotel?'

'Sure. He'd used the hotel as security against a loan. The liquidators grabbed it. It was one of the few assets they got their mitts on.'

As if shaken by the memory, Jake missed a six-foot putt that didn't look too difficult from where I was standing. 'That's why I'm back on the tour,' he said as we walked away from the green. 'I need the money. Mind you, I'll be eligible for the Seniors' Tour in a few years' time and then I'll really clean up. Maybe I'll go to the States and become a dollar millionaire. In my first season, of course.'

'You've got the game to do it, Jake,' I said. 'By the way, what happened to Freeman?'

'He did less than a year in the slammer. In an open prison, with all the other white-collar crooks.'

By the end of the round Jake had secured another birdie and stood at two under par. To his great satisfaction it started to pour with rain again and his unexceptional score looked much better than that by the end of the day's play.

On my return home I found a message from Toby, who asked me to accompany him on a visit to Harry Goodison's office in

Salisbury on the following evening. He gave the address and stated the time of the meeting as five o'clock.

'I've checked Jake Bowden's starting time,' he concluded, 'and you'll make it easily, even in that bone-shaking German machine of yours.' My Porsche did indeed have nearly 150,000 miles on the clock, but there was no need to be so dismissive of the faithful old vehicle. 'The purpose of the mission,' Toby went on in his pseudo-military tones, 'is to try and get a lead on who set up those golf-club thefts. "Once more unto the breach, dear friend",' he ended, not inaptly.

The weather continued foul during the next day and some of the players grew frustrated by the problems it imposed: the slippery grips on their clubs, the discomfort of damp clothing, and the unpredictable behaviour of the ball as it flew out of the wet grass. The game was difficult enough already, as Jake said emphatically when his ball plugged in the sodden sand of a greenside bunker. Nevertheless, he hacked it out to within a few feet of the hole and stroked it home with aplomb for a par. His determination, allied to the solid foundations of his game, enabled him to keep his round together and to capitalize on the few moments of good fortune which came his way. He also managed to remain cheerful which is a considerable help in such conditions. By the end of the second round he was lying in a very satisfactory position in the top twenty.

# Chapter 9

Despite the rain, Jake had wanted to practise his putting when his round had ended and in consequence I was about half an hour late for the meeting.

Harry Goodison's offices occupied what had once been a cinema in a street about a mile from the great cathedral with its beautiful soaring steeple. There was nothing beautiful about the old cinema front and I could still identify its original name under the thin coat of paint. A receptionist, elegantly attired in a dark grey suit, led me along several corridors, through many doors and up three flights of stairs to Goodison's office. It was just as well that it was a large room. Prints and pictures were stacked around the walls, the chairs overflowed with books, old catalogues and magazines, and bundles of golf clubs lay in every available space.

'I'm sorry about the chaos,' the auctioneer said to me. 'We're preparing for the annual sale before the Open. Find yourself a chair.'

I moved a few armfuls of books and sat down on a chair which creaked alarmingly.

'Harry has just given me a very learned dissertation on the history of long-nose wooden clubs,' Toby said. 'What I didn't realize was that they were making fakes even in the old days. Apparently long-nose clubs were being sold from Old Tom

Morris's shop in St Andrews as late as 1910 when they'd been out of fashion for decades.'

'They would have been replicas, not fakes,' Goodison corrected him. 'I doubt there was any intention to deceive. We ourselves do a good trade on the side with replica clubs and they're very nicely done but we wouldn't dream of implying that they're anything other than repros.'

'But there must be some crooks in the business,' I said, 'who'll try and fake clubs and balls.'

'Maybe,' Goodison replied. 'But the difficulties outweigh the rewards, I think. If you try to make an iron club, you've got the problem of ageing the material. The effect of ageing is random and therefore almost impossible to fake. If you find an old iron tool, a billhook let's say, you might be able to shape a clubhead from it and get away with it. But it would be a difficult process. And for what reward?'

'You tell us,' Toby suggested.

Goodison shuffled through a catalogue. 'Oh, fifteen hundred quid for something rare like a rake iron. You'd be better off trying to fake some Hugh Philp woods. But wood and other organic matter can be dated. The Carbon 14 test. But the process is fallible, so you'd stand a chance and Philp woods can go for several thousand at auction.'

'What about golf balls?'

'Featheries would be the best bet. Again, you'd have to find someone very skilled to make them. It's a painstaking process but the rewards are considerable if a top name's on the ball.'

'Allan Robertson or Tom Morris,' Toby said.

'Yes, or John Gourlay or Thomas Alexander. They both came from Musselburgh. But if I was going to do some forgeries, I'd do paintings. Not watercolours but oils because they're easier to fake.'

'Or go into the theft business and flog the ill-gotten objects abroad,' Toby said.

'You're still worrying away at that theory, are you, Toby?' Goodison said. 'I really don't think it'll get you anywhere. I'm sure my assistant, Jonathan, was right to say that those thefts were the work of a few yobs who saw the clubhouses as soft targets.'

'You know, I suppose, that those yobs put the steward at Royal Dorset into hospital, do you?' Toby said sombrely. 'He's in intensive care.'

'That's terrible,' Goodison said.

'Yes. Anyway, indulge my fantasies for a moment, Harry. If the booty went abroad, where would it go?'

'Honestly, Toby, I wouldn't have a clue. You know as well as I do where the golf markets are. America, Japan, Australia and one or two other parts. I'm an auctioneer, so I know the dealers and, yes, one or two of them sail close to the wind. But I wouldn't categorize any of them as crooked, I assure you. When you meet some of them, you'll see that. Poynton's are holding an auction just before the PGA Championship. Speak to Charlie Ito. He knows the Japanese market inside out and he's very knowledgeable. Then there's Julius Kincaid from Boston. He'll be there because Poynton's have got some good stuff in their sale. Talk to him, too, Toby.'

Toby nodded and Goodison rose to his feet. 'I've got some catalogues together for you but they're in Jonathan's office. I won't be a moment.'

As Goodison rose to his feet, so did I and stretched my legs and arms. 'Sorry, I've been in the cold and the rain all day. I'm getting a bit stiff.' He nodded and made his way to the door. I took my chance and walked swiftly round to his side of the desk. I had no idea what I was looking for, I was merely aware that people sometimes left remarkably confidential material lying around in their offices. Maybe there was something that would help Toby's investigations. The ace reporter himself was looking nervous and darting anxious glances at the door. Papers covered every square inch of Goodison's desk and seemed to be the normal mixture of correspondence, telephone messages, memos from other people in Goodison's firm, and invoices.

Harry's desk diary lay open and I saw his meeting with Toby listed. There were notes and reminders at the top of the page. We both heard the auctioneer returning along the corridor and Toby gestured urgently in my direction. I just had time to register one item, which was starred in red ink – 'Speak WW re diaries.' It was obviously important to Harry Goodison, even if it was meaningless to me.

Jonathan Wright was in Goodison's wake and stood just inside the doorway while he gave Toby a bundle of catalogues and magazines. Wright was wearing an expensive-looking grey suit, a pale green shirt and a colourful tie. A pair of black loafer shoes with tassels completed the ensemble. His nod of greeting towards me and Toby was so brief as to be almost imperceptible. He did not speak.

'Here we are,' Goodison said to Toby. 'These will help you on current values.' He remained standing. 'Jonathan and I are late for a meeting with a client, Toby, so I hope you'll forgive me.'

The receptionist had already appeared in the doorway and she led us down the labyrinth of corridors and stairs to the front door.

Our cars were parked side by side and Toby paused by his and said, 'What did you make of that?'

'Your pal Goodison wasn't as forthcoming as I'd hoped. In fact, he was quite eager to get rid of us.'

74

'Especially when Mister Wright came on the scene. He seems a bit sensitive when the conversation turns to fakes or forgeries, doesn't he?'

'Just like Sir Nicholas Welbeck,' I said. 'He put me down sharply when I had the temerity to mention Tom Keating.'

'I read about a London art-dealer the other day,' Toby said reflectively, 'who estimates that at least fifty per cent of all works of art which come on the market are of questionable authenticity.'

'No wonder that the likes of Goodison and Welbeck get sniffy about fakes, then. They're in the antiques business so they have to defend its integrity or the punters will get anxious and then their business will be in the mire.'

'I see that, of course. But usually old Harry is very up-front, very chatty. But now he almost seems to defer to that slime-bag, Wright. And Harry is the boss, after all.'

'He's obviously grooming Wright to take over.'

'God help the firm then. I'll see you at the Catesby tomorrow, young man.'

'You don't fancy a beer when we get back to London?'

'Better not. I've got to go out.' Toby looked a little furtive.

'An assignation? Perhaps some bridge-mending with the beautiful Isobel?'

'That's my business,' Toby said, as he heaved himself into his car.

# *Chapter 10*

Despite one or two wobbles during the early part of the final round, Jake's resolution held fast over the closing stretch of the Catesby Classic. On the last day the dreary onslaughts from the rain at last ceased and there was a consequent improvement in the scoring. Jake had a splendid finish, three birdies in the last five holes, and this gave him a share of tenth position.

Smiling broadly as he looked at his cheque, which gave him prize money of well over £10,000 and me a very nice bonus of just under a thousand, Jake confirmed that he wanted me to caddie for him in the PGA Championship which began in less than three weeks.

I helped him take his various bags over to his Mercedes and he said, 'That was a good week's work, Chris, and we could have many more. We make a good team, my old son.'

I thanked him and he reached into the recesses of the car's boot and pulled out several old golf clubs. He eyed them for a moment and handed me one. 'It's yours,' he said. 'An extra bonus. It's a niblick, as you can see, by Forgan. It's not worth a lot but it's a nice example. I do a little sideline in old clubs. Stick it on your office wall.'

Jake slammed the boot shut, waved a farewell and eased the big car towards the exit. I looked at my unexpected gift. It had a large head, with holes punched into the face. Forgan's name and the Prince of Wales feathers had been stamped on the back. The club had been reshafted, as it would have been on several occasions during its playing days. It was a nice gesture by Jake, who seemed to have a generous nature.

During the night a thunderstorm, complete with full sound effects, jagged spears of lightning and torrents of rain, woke me. I watched its dramatics for some time through my bedroom window and hoped that the storm was localized and had missed Royal Dorset. We had recently rebuilt two of the greens in their entirety. What kept me awake, apart from the storm above west London, was the dire thought that the two layers of topsoil, which had only been seeded a few days before, might be washed away.

I gave up trying to sleep shortly after five o'clock and made myself a mug of tea. An hour later I was in my car and heading for the Dorset coast. In the relatively light traffic I was outside the clubhouse in about ninety minutes. I had begun to fear the worst as soon as I left the main roads. The narrow country lanes showed clear evidence of the nocturnal downpour; ditches were filled with water and the road surfaces were obscured by floodwater and patches of mud.

I dived into my office, donned some Wellington boots and headed for the thirteenth and fifteenth greens. They lay less than a hundred yards apart and, at first glance, looked as though they had made a determined effort to merge. The head greenkeeper, Dave Gray, was already examining the damage. Like many people whose work depended on the vagaries of nature, Dave was a pessimist.

He shook his head gloomily as we exchanged greetings. 'Another two or three weeks and we might have been OK,' he said. 'What a bastard. We'll have to start again.'

'We'll get the contractors in,' I reassured him. 'The basics are still there. It's just a matter of rescuing as much topsoil as we can, contouring the greens to the same pattern and re-seeding.'

Dave grunted. 'It'll put the programme back by weeks. And I'll get all the moans and groans from the members.'

'We all have our crosses to bear,' I said. 'I'll go and see the Secretary and let her know the extent of the damage.'

'I hope the insurance policies are all in place,' Dave muttered.

Anxious to get the renovation of the greens under way as soon as possible, I strode off in the direction of the clubhouse. I was able to look more closely at the damage caused by the sudden and fierce downpour. No drainage system could have coped. There was flooding in many places and streams of water had gouged out great channels in some of the bunkers. Several gravel paths had had their top surfaces ripped away and deposited elsewhere.

Halfway up the first fairway I spotted Helen walking briskly towards me, her green Wellington boots flapping under her loose tweed skirt.

'What's the damage?' she asked without preamble.

'Plenty, but the real disasters are to the new greens.'

'Washed away?'

'Afraid so. Dave is already worried about the insurance.'

'It's all in place,' Helen said, 'but undoubtedly not enough of it. The last Secretary scrimped on the premiums.'

'So the members will have to make up the difference?'

Helen shrugged. 'We've got money in reserve but not much. I'll catch you later.'

# Chapter 11

Over the next couple of weeks I had to devote myself to my job at Royal Dorset. It is always frustrating to have work you have already done suddenly undone and I had to make a real effort to motivate myself to tackle the new and unwanted problems which the storm had caused. I deliberately pushed the question of the search for Mrs Bradshaw's absconding tenant to a dusty corner of my mind. I hoped that she would abandon her thoughts of revenge and let me off the hook.

The thefts of the golfing treasures seemed to be a dead issue, too, despite Toby's efforts in the *Daily News* to keep it alive. In one article, he attacked the police for 'lack of action on a matter of public concern'. It's always a popular move to have a go at the upholders of law and order but, in the context of a bloody civil war in central Europe, Britain's continuing economic malaise and the leadership crisis within the Conservative Party, the theft of a few paintings and some old golf clubs was certainly not a matter of urgent public interest.

The death of the Royal Dorset Golf Club's steward, however, put new urgency into the affair. Helen called into my office one morning to tell me that Mike had never recovered consciousness. An inquiry into a series of robberies had become a murder hunt.

\* \* \*

81

I had promised to carry Jake's clubs at the PGA Championship which was scheduled for a new course in Oxfordshire, built at enormous expense by a Japanese consortium. On the Monday of that week, Toby called to remind me that I had agreed to join him at an auction of golfing memorabilia to be held at the Fairway Hotel near Oxford on the day before the tournament began.

'I'll buy you lunch in Oxford,' he said grandly.

'At Le Manoir?' I teased him, mentioning one of the most sumptuous restaurants in Britain.

'My dear boy, I can't run to that.'

'Toby, I'm really short of time. I'm caddying for Jake at the PGA and I must play fair and do a couple of practice rounds with him. I don't know the course at all.'

'It's an easy track,' Toby said dismissively. 'The auction's on Wednesday and I'm sure you can persuade Jake to practise in the morning.'

'Well . . .'

'Come on, Chris, I'm meeting Charlie Ito at the auction and you did promise to lend me your help. It could be a big story.'

'I don't see why you're so keen. The death of poor old Mike has turned it into a nasty affair. Surely it should be left to the police.'

'Perish the thought. It may've become a dirty business but my instincts tell me that there are some juicy ramifications to it. If I can uncover them, I'll not only have a bloody good story for the *News* but also a diverting tailpiece to my book.'

'Now we get to your real motivation,' I said. 'OK, but I'm glad that there's no pro-am on Wednesday because Jake would've insisted on my being around.' The PGA Championship was regarded as too important to merit the distractions of a pro-am and it had been dropped some years before.

'You know my opinion of pro-ams,' Toby sniffed. 'A circus for jaded has-beens from showbiz and fat businessmen in unsuitable clothing who couldn't hit a donkey's arse with a banjo, let alone a golf ball with the appropriate club. They make a mockery of the game.'

'You've suddenly become rather puritan, Toby. Quite the Bernard Darwin, eh?'

'I'll find you at the course on Wednesday,' Toby said sharply and put down the phone.

Wednesday's practice round was slow. The professionals were trying to assess the course and plot their way around it before battle commenced on the following day and the caddies were checking and re-checking the measurements of the course and the lines on the greens. I had to admit that Jake was more relaxed about the process than some of the golfers for whom I had worked in the past. I was determined, however, that I would have every detail of the course at my beck and call, and as many of its nuances as I could manage in the available time.

It was nearly one o'clock before Jake putted out on the final green. From the verandah of the clubhouse, Toby waved anxiously at me. The auction began at two o'clock and I knew that he wanted to corner Charlie Ito, who was leaving for New York on the following day.

Jake was aware that I needed to leave promptly and told me not to hang about. 'See you tomorrow at eight,' he said. He was due to start his round at 8.30.

'Is that enough time to warm up?'

'It doesn't take a Roller long to warm up, my son,' he said cheerfully. 'If I don't know how to hit it now, I won't learn from an extra hour on the practice ground, will I?'

His relaxed attitude suited me and I hastened in Toby's direction. He bustled towards me, handed me a paper bag and said, 'We'll have to skip lunch. This will keep the wolf from the door. A salmon sandwich on brown bread.'

'Courtesy of the sponsor?'

'Of course. Now, come on, I don't want to miss Charlie Ito.'

It took us a little more than half an hour to travel to the Fairway Hotel, an agreeable modern building of deep-red brick and timber on the outskirts of Oxford. A large number of people filled the entrance hall and the lounges. We made our way to the Grosvenor Suite where Poynton's sale was to take place.

'Can you see an eighteen stone, five feet tall Japanese gentleman?' Toby muttered to me. 'He said I couldn't miss him.'

'No, I'll bet. Did he say he'd be carrying a Poynton's catalogue?'

'Very funny. But keep a look out for him, please.'

We both did but there was nobody at the auction who remotely resembled Charlie Ito's description of himself.

The large room, its lofty ceiling distinguished by a splendid chandelier, was packed with people. Every seat was taken, its occupant's attention already focused on the auctioneer's rostrum at the far end; on either side, trestle-tables were stacked with a variety of golf clubs. Halfway along the room six girls and a couple of young men, each equipped with a telephone, sat behind a table.

Toby and I stood behind the last rank of chairs, and, as two o'clock approached, the standing room began to fill at our backs.

'Nearly six hundred items,' Toby said, brandishing his catalogue.

'They'll have to move along fast to shift them, won't they?'

'They do. And you'll notice that when the important pieces come up, there'll be only two or three people in the bidding. That's when they get into the act.' Toby gestured towards the people with the telephones. 'They're acting on behalf of overseas dealers or for bidders who want to remain anonymous.'

'Museums?'

'Could be, or rich individuals who might only be interested in one item.'

On the dot of two o'clock, the auctioneer, a thin, bespectacled man in a dark suit, mounted the rostrum, greeted us all, and began the sale. His resonant voice gave him an air of authority and he rattled through the early items. Miscellaneous and unnamed clubs were knocked out at a great pace, the process helped by the auctioneer's familiarity with the names of many of the bidders.

The sale of a John Gray lofting-iron provoked a flurry of activity and it eventually went for nearly a thousand pounds. We only noticed Welbeck in the front row when the auctioneer referred to 'Sir Nicholas' and we then picked out his fine head of silver hair. He dropped out of the bidding for the lofting-iron early.

'What a creep,' Toby muttered and then, 'Where the hell is Charlie Ito?'

However, Welbeck did stay with the bidding to acquire two patent rake-irons for nearly two thousand pounds apiece. His main opposition was an American sitting by the wall not far away from us. A pair of square-shaped, rimless glasses perched on his prominent nose. His head was almost totally bald, except for a few wisps of white hair above his ears. He could have been any age between fifty and seventy because his pink face was virtually unlined, but I was to learn later that he was nearer eighty than seventy. For much of the time that I observed him he had his arm around a slim dark-haired woman in a dark green dress which hugged her figure. And it was well worth hugging. The auctioneer acknowledged a decisive bid for a Forgan long spoon to Mr Kincaid.

'Julius Kincaid,' Toby said in my ear. 'A big-time collector from America, as you can tell from his clothing. I was told he might be here.'

'Is that his wife?'

'No idea. But it if is, it's probably not the first Mrs Julius Kincaid.'

As I studied the American couple again, the woman looked around the room, caught my eye and grinned at me. Wide eyes, a lightly tanned skin and a generous mouth with bright red lipstick. Yes, she had all the right attributes. No wonder Mr Kincaid kept a protective arm around her. I grinned back.

Kincaid was in action again when a Wilson putter was offered for sale. It didn't look special to me, until the auctioneer said, 'This is the putter used by Sam Snead when he won the first Open after the Second World War, St Andrews in 1946.'

'Oh yeah,' I began cynically.

'And we have a letter from Mr Snead which confirms the authenticity of the club.'

'Provenance,' Toby said, 'it's got provenance.'

Some brisk bidding took the price up to £800 and then everyone dropped out except Welbeck and Kincaid. The American bought the putter for £1550.

'Sir Nicholas won't like it,' Toby said happily.

Welbeck liked it even less when Kincaid acquired six woods made by Hugh Philp for not far short of £20,000. The most expensive was a play club with a lovely shallow head made of dark brown thornwood – a work of art in its own right. It was obvious, even to someone unversed in the auction process, that

Kincaid was determined to buy those clubs, whatever the opposition.

'Twenty grand is just loose change to him,' Toby said. We saw the American get up and move towards the exit. He was a tall man, well over six feet in height, and towered above his companion. 'Come on,' Toby said urgently, 'I want to talk to him. Since we've had a no-show from Ito, he'll do very well as a substitute.'

Intercepting the Americans near the exit, Toby produced a business card from his pocket with a flourish and said, 'Mr Kincaid, may I introduce myself? Toby Greenslade, chief golf writer on the *Daily News*.'

After introductions all round, which established that his wife – 'my little lady' – was called Amy, Toby asked if he could make an appointment.

'Now's fine with me,' Kincaid replied. 'Let's go and have some of your famous English tea.'

'I'd been hoping to talk to Charlie Ito,' Toby said, when we had all settled in a corner of the hotel lounge. The Kincaids, hand in hand, occupied a sofa. 'But he hasn't turned up yet.'

'And real grateful I was for that small mercy,' Kincaid said. 'No way would I've got those Philps so cheap if old Charlie had been around. He's my keenest rival for stuff like that. An interesting guy. I've never fathomed him, though, have I, hon?'

'You don't have to, darling,' Amy said as she squeezed his hand and smiled. Her husband obviously loved the attention she gave him and I couldn't fault his judgement.

'What about Sir Nicholas Welbeck?' I asked. 'How do you get on with him?'

'Are you in the golf business, Chris?' Amy asked and gave me the full wattage of her smile.

'Not on the antiques side. I work for a golf architect.' I told them about my current work at Royal Dorset.

'Trent Jones is a real close friend of mine,' Kincaid said. 'A great designer, don't you think?'

'Well, I, er . . .'

Toby saved me from a white lie by interrupting. 'You were going to tell us about Welbeck, Mr Kincaid.'

'Julius, please, call me Julius. Sir Nicholas, yes. Say, did he buy that title?'

'No, he's the real thing,' Toby said, laughing. 'He inherited the baronetcy from his father.'

'But he ain't gonna pass it on, is he?' Amy said.

'No, but he has a younger brother who'll inherit if Sir Nicholas dies without issue,' Toby said.

'And we can safely assume that,' Julius said. 'I see him around all the auctions. Real smooth, sets himself up as the number-one pundit but I think he's a big bag of wind. I won't deal with him any more.'

A waiter arrived with tea and a selection of sandwiches, scones with cream and jam, and fruit cake.

'I love teatime,' Amy said, as she piled a plate with sandwiches.

Julius gave the waiter a note and waved away the change.

'Shall I be mother?' Toby said, as he laid out four cups and began to pour the tea. Amy giggled.

'Why won't you deal with Welbeck?' I asked.

Kincaid sipped at his tea and said, 'I really don't trust him. I have my reasons but it wouldn't be fair to get into all that at present.'

'You heard about the robberies over here?' Toby asked.

'Sure. Very sad. That Francis Grant painting was a fine piece of work. And, of course, in a golfing context it was invaluable.'

'Julius, I have a theory,' Toby said. 'All those antiques and paintings were stolen to order and are probably out of the country by now. What do you think?'

'Well, I haven't got any of 'em, have I, hon?' He laughed loudly. 'It's an interesting theory, but perhaps a journalist's theory. Don't think me rude, Toby. There are some unscrupulous dealers around but I can't think of anyone who'd have the balls to organise a hit on three golf clubs in one night. If you find him, Toby, I'd sure as hell like an introduction.'

Amy nudged her husband. 'Come on, darling, we must get back to our hotel. Time for your afternoon sleep.'

Kincaid stood up, and produced a sheet of paper from his jacket pocket. 'Here's my itinerary, Toby. I'd like to talk some more. Call me any time. And you're at Royal Dorset, Chris, is that right? I'll be in touch. Amy and I'd like to play the course. Give my regards to Charlie Ito when you catch up with him.' With a wave Kincaid headed for the door, still hand in hand with Amy.

'"Once in love with Amy, always in love with Amy",' Toby crooned softly.

'Can you blame him. What a body,' I said.

'Yes, quite. And an age difference of about forty years. Ain't love grand? I'm going to check if Ito's arrived at the auction yet.'

When Toby rejoined me in the entrance hall, he shook his head and made for a telephone. 'No answer from his apartment,' he said gloomily a few moments later. 'Let's get back to London. We'll knock on his door. You never know your luck.'

# Chapter 12

Under Toby's direction I parked the car in a Bayswater side street. We walked back to the main road and Toby indicated a modern building. Each of the flats at the front had a long balcony overlooking Kensington Gardens.

'Nice view,' I said.

'Especially for Charlie. He's got the penthouse.'

We strolled through the glass doors and towards the reception desk. A middle-aged man in a blue uniform was watching a repeat of *Cheers*.

He dragged his eyes away from the television momentarily when Toby said that he'd come to see Mr Ito. The man's thumb jerked towards the lift doors. 'Sixth floor, chum. Turn left. Penthouse A.' His gaze returned to the small screen.

'You simply can't get the staff,' said Toby as we headed for the lift.

The door of the penthouse was substantial and had a spyhole in its centre. Neither a ring on the doorbell nor a bang on the door brought any response. There was no letter-box through which to peer.

Toby shrugged. 'There's no future here. Let's go to a pub.'

'Hang on.' I reached in my trouser pocket. Attached to my keyring was a cylindrical piece of silver. When I twisted one end, a pointed piece of metal, nearly an inch in length, protruded. It was a toothpick but my brother, Max, had shown me how to put it to other uses – to pick locks, for example. It was easy to circumvent a conventional lock though I couldn't handle a proper mortise. It was worth a try.

As I stuck the pick in the lock and began to manoeuvre it, Toby shifted uncomfortably. 'Chris, er, there's no point. If he's not here . . .'

'If he's not here, we might just as well have a look around.' If Toby was on the track of a story, I was ready to enter into the spirit of the chase. I fancied a nose around anyway.

There was a click and I pushed the door open. 'Someone's left the door open, Toby.'

We walked softly into a large oblong hallway with several gilt tables against the walls, some formal chairs in a similar style and two armchairs upholstered in white leather. A number of oil paintings in heavy frames decorated the walls. A corridor ran off to the left and a pair of double doors faced us. Two large suitcases lay on the floor, their contents strewn hither and thither.

'Was he packing or unpacking?' I asked. My voice sounded very loud in the unnatural quiet. For once, Toby said nothing.

I pointed at the double doors and he nodded. I knocked politely and waited. I tried again. 'Hello. Is there anyone home?' Gingerly I eased open the doors and stepped into a room whose huge picture windows looked over the lush terrain of the royal park. The view was worth a million quid of anyone's money.

Charlie Ito had obviously been sitting looking at it when he fell asleep. I could make out the top of his head, scantily covered with thin strands of grey hair, as he slumbered in a tan-coloured leather armchair. He was so fat that his body overhung the chair on both sides.

Toby had stopped just inside the door but I moved quietly

towards the Japanese dealer. There was a stillness about him which made the skin of my face feel suddenly cold. As I reached out to nudge him gently awake, I saw the rich and random patterns of red on his white silk shirt. When I stepped in front of him I saw the blood on the floor. His left ear had been cut away from his head and was hanging, like a piece of raw pork, over his neck. Judging by the rips in his shirt he had been stabbed several times in the stomach and under the heart. His wrists were resting in his lap, tightly bound with wire, as were his ankles. Four of his fingers were unnaturally askew, broken prior to his death. No wonder his face was twisted in a final unnerving rictus of agony. Poor old Charlie Ito had done his last deal.

Toby hadn't moved from his position by the door. 'What's happened?' he asked, his voice hoarse with foreboding.

'You'd better see for yourself. It's not pretty,' I warned.

His face suddenly paler than usual, Toby advanced across the carpet. I felt as bad as he looked but, to his credit as a journalist, Toby fumbled a small notebook from his pocket and walked slowly towards the corpse. He peered past me and muttered, 'God Almighty. Who could've done a thing like that?'

'Whoever it was, I don't want to bump into him in a dark alley. The sick bastards tortured him before they finished him off.'

Busily writing in shorthand, Toby grunted. 'What should we do?'

'Only one thing we can do. Call the police.'

'I suppose you're right,' Toby said doubtfully. 'They'll have quite a few leading questions for us, won't they? Why were we here? How did we get in? It won't be pleasant.'

'There's no alternative, Toby. The doorman will probably

remember us anyway, even though his few brain cells were concentrated on the telly.'

'I've got one hell of a story here and I want to write it.'

'In which case you'll have to sit tight and go through the wringer with the police. Not that there's a problem – we can account for our movements throughout the day. He must have been killed some hours ago. Look at the blood. It's dried up quite a bit.'

The fearless reporter shuddered. 'I'd rather not, if it's all the same to you. You'd better dial nine-nine-nine, hadn't you?'

'After I've had a look around.'

'Do be careful, Chris. Surely you should leave that to the boys in blue.' Toby moved nervously into the middle of the room. 'There's a phone over there.'

'Give me two minutes,' I said.

With a handkerchief wrapped around my right hand I went through another set of double doors into a dining room. It also looked over the park and a huge oak table ran down its centre. A dozen elaborately carved wooden chairs were stationed around it. A cupboard, filled with a variety of silver plates, serving dishes, jugs and goblets, was undisturbed, as was a dresser displaying sets of ornate china. A sideboard was covered with bottles of spirits.

Careful to use only the hand protected by my handkerchief, I passed through a door into the main corridor, glanced briefly into a large and tidy kitchen and then went into the first room which led off the corridor. It was a guest bedroom and was in pristine order, as was the adjoining bathroom. Next door was an office with a photocopier, a small filing-cabinet and a desk with a telephone and a fax machine. The in-tray of the fax was empty and the telephone answering machine was switched off.

The drawers of the cabinet had been opened and several

files had been taken out, rifled and then thrown on to the floor. I recognized a Poynton's catalogue. I bent down and carefully turned the pages. Some of the items were marked, particularly the Hugh Philp long-nose woods which had been bought by Kincaid. Someone, and I assumed it was Charlie Ito, had put prices alongside the auctioneer's estimates. They looked like Ito's own assessments of what he might have to pay. It was obvious that he had intended to be at the auction and that Kincaid would have had strong opposition.

Some of the drawers from the desk had also been searched. I wondered what the killer had been seeking and whether he had found it. I poked at some of the documents on the floor with my foot but, since I didn't know what I was looking for, soon gave up. There was nothing useful like an address book or a diary lying around – not that I expected it.

The master bedroom next door had been trashed. Clothes from the two large chests had been thrown over the bed and onto the floor and the fitted wardrobes had also been half emptied. Jackets and trousers, suits in a variety of patterns and colours, dozens of cream silk shirts were strewn about. I looked around briefly, glanced at the bathroom and headed back to the living room.

Toby was sitting in an armchair well away from Ito's corpse. 'Well?'

'Nothing. I'll dial the emergency number. There are plenty of silk shirts in Ito's bedroom if you want to add to your wardrobe, but nothing else of interest that I can see.'

Toby attempted a smile. 'You could fit two of me into one of Charlie's shirts.' He shook his head dolefully, though it was good to see that his face had recovered some of its normal robust colour. 'Who could've done this?' he said quietly. 'It's so . . . so brutal. Was it some yobs, do you think, who assumed there'd be plenty of cash in a place like this?'

'Why would Ito have let them in? Even that doorman would've noticed that something was wrong if a couple of hooligans came calling. No, it doesn't have any of the hallmarks of a random hit for cash to buy drugs or whatever. I'm convinced that Ito knew the killer or killers and let them in. They were looking for something and tried to torture the information out of the poor sod. They went through all his files and other papers. What we don't know is whether they found what they were looking for.'

I told Toby about the Poynton's catalogue. 'He certainly meant to be at the auction. The police should be made aware of that.'

The emergency services went into action with a will when I told them I'd found a dead body. It was no more than a few minutes before we heard the sound of sirens approaching along the Bayswater Road.

The tortuous business of being interviewed by the police and of making a formal statement took even longer than I had anticipated. The detective-sergeant who questioned me was intensely interested in how we had gained access to the flat. I stuck to my story that the door had been left on the latch and had yielded to a mere push on my part. A dark and thin-faced man, with pronounced bags under his eyes and the sort of bandido moustache that went out of fashion in the seventies, he countered my explanation with a look of amused scepticism and a shake of his head. I hoped that Toby was sticking to the same story.

Sergeant Hopkins seemed to lose interest when I gave him a full account of where I'd been and with whom during that day.

'I suppose your mate, the journo, will confirm all this?' I nodded. 'And we can contact these other people?' I nodded again. 'That probably lets you off the hook, then.' He seemed annoyed by the thought. 'Probably some junkies from down the road,' he jerked his head in the direction of west London. 'They keep a look-out for rich bastards. A fat nip like him would've made an ideal target.' Hopkins obviously hadn't yet got around to attending any political correctness courses.

He snapped shut his notebook and warned me that I'd be required again.

## Chapter 13

The front page of next day's edition of the *Daily News* did not even carry the story of Ito's death. Instead, it was taken up by the lurid revelations of a woman who claimed to have supplied drugs and 'very special' services to a number of MPs, showbiz personalities and even some minor royals.

The surprisingly restrained headline above Toby's report on an inside page read, 'Japanese art dealer's mysterious death' and, contrary to the tabloid newspaper's usual style, Toby's part in the discovery was not mentioned. The account was brief and factual. I guessed that Toby felt anxious about our enforced entry to the apartment and wanted to play down his role in the affair for the time being.

I was able to linger in my flat because Jake Bowden had drawn a late starting time, just after three o'clock, for his first round in the PGA Championship. It wouldn't worry him but I knew many other pros who, under the same circumstances, would curse their bad luck and complain that all the other players would have trampled over the greens and left spike marks around the holes – so how could they be expected to putt in such conditions? They'd moan that the round would be played so slowly they would run out of daylight over the last few holes and wouldn't be able to see properly. All they'd succeed in doing was talking themselves out of playing well.

However, such a start suited me because it gave me the opportunity to wander around the course and chat to a few friends. One of my pleasures was the tented village where you could look at the latest equipment, all of which was pretty much guaranteed to improve your game by several strokes a round. It was fantasy time again and I surrendered to it.

Near the entrance to the massive tent I narrowly escaped being run down by a remote-controlled caddie cart and then I was confronted by an Aladdin's Cave of golfing equipment. As well as the manufacturers of clubs and balls, shoes and clothing, caddie carts and buggies, there were travel companies promoting a dazzling choice of exotic golfing destinations, time-share operators offering unrepeatable bargains and several stalls heaped with golf books and videos. Most of the golf magazines were represented and, to my surprise, so was Sir Nicholas Welbeck. His stand was in a corner of the tent, with his name in discreet lettering above it. Everything was understated. At the back of the stand there was one display case which held about twenty antique clubs in a fan shape. A selection of ancient golf balls, both featheries and gutties, had been placed between the clubs. The only item of furniture, apart from two uncomfortable-looking chairs with spindly legs, was an antique desk, behind which sat a man of about my age; I assumed that he was one of Welbeck's assistants. Sitting bolt upright, his gaze settled in the middle distance, he was as elegantly attired as I remembered Welbeck to have been. I recognized the Old Wykehamist tie, but only because one of my former colleagues at Norton Buccleuth used to wear it every day of his working life.

I strolled on to the stand to look at the display.

Moments later I felt his presence at my elbow. I turned as he said, 'They're not for sale, sir. They're from Sir Nicholas's own collection.' He offered me his hand. 'I'm Jamie Tilden, Sir Nicholas Welbeck's assistant.'

Like his employer, Tilden had a drawl in his voice. Although he was my height I had the distinct impression that he was doing his best to look down on me. Two can play at that game – I made my back as straight as I could and raised my chin slightly.

'So, if you're not selling anything, why are you here?' I asked innocently.

'Sir Nicholas likes to maintain a presence at some of the major tournaments. He is *the* authority on golfing art and antiques.'

'He's a dealer, is he?'

'No, sir. We advise a limited number of clients on investing in golf artefacts. We do valuations, of course, and Sir Nicholas knows the whereabouts of virtually every significant work of golfing art in the world. In fact he probably knows the owner personally.'

'Could he lay his hands on those paintings that were nicked from Royal Dorset and Winterbourne, then?'

The merest flicker of a smile frosted Tilden's handsome features. He sauntered over to the desk, opened a drawer and returned with a booklet in his hand. The cover showed a painting of a golfer in a red jacket and the border was trimmed in dark green and gold.

'This will tell you about Sir Nicholas and the services we can offer, sir. Thank you for dropping in.'

Although politely phrased, it was a dismissal and I saw no reason to stay, especially when I looked down one of the aisles and thought I recognized Laura Stocker. Her company was infinitely preferable to that of the supercilious Jamie Tilden. I walked slowly towards her. Yes, it was the same lissom figure and she was wearing a pair of black jeans, as when I'd last seen her. She was talking animatedly to someone on the stand. I saw the glint of the stud in her nose as she turned her head. A couple of cameras slung around her neck suggested that she was on an assignment of some kind.

I had thought about her in vaguely lascivious terms on several occasions since our first encounter. I had wondered whether to try and contact her. Toby's strictures about her being involved with some man in the City had put me off; I didn't want any complications. Anyway, here was my chance to establish to my own satisfaction whether the complications would be worthwhile.

I walked on to the stand, which belonged to one of the golf magazines, and said cheerfully, 'Hello, Laura. We met at . . .'

'Royal Dorset,' she finished for me, with a smile. 'You're Chris. A friend of the lovely Toby.'

I hadn't heard Toby described as lovely before and I smiled back. We stood there for several moments, grinning at each other like a couple of shy adolescents.

'Are you working on something here?' I asked at last.

'For the magazine.' She nodded at the woman to whom she'd been talking. 'This is Jilly Holland, the features editor. I'm doing a piece for her – "a day in the life of a tournament". I'll catch you later, darling.' She fluttered a kiss in Jilly's direction, clasped me by the arm and said, 'Let's have a cup of coffee, shall we?'

'I've just got time,' I said. 'I'm due on the practice tee in ten minutes.'

As we drank our cups of grey and insipid coffee at a nearby refreshment booth, I explained that I had a second occupation as a professional caddie. A few minutes later she had agreed to have dinner with me that evening and I had agreed that I would accompany her to a gig at a west London theatre first.

'It's a sixties revival evening,' Laura said. 'Get your bopping gear on.'

'I'll borrow some from Toby.'

Jake had one of those infuriating days when he might have recorded an exceptional score; a bit of luck early in the round could have seen him finish at four or five strokes under par. Maybe he was nervous because he was in the same group as one of Europe's leading golfers, a taciturn Scot who spoke only to his own caddie. Such was the density of their accents that I gave up trying to interpret their remarks. When Jake stood at one over par on the seventeenth tee and pushed his tee shot perilously close to an out-of-bounds fence on the right side of the fairway, I feared the worst. However, his ball lay just in bounds and in a reasonably good lie. A few feet either side and he would have been in thick heather and reaching for a wedge with which to hack back to the fairway.

The green lay 280 yards away on the par-five hole. I handed Jake a five-iron. With a quiet punt up the fairway, followed by a short iron to the green, a birdie was still a possibility. Shaking his head, Jake said, 'Give me the three-wood. I can chase it close.'

He sounded confident enough and I had no wish to implant any doubts where none existed.

'Watch this,' Jake said with relish. I could hardly bear to. But Jake hit a wonderful low shot which hooked from right to left, shot through the only opening in a line of bunkers a hundred yards from the green and finished about twenty yards short of the fringe.

'A career shot,' said Jake in an appalling parody of an American accent. 'I nearly over-pured it.'

'Great shot,' I said, with feeling. 'Lousy jargon.'

When we got to the ball I expected Jake to choose one of the three wedges he carried and float the ball up to the hole. Instead he grabbed an eight-iron. 'We need the points,' he said.

He squatted down and surveyed the line of his shot. I walked on to the green and looked at the lie of the ground over the last ten feet. 'It'll run in from the left,' I told him. 'Give it about a foot.'

'Hold the pin, will you, Chris?'

I would have bet even money that he was going to hole that shot. And I would have won. From twenty feet away it looked a certainty and it duly fell into the can from the left side.

'A sodding eagle,' I heard the Scot mutter in disbelief to his caddie.

'Daylight bloody robbery,' the caddie replied. I understood them that time.

Jake's play on that hole saved his round and he finished at one under par; well down the field but with no reason to feel dejected. On the contrary.

# Chapter 14

The Victorian theatre near Shepherd's Bush had seen better days but its sizeable interior was ideal as a pop-music venue. It was pop music with a difference, however, since most of the fans were well into the middle years of their lives; some of them had brought their teenaged children along.

I was thankful that there was a bar at the back of the theatre and, on Laura's instructions, I bought a six-pack of Red Stripe. Laura was wearing what I guessed was a sixties-style dress, close-fitting and with a flared mini-skirt. It showed off her legs to supreme effect; until then I had only seen them encased in jeans.

Four men with grey hair and glasses comprised the first act. They made a deafening noise on their amplified guitars but were quiet compared to the next group, whose American lead singer ('a rock legend' said the posters) wore a wig of some magnificence, in the 'DA' style.

Laura dragged me away from the bar into the main body of the theatre where several couples – male and female, female and female and, in one case, male and male – were jiving.

'Put your beer down,' Laura shouted in my ear, 'we're jiving.'

'I'm not sure I ever learned,' I shouted back.

'Just catch me on the way round,' Laura said confidently. So I did and watched her joyfully wheeling and spinning, strutting and turning. I got giddy as I tried to keep track of her gorgeous legs.

'What did you think of it?' asked Laura later, as we settled into a bistro not far from the theatre.

'It was different and, er, refreshing,' I replied.

'Don't go overboard, Chris.' She laughed at me. 'I love sixties music and some of those old guys can really play.'

'I'm sure they'd be glad to hear that.'

'Don't be stuffy. You're not much older than me but you seem to lead a sheltered life.'

I thought back to breaking into Ito's apartment and finding his body. I said nothing.

'So I'll be good for you,' she continued. That was promising, I thought.

Over the course of the meal I discovered that she'd had a conventional upbringing: boarding school in Surrey and a place at Manchester University to read the history of art. 'I hated it,' Laura said. 'Too constricting. I left after a year. My parents took it well, even though they swallowed hard when I said I wanted to be a professional photographer.'

'Why?'

'I think my dear old mama had visions of my doorstepping politicians and tarts . . .'

'They usually go together.'

'. . . of my doing the paparazzi bit.'

'So you want to be a serious artist?'

'Don't be sarcastic. It can be art, you must know that.'

I nodded and gave her my sincere look.

'Is that your sincere look?' Laura asked, with a smile. 'And are you about to ask me back for coffee?' She arched her eyebrows comically and fingered her nose-stud.

I wondered briefly what had happened to the man in the

City with whom, according to Toby, Laura had a liaison.

As if telepathic, Laura said, 'I'm between engagements, you might say. As long as you're not married . . . well, I know you're not.'

'Because Toby told you.' She nodded and grinned.

'I do have some sixties records back at the flat,' I said. 'My father gave them to me.'

'That'll be fun,' Laura said. 'How about Saturday night? You see, I've got to be at the course tomorrow at five o'clock.' She glanced at her watch. 'Today at five o'clock. I also happen to know that you tee off at eight o'clock.'

'You do your research, don't you?'

Laura shrugged. 'There's no point in rushing. We'll give those records a spin next time.'


The effect of his eagle the previous day stayed with Jake during his second round. Any worries that we might have had about his missing the cut (which is always made at the halfway mark) disappeared when he managed four birdies in the first ten holes. Two more over the closing stretch put him in the clubhouse at seven under par. We guessed that, by the end of the day, he would be in the top half of the field.

When Jake came out of the scorer's trailer after handing in his card, I expected him to head for the practice ground or the putting green. To my surprise he said, 'I'll see you tomorrow. I've got a bit of business to sort out. I always take some punters to the Algarve after Christmas. Forty of 'em and their wives, mostly from the local club. It's a nice little earner and I've got to go over a few details with the travel agent.'

Jake gestured towards a golfer who was heading purposefully towards the practice ground. He was one of the luminaries of the European Tour who had won dozens of tournaments, including a couple of majors. 'Look at him, he's off to beat his brains out on the range. He's got a coach, a fitness trainer, a dietician, a personal manager and a publicist. If I were him, I'd lighten up and relax. I know when my swing's in good nick but he needs seven people to tell him.' Jake clapped me on the shoulder and walked away.

Glad to make an early escape, I began to walk towards the caddies' quarters. A sandwich and a cup of tea was all I needed and then I could return to London and catch up on some of my work for Calvin Blair.

'Over here, Chris.' There was only one voice like that – a unique blend of fruitiness and authority, rather like a good claret. Toby was waving to me from the entrance to the sponsor's tent, a venue from which he rarely strayed. It was his claim that all the best gossip was to be heard in such surroundings.

'My dear boy,' Toby said, 'I have some amusing news for you. Come and have a celebratory glass with me. I see that you coaxed an excellent round out of the old warhorse.'

'Jake is younger than you, Toby,' I pointed out with relish.

'I dare say but he hasn't had my tough life.' He waved at one of the pretty waitresses and, despite the attentions of many other guests who were vying for her services, she walked straight over and filled two glasses with champagne. He has a knack, an invaluable one in such situations.

'Up she goes,' said Toby.

I drank with him. 'You were very modest in your account of Ito's death. I expected rather more journalistic licence. Where was the fearless correspondent battling it out with the sinister forces of evil?'

'That might have been a mistake, dear boy, in the circumstances.' His glass was only half empty but was swiftly replenished by the same attentive waitress.

As the lunchtime crowd arrived in numbers we were hemmed in by a motley collection of journalists, public relations people representing the sponsor, radio and television executives, agents and business managers, equipment manufacturers and administrators from the European Golf Tour. I knew many of them, if only on a nodding basis.

'What are we celebrating?' I asked.

'Sir Nicholas Welbeck's tragic loss.'

'What?'

'His house in Chelsea was burgled in the early hours. Not much was pinched except for half a dozen paintings – including his greatest treasure, a seventeenth-century landscape painting, done by some Dutchman or other. Van der . . . Van Himst?'

'He was a footballer, Toby.'

'Well, never mind. Anyway, it's extremely valuable.'

'How much?'

'The buzz in the press tent says in excess of half a million quid.'

'Bloody hell. If we were supporters of the conspiracy theory, we'd have to tie that theft in with the ones at Royal Dorset and the other clubs, wouldn't we?'

'Yes. It's beginning to look that way.'

'And what about poor old Charlie Ito?' I said. 'Is he connected in some way?'

Toby shrugged and told me to drink up. 'I suggest we start with the obvious. Let's go and interview Jamie Tilden, Welbeck's assistant.'

We weren't the only people to have that idea and there were a dozen journalists on Welbeck's stand when we arrived. Tilden was flushed by his efforts to answer the questions which were being shouted at him.

'Who's the Dutch artist, Jamie?' asked one voice.

'Van der Neer,' Tilden replied.

'Spell it, will you, Jamie?' He did so.

'How much is it worth?'

'Sir Nicholas cannot put a value on it.'

'Come on, give us the ballpark figure. A mill? Two?'

'A conservative estimate would be half a million pounds,' Tilden said. 'But it's only an estimate. The other pictures were also valuable. Two Thomas Hodges, two Frances Powell Hopkins and a Charles Lees.'

'Insured, Jamie?'

'Sir Nicholas will issue a statement later today, gentlemen. That's all I can tell you.'

We watched as some of the journalists tried to extract more information from Tilden but he rebuffed them and, grumbling, they gradually ebbed away from the stand.

As we turned to go, Toby said, 'Let's go and finish our lunch. I can't feel sorry for that pompous arsehole, by the way. Couldn't have happened to a nicer fellow.'

Toby has no idea how far his sonorous tones can carry – well past the distance John Daly can hit a driver by my reckoning. He doesn't do *sotto voce*. Instinctively I looked in Tilden's direction and caught his stony glare. I guessed that if Toby had harboured any faint hopes of obtaining Welbeck's blessing for his book, they'd just been killed stone dead.

# *Chapter 15*

On the following day the newspapers gave full coverage to the burglary at Welbeck's house. One of the broadsheet papers had a front-page photograph which made Welbeck look like one of Britain's foremost ambassadors, or maybe the Governor of the Bank of England. Someone very important, someone with gravitas. The article referred to him as the world's leading authority on golfing art and antiques, and a considerable collector in his own right. Among several quotes from Welbeck was one about his irretrievable loss – the Van der Neer was a work of genius on which a value could not be placed. Whatever the settlement with his insurers, it would not compensate him.

Toby's short piece about the burglary merely referred to Welbeck as a dealer in antiques.

Jake was due to tee off just before midday so I got to the course at ten o'clock, fetched a cup of coffee and went to look at the players on the putting green. It's always interesting to observe new techniques and I noticed that several players had switched to putting with their left hands below their right. The theory was that it gave them more control over the short putts; if they believed it hard enough, then it probably did.

Jack Mason hadn't altered his putting style in ten years, nor his putter, but he had an exceptionally smooth action, just like

Jake. As I chatted briefly to him, I heard the whirr and click of a camera's motor-drive. I turned to see Laura with a Nikon to her eye.

'Caught for posterity,' she said, 'and maybe for the magazine. "Chris Ludlow, course designer and moonlighting caddie shares some technical secrets with Ryder Cup player, Jack Mason." What d'you think?'

'I think your editor will spike it. But I'd like a copy anyway.'

'I'll have it ready for tomorrow night, Chris.' She began to walk away and then said, 'By the way, Toby is looking for you. He seems a little *distrait*.'

'Toby *distrait*?' Jack said. He consulted his watch. 'He can fix that easily. The bars are open.'

'Don't be unkind.'

'Tell me, Chris, why is a beautiful girl like that bothering with a bloke like you?'

'Looks, charm, intelligence.'

Shaking his head in mock-wonder, Jack turned away. He holed six ten-foot putts in succession.

With time to spend before I met Jake on the practice ground I headed in the direction of the press tent. What could have upset Toby's equilibrium?

The tent was quiet since the real action on the course had not yet begun; the main contenders for the championship would begin their rounds after one o'clock. A few journalists were talking on the telephone and others were chatting. Toby tapped away at his lap-top computer.

'Oh, there you are,' he said grumpily as I arrived at his side. 'I've been looking all over the place for you.'

'Well, here I am. This is the last place I'd normally expect to find you,' I said nastily. 'What's the problem? An attack of conscience?'

'The problem, Chris, is that I have already spent two hours today being grilled by our friend, Inspector Rattray. The bastard got me out of bed at seven o'clock. He insisted I went down to the local nick for an interview.'

'Bright lights and rubber hoses?'

Toby ignored my remark. 'His thesis is that I'm the common factor in all this mayhem in the golf antiques business. I visited the three clubs that were turned over, I knew precisely what they owned, how much the good stuff was worth and where it was located in each clubhouse. Unfortunately, I was also present when Charlie Ito's body was found. Thanks to you. As I said at the time, we should've kept well clear of Ito's apartment.' I recalled that the visit was Toby's idea but facts don't usually bother a journalist.

'If you're on the track of a big story, you have to take risks.'

'Maybe. But Rattray thinks I know more about those thefts than I've admitted. Not only that but he accused me of being implicated in the robbery at Welbeck's house.'

'He's having you on.'

'That's OK then,' Toby said with heavy sarcasm. 'But you didn't have to sit through all the questions and nasty innuendoes. "I expect you're a bit short of money, Mr Greenslade, aren't you? What with two ex-wives to support." All that bullshit that coppers go in for.'

'It's conjecture, Toby.'

'Quite. And have a guess at who's stirring it up.'

'Sir Nicholas Welbeck, baronet?'

'Exactly. Rattray is apparently in charge of all these investigations, though he was careful to tell me that he's liaising with a special Art and Antiques Squad at New Scotland Yard.'

'Three men and a dog, or so I read the other day. They clear

113

up less then ten per cent of their cases.'

'Rattray told me that he'd had a long interview with Welbeck. A very interesting interview. Apparently Welbeck emphasized, on several occasions, the coincidence that I'd visited those three clubs in the last six weeks or so. He also said that I'd been badgering him for access to his collection. Now, that's a bloody lie.'

'Well, you did ask for it, Toby.'

'Who? Me?'

'You referred to Welbeck as a pompous arsehole.'

'I said it to you.'

'Tilden heard what you said and undoubtedly reported back to his lord and master. Your voice can be heard six blocks away.'

'Hrmph, I wouldn't say that,' Toby grunted. 'I admit I enunciate clearly, unlike most of the non-professionals who pontificate on radio and television these days. The likes of Henry Longhurst and John Arlott would turn in their graves.'

'Look, Toby, I've got to go,' I said, anxious to avoid another virulent outbreak of nostalgia.

'The problem is that Rattray takes Welbeck and his comments seriously,' Toby said thoughtfully. 'He's impressed by him. He kept referring to him as "very distinguished" and mentioned his vast knowledge of golf and its history. It made me want to puke.'

'He has got some front, you have to admit it.'

'I do.'

I began to move away. 'Chris, before you go, I've got something very intriguing to tell you.' He looked around at the other journalists. 'Tents have ears. I'll walk with you to the practice ground.'

As we moved past the tables towards the exit, one of Toby's

fellow journalists shouted out: 'Where're you going, Toby? The cricket's on the box in a couple of minutes.'

Toby waved airily in his direction and we made our way towards the practice area. The Saturday crowd was beginning to build up: there were all sorts and conditions of men and women, a cross-section of the British public from excited youngsters with their autograph books at the ready to elderly men and women with shooting sticks and sensible clothing. All the paraphernalia of a day out at the golf was on display: umbrellas and waterproof jackets, flasks of tea and bags of food, binoculars and periscopes. A few people, anxious not to miss anything, carried metal ladders or plastic beer crates on which to stand.

'There's something on the grapevine,' Toby said in my ear. His muted tones couldn't disguise his excitement. 'I haven't got anything like the full story yet but there's talk that diaries by a very famous golfer are about to come on the market.'

'A golfer's diaries? I can't see the money rolling in for those. How he shot a sixty-six at the Open and then followed it with a seventy-six and missed the cut. We're not into bestseller territory with material like that, are we?'

'No, Chris,' Toby snapped. 'Hear me out. These diaries are about the man's innermost thoughts and feelings – particularly his sex life. They're said to be dynamite.'

'Who . . .?'

'That's one of the problems. I don't know. What I have gathered is that the diaries have come from an unusual source and are being offered on behalf of an anonymous client, by one Nick Adams.'

'What – Nick Adams the publicity agent?'

'He calls himself a public relations consultant and he doubles as a literary agent. He's made a fortune selling sleaze to the

115

tabloids and to television. If you look behind any of the big bonking stories of the last decade you'll probably find Nick Adams pulled the strings. The cabinet minister and the call-girl, the admiral and the rent-boys, the TV star and the model, the princess and the polo player. Most of those kiss-and-tell stories come from Adams.'

'Nice chap.'

'You know how that stuff sells newspapers, Chris. There's a thriving market and Adams exploits it to the last penny. It's much cheaper and easier for a tabloid editor to buy in such dross than to do a real investigative job. You spend a fortune on surveillance and teams of reporters and you might end up with nothing you can use. Much better to pay the tart in question, spend a day photographing her in her underwear and get an inventive reporter to do the story. Bingo, you're there.'

'And the public couldn't care less whether it's true or not, as long as it involves a TV star, a footballer, one of the royals or, at a pinch, a top politician.'

'Precisely. Bread and circuses. Some balm to soothe their humdrum lives.'

'We all enjoy a bit of scandal, Toby, especially if it attaches itself to someone we suspect of hypocrisy. What I'm getting at is why should anyone be interested in a golfer? Golfers are not especially high up the scale of public interest, are they?'

'I agree but I've discerned more than a hint of excitement in the air. It's something big and undoubtedly dirty.'

We were now close to the practice ground and I could see Jake talking to one of the technicians who manned the equipment caravan. It was present at all professional tournaments in case a golfer needed a repair or a readjustment to his clubs. I hoped Jake wasn't going to mess around with any of his wedges.

'It must be one of the all-time greats,' I said. 'Palmer, Nicklaus, Player?'

'I don't know but I'm going to find out. See you later. Have a good round.'

# Chapter 16

In a slight daze as a result of Toby's story, I watched Jake go through his warm-up routine: chip shots, full wedges, short and medium irons, a few long irons and finally half a dozen hits with his woods. Then it was back to his three wedges and he hit all kinds of cut-up and running shots. I could think of very few golfers with his repertoire.

As we walked to the first tee Jake said, 'You're looking very serious today, Chris. What's up? Sex life a bit quiet? You're not a name at Lloyd's, are you?'

'Yes to the first, no to the second. I'm sorry. I've just heard a very odd story.'

'Yeah. I saw you talking to Toby. He's got a million of 'em. Can I hear it?'

'It's not much of a story, not yet anyway. Tell me, Jake, who are the really great golfers in your opinion? Ignore the current players, I mean the legends who made golf what it is today.'

'Off the top of my head I'd say Hagen, Sarazen, Bobby Jones, Snead and Ben Hogan of course. Then there's our own Henry Cotton. Palmer and Nicklaus. Oh, and Peter Thomson. Player and Trevino maybe. Those sort of guys. Why?'

'I'll tell you later,' I said thoughtfully. We approached the tee and I reached into Jake's bag and handed him his driver. 'Right, Jake, back to business.'

119

'Relax,' he said, 'it's only a game.' He hit his first drive solidly down the centre of the fairway.

Throughout the round I watched enviously as Jake made the game look easy. I had very little to do beyond computing the distances to the greens and handing him the clubs he required. It was just as well because my mind kept returning to what Toby had told me. Jake had listed most of my golfing heroes and I hoped it wouldn't be one of these who would be revealed as a sex-crazed adulterer or worse.

Although Jake made the game look easy, his skill was not reflected in his score. The putts would not drop. He shrugged his shoulders and smiled occasionally at his ill luck, as his ball stayed inexorably above ground when it might just as easily have toppled into the hole. Nevertheless he finished at three under par for the round and ten under for the tournament.

'They'll all go in tomorrow,' Jake said, as we parted company.

'You bet,' I said enthusiastically. If they did, I reckoned we'd both have a very good pay day.

I didn't need the deductive powers of the great Sherlock Holmes to locate Toby. I walked to the sponsor's tent, mentioned the Greenslade name and was admitted to the bar. It was crowded and many of its occupants were full to the brim with the sponsor's generous hospitality. At intervals the hubbub was punctured by erratic bursts of laughter from the various groups of guests.

Toby had a secure bridgehead on a corner of the bar and was holding court. He waved me over and introduced me as 'one of Britain's bright young course designers' before drawing me away from the bar. Because of the noise, we were able to speak in comparative privacy. 'I've been busy on the phone while you've been meandering around the golf course with Jake,' said Toby. 'I spoke to my editor about those diaries. I decided the quick way to find out what was going on was to get him to wave his cheque book under Adams's nose. His ability to do that is legendary. Indeed, it's his only claim to journalistic expertise.'

'And he got hold of Adams?'

'Yes. At his country house in Somerset. My God, the wages of sin. Adams told him that he was inviting sealed bids for various rights in those diaries. Publishing rights, TV and film rights and, naturally, newspaper serialisation rights. My editor asked for some material so that he could judge its value and Adams said that he could see the same as everybody, which is twenty or thirty photocopied pages. Based on the first bids Adams will draw up a short-list of three newspapers and they can examine the diaries in detail.'

'I'm fascinated by the business mechanics, Toby, but who the bloody hell is the golfer?'

'A legend.'

To irritate me, Toby finished his glass of champagne and surged towards a gap at the bar. I became aware of two men in pinstriped suits on my left, both 'well-lunched'. They were chatting about a golf day to which they had been invited the following week.

'Hope the weather holds,' the shorter man said. 'St George's is too much for me when it's windy.'

The other man agreed. 'Welbeck usually plays, doesn't he? Did you read about the burglary? Apparently the old bugger lost some of his favourite paintings.'

'I'll bet he comes up smelling of roses,' the shorter man replied. 'D'you remember that business in New York, when he was working for Browning's? A bit of unpleasantness, as I recall, but it was brushed under the carpet.' My ears were tuned desperately to the conversation but that was all I heard because the taller man suddenly spotted another of his acquaintances and bellowed a greeting. They both moved away.

Toby returned and handed me a beer. 'The golfer in question was synonymous with everything that was good and honourable in the game. He was a true champion.'

'Arnie?'

'No. The man I'm talking about is dead.' Toby was enjoying the teasing and I refused to say anything. 'He was one of the greats, a nonpareil one might say and a complete gentleman. And his reputation has remained untarnished. In fact, as the years have rolled by, his prestige has increased rather than diminished.'

I looked hard at Toby as, with a self-satisfied smile on his face, he put away a slug of champagne. 'You're not referring to an American who won thirteen major titles in the space of eight years, are you?' I asked quietly. 'Who did the Grand Slam of both the American and the British Opens and the respective amateur titles in the same year and then retired?'

'You've got him,' Toby said.

'Bobby Jones? I don't believe it.'

Toby shrugged but I knew that he must share my disbelief. To every generation since his heyday in the 1920s, Jones had been an idol, the gentlemanly amateur who outshone every other golfer not only by his achievements but by his demeanour. He had retired at the peak of his ability and founded one of the three greatest tournaments in golf, the Masters at Augusta.

I tried again. 'Jones was happily married to the same woman all his life. He was the epitome of the southern American gentleman, Toby, a man of honour. I think Adams must be taking the mickey.'

'You haven't heard the whole story. Adams consulted a

renowned authority on golfing matters, someone who could give an expert opinion as to the authenticity of the diaries.'

'Don't tell me . . .'

'Yes, Sir Nicholas Welbeck has confirmed that the diaries were without doubt written by Bobby Jones. The handwriting is authentic and so is the style and he confirms that all the background information in the diaries is correct. References to tournaments and players in the twenties and thirties, to his friends and to current events are all accurate.'

'But you said the diaries have details of Jones's sex life?'

'Yes. Therein lies their value. It seems he had a number of extra-marital affairs. In particular with someone he refers to as S.'

'I still don't believe it.'

'I'm surprised at your naïve attitude, Chris. We all know people who lead double lives and celebrities seem more prone to excess than ordinary people. Every year there are dozens of books which purport to tell the truth about someone or other who didn't appear to have a stain on his or her character.'

'They're mostly muck-raking memoirs about dead people, conceived and written with only one motive.'

'Money. Yes. And you should hear what the projections are for the Jones Diaries. Half a million for newspaper serialisation over here and maybe twice as much for the publishing rights. Of course the American rights are worth much more, and then there's the film and television rights. There could be up to ten million quid at stake here.'

'And all resting on the opinion of Sir Nicholas Welbeck. I wonder what sort of a cut he's negotiated for himself.'

Toby lifted his arms in a gesture of horror. 'How can you impugn the reputation of such a man? The doyen of the golfing art world! Really, Chris.'

123

'Do you know anything about his time in New York? He worked for Browning's apparently. I overheard someone talking about some sort of scandal there.'

'That must've been the late seventies or very early eighties. It doesn't ring any bells with me but I'd love to hear more.'

'I'll have a word with Andrew Buccleuth. He moves in artistic circles, so he's bound to know someone who knows someone.'

Jake began his final round in the PGA Championship only four shots behind the leaders. It was a cool and blustery day with rain in the air and club selection was more difficult than usual. Between us we made a mess of the first short hole, which called for a shot of around 175 yards into the prevailing wind to a plateau green. Jake wanted to hit a five-iron but I counselled a four-iron since all the trouble was at the front of the green, whereas the ground at the rear was relatively flat. With a doubt about the wisdom of my club selection in his mind, Jake didn't go through with his shot as he normally would and carved his ball well right into a grove of trees. He played a miraculous shot to bounce his ball on to the back of the green but a stroke was dropped.

As we walked away from the green, I began to apologize to Jake for putting negative thoughts, the enemy of all golfers at whatever level of skill, in his mind.

'Not your fault, Chris. Bloody awful shot.' He glanced at the scoreboard by the sixth tee. 'I'm losing ground. We need some birdies if we're to have a good pay-out. We'll agree on the club and the shot required and I'll commit myself to them, OK?'

Jake squared his shoulders and jutted his formidable chin. I had no doubts about his resolution and, from the sixth to the fifteenth holes he recorded five birdies and one more dropped shot to take his score to thirteen under par. Another birdie at the long seventeenth hole gave him a final round of four under par.

It was a sterling performance in difficult conditions. When all the scores were in we saw that Jake had hauled himself into sixth place to win prize money of over thirty thousand pounds. With his face creased by a broad smile, he said, 'It's the biggest win I've ever had.'

My grin was as wide as Jake's, since my share came to over two grand.

We had a couple of glasses of champagne to celebrate and then I crawled back to London amid the heavy Sunday evening traffic. By the time I got to my flat I was already half an hour late for my date with Laura.

'Come over to my place,' she said, when I telephoned her. 'I've got plenty of food and wine.'

' With an unspoken agreement we didn't linger over the food. It's surprising how quickly you can eat steak and salad when you have more pressing needs in mind.

I drove home at six o'clock the next morning with a mild hangover, a tired body and a contented mind.

# Chapter 17

Monday is traditionally a day off for the Secretary of a golf club who is expected to be in attendance during the weekend when the members are out in force. But Helen Raven was outside the Royal Dorset clubhouse when I arrived.

She was shaking hands with a man in a grey suit who was clutching a briefcase in his left hand. As he strode away across the car park, Helen turned her attention to me.

'You look a shade tired but triumphant,' she said cheerfully. 'Were you out late celebrating Jake Bowden's success?'

'Sort of. It did get out of hand, I'm afraid.' I gestured at her visitor, who was gunning his Vauxhall Cavalier towards the main road. 'Who's that?'

Helen sighed. 'The loss adjuster from the insurance company who wasn't the bearer of good news. He described our cover as derisory. The pay-out for the storm damage is reasonable but the paintings and the antiques were hopelessly undervalued.'

'Your predecessor dropped the club in it, then.'

'I'm afraid so, though I sympathize because I'd no idea what we were sitting on until Sir Nicholas told me. And now I read that his house has been burgled, too.'

'Yes, but his insurance was up to date.'

'I'm glad. Such a charming man.'

I nodded noncommittally. 'Your friend Inspector Rattray

127

thinks Toby is implicated in these thefts.'

Helen laughed. 'What nonsense. Toby may be a journalist but anyone can see he's harmless. Rattray probably thinks he's holding back some information and he's trying to frighten him.'

'Well, he's succeeded. Poor old Toby is very agitated.'

'I can imagine. The average policeman can be a nasty piece of work.'

'Is that why you opted out, Helen?'

She looked sharply at me for a moment. 'Not exactly. I was prepared for all the unpleasant aspects of the job and, because I'm a woman, I knew I had to demonstrate that I was tougher than anyone else. That in itself was very wearing. But it was the extreme prejudice against me and all the other women in the force that got me down. I thought I could overcome it and I had great ambitions to go all the way to the top. But in the end I was defeated. I remember the shock when a senior officer told me that I'd never get beyond the rank of chief inspector. "Over my dead body," he said and I couldn't believe the malevolence I saw in him.'

Suddenly Helen sat down on a solid wooden bench. It had been donated by Giles Kemp-Bastin, MC, 1916-88, 'who loved this course'. She looked reflectively over the emerald green expanse of the putting green. The shadows of that past defeat lay across her attractive face. 'I gave up. I'd battled away for twenty years and suddenly I realized I'd had enough. So I decided to accept an early retirement.'

'Do you regret it?'

'Not now. I was consumed with anger and frustration for a while and a feeling that the work I'd put into my career was all wasted. The worst thing was that the demands of my work messed up my marriage.'

'But you have your two children.'

'Yes. They're at boarding school. Nice young boys.' She turned her head and smiled at me. 'I tried to get the bastard who blocked my promotion but he managed to slither out of trouble. He was a commander and he abused his position. He was fond of the booze and arrogant enough to use his car when he went out on a spree. I knew he'd been stopped on two or three occasions but he'd flashed his warrant card and got away with it. Last year, just before I left the force, I set him up. He was at a colleague's farewell party and I tipped off someone I knew, someone who'd had his promotion prevented by the same man because he was a Roman Catholic.'

'A Catholic,' I said in astonishment. 'I don't get it.'

'The commander's a mason, so he doesn't like Catholics. Nor blacks of any shade, nor spicks or any other greaseballs – and especially not women. Anyway, my friend stopped his car and, despite all the threats and the bullying, he breathalysed him. He was positive, of course.'

'What happened? Was he disciplined?'

'No, someone managed to lose the blood samples, so he got away scot-free.'

'Didn't anyone in higher authority think that highly suspicious?'

'Not at all. It was a bloody good result for the guv'nor, my son,' Helen said in an excellent parody of any one of a thousand police television series.

The sense of injustice engendered by Helen's story switched my mind to Mrs Bradshaw and our search for Paul Stacey. 'Is your policeman friend still in the force?'

'Yes. At least something good came out of it. He was transferred and got the promotion he'd been denied.'

'Could he help to find a missing person?' I explained the background.

'The police computer would have some details if he's got a record but from what you've told me about him he sounds far too clever to have been caught doing anything illegal. Anyway, the computer wouldn't necessarily have a current address. That's what you want, isn't it? So you can deliver a summons?'

'Ideally, yes.'

'You might find him from the electoral roll. Do you know what part of the country he lives in?' I shook my head. 'So that's no good. But you said he's a solicitor – have you tried the Law Society?'

'No good.' The woman in their Press Office, though helpful, made it clear that their information only covered solicitors' practices. They could not provide personal data on individuals.

'A smart move would be to get some electronic surveillance into those offices in the Strand. It's a pity that they know who you are. You could've gone in there to service the photocopier or the coffee machine and given them a new wall plug. Inside would be a transmitter. Easy. The best bet now is an intercept on their telephone lines. The problem is that it can only transmit over a limited distance, so you probably need an expert who can set up a bug with an ultimate infinity receiver.'

'Sounds like a gadget from *Star Wars*. Expensive? Illegal?'

'Yes,' Helen said comfortably, 'right on both counts. With an infinity receiver you can dial in and listen to conversations which are actually taking place in the office at that time, or you can record telephone conversations and listen to them later.'

'Helen, I'm not into James Bond territory. I'm just trying to get a few grand that's owed to Mrs Bradshaw.'

She nodded and continued enthusiastically, 'I'll bet Reynolds has got a mobile phone. So, get the number and hire a Celltracker.'

'A Celltracker?'

'It'll lock on to his signal and you can listen in to his calls.'

Helen's secretary appeared at the clubhouse door and waved to her. 'It's the Captain on the phone for you, Helen,' she said.

Helen groaned, turned on her heel and said she'd see me later.

My telephone was ringing as I unlocked the door to my office. It was Jake, to discuss whether I could caddie for him in any of the tournaments leading up to the Open Championship. I promised to ask Calvin for some more time off.

I was about to put the phone down when Jake said, 'You'll never believe this, Chris, but that bastard who rolled me over a few years ago has come out of the woodwork. Charles bloody Freeman. He had the nerve to ring me this morning.'

'He probably read about the prize money you won.'

'I think you're right, old son. He wanted to set up a meeting. He feels guilty about what happened and wants to try to make amends. He's got a foolproof scheme, something in the property game again, and he just wants a few private investors. Smooth bastard, he almost had me believing him again. It's all kosher, he said. He's got an experienced solicitor on board and it can't fail.'

'But you told him to get stuffed.'

'Too bloody true. Make sure you warn your City friends, Chris, about these thieving buggers.'

'What're they called?'

'R S Developments. Steer well clear.'

'Bloody hell,' I said softly.

'What?'

'Freeman didn't happen to tell you the name of the solicitor, did he?'

'Yeah, he did. He wanted me to meet him too. Paul something.'

131

'Paul Stacey.'

'Yeah, that's the chap. Paul Stacey.'

'Jake,' I said urgently. 'Will you do me a favour? I'll explain everything to you later but will you get back to Freeman and make an appointment. And make sure that Stacey is there. Tell them that you'll have your business manager with you.'

'I don't have a business manager. You know that.'

'You do now. Me.'

I heard Jake's rumble of laughter. 'I don't know what you're up to, old son, but I'll set him up. You'd better have a good story ready.'

After spending an hour with the head greenkeeper, I settled down in the office to make inroads into the paperwork which had accumulated. Much of it was junk mail but I tapped out replies to a few of the letters. It had been on my mind to get in touch with Andrew Buccleuth and a few minutes before one o'clock was a good time to try my old employer.

When I got through to his office, I was greeted by the steely tones of his personal secretary, Veronica. She regarded it as her mission in life to protect Andrew from anyone who might waste his time, irritate him or disrupt his business life. From her vantage point, ninety-nine per cent of his callers had therefore to be kept at bay; it was easier to get through to the Dalai Lama than to Andrew.

'Ah, Christopher,' she said when I announced myself. Only my mother used the full version of my name – and rarely. Veronica's headmistressy voice implied she expected I was about to commit some misdemeanour and, whatever it was, she knew just how to deal with it. Andrew had told me she had mellowed since her marriage a couple of years previously but I could hear little evidence of it. 'Mr Buccleuth is in conference and then has a lunch date. I can give him a message.'

She took my number and I heard Andrew's cheerful tones as he asked her who was on the line.

'It's Mr Ludlow,' said Veronica.

'Oh, fine. Put him through,' Andrew said.

'Very well,' she said frostily. 'Mr Buccleuth is free for a moment and can talk to you, Christopher. I'm transferring you now.'

'Veronica's in fine form,' I said caustically when Andrew picked up the telephone.

'Isn't she?' Andrew said. 'She's off to Cumbria with her husband next week. A walking holiday.'

He then talked enthusiastically about a new set of irons he'd bought. Andrew was fanatical about golf. He devoured every magazine and tried every tip that he read; he was also susceptible to every 'new and improved' golf club that came on to the market. During the time I'd known him he must have averaged a new set of clubs every year and he had nearly a hundred different putters. He was a club professional's dream.

'And I've gone over to three wedges,' Andrew continued, 'just like your man, Jake Bowden. Conventional one, sand wedge and a lob wedge. Should help me, don't you think?'

'If it makes you more confident, Andrew, of course.' I changed the subject. 'I need a few names. People who know Sir Nicholas Welbeck. I need to dig into his background.'

'It's impeccable, as you must know. A fine golfer and a man of great taste and judgement. He's very well connected. He's occasionally advised the royal family about aspects of their art collections.'

'Fine, so he's a top man. But do you know anybody at Sotheby's who would talk to me about him? Even more important, I need a contact at Browning Fine Arts in New York.

133

Welbeck worked there for a while.'

'What are you up to, Chris? No, don't tell me. It's better I don't know. I'll find some names for you by the end of business today. We must have a game soon. Come over to Swinley Forest. I'll fix it up.'

Andrew kept his word. In the middle of the afternoon he gave me the telephone number of Neville Thorneycroft who had recently retired from Sotheby's in order to begin a new career as a writer. 'His family have been clients of this firm for decades,' Andrew emphasized. 'He's rich and pretty sharp. Handle him carefully.'

According to Toby, anyone contemplating a career as a writer would have to be rich – or nuts.

I got through to him just before I finished work for the day. The initial numbers for his telephone told me that he lived in the Hampstead area of London. Thorneycroft's voice was high-pitched and precise. He sounded wary, even when I mentioned Andrew's name, and kept repeating what I'd said to him.

'You used to work for Andrew Buccleuth, you say? And you want to ask me some questions about Sir Nicholas Welbeck? I can't tell you anything you can't find out from *Who's Who*.' When I remained silent, he added, 'A press-cuttings library would no doubt serve you well.'

'You were at Sotheby's with Sir Nicholas,' I said. 'What was he like to work with?'

'Sotheby's isn't like a typing pool, you know. We had our different departments. If I recall correctly, Welbeck dealt primarily with twentieth-century paintings. I would have been in the porcelain department then.' He paused. 'Give me your number. I'll call you back.'

It was obvious that he was checking me out with Andrew and I had no qualms about that. When he rang back a few minutes later, he seemed slightly less remote.

I had been irritated by his patronizing manner and decided to go on the attack. 'I heard there was some bother with Welbeck,' I said with an assurance I didn't feel. 'The provenance of a painting, was it? Something like that.'

It was a guess but it struck home.

'Who told you that?' Thorneycroft's voice suddenly became thinner and sharper.

'Gossip. And Andrew confirmed it.' I hoped Andrew would forgive me if he found out I'd used his name to tease information out of Thorneycroft.

'First of all, Mr Ludlow, I would emphasize that stories about questionable attributions, and forgeries, are legion. And usually wildly exaggerated. I realize that experts are fair game but the majority of them are men and women of probity and they act in good faith. Sometimes they become, oh, over-enthusiastic, let us say. Even the great Rembrandt was a victim of this tendency. Earlier in this century paintings and drawings by his pupils were attributed to the Master. Inevitably there was a strong revisionist tendency by a group of Dutch experts. They reduced the attributions to Rembrandt by half and wiped millions off the values of his paintings. Even Her Majesty suffered when one of her Rembrandts was attributed to one of his apprentices.

'No doubt you know the old joke about the Picassos,' he continued. 'There are nine hundred genuine ones and nine thousand of them are in America.' His laugh had an odd reedy quality.

'However, to get to the point. Welbeck became something of an expert on the work of Henri Matisse. In fact, the Queen was impressed enough to consult him about some of her works by that artist. In the mid-seventies, a hitherto unknown work by Matisse came on to the market, a self-portrait. There was great excitement and also some uncertainty about its authenticity.'

'Why was that?'

'Partly because of the dealer who claimed to have acquired it – Piet Mulder, also known as Patrick Moloney, also known on occasion as the Baron de Murat. He been knocking around the art world for years and nobody took him very seriously. He insisted that he was acting on behalf of a friend of Matisse and he had some back-up – letters from experts confirming the painting was a genuine Matisse, and letters from members of the family. Then Mulder pulled off his master-stroke. He persuaded Welbeck to look at it. Welbeck, wearing the mantle of the Queen's expert on Matisse's paintings, was flattered and only too ready to oblige.'

'And he passed it as the genuine article.'

'Oh yes. And it didn't even go to auction. Presumably on Welbeck's advice, the Queen bought the work.'

'For how much?'

'No one knows. No doubt for a considerable sum. Works by Matisse have been known to fetch millions. Sotheby's were not amused and Welbeck left their hallowed portals soon after. And doubts still remain about the Matisse but since it's in the possession of Her Majesty . . .'

'And doubts perhaps as to whether Welbeck acted in a totally disinterested way?'

'I wouldn't dream of speculating about that.' He laughed his scratchy laugh again. 'But Browning's in New York will no doubt have an opinion about Sir Nicholas. I expect Andrew has given you a name there, too.'

# Chapter 18

Before I called the Browning office I wanted time to mull over what Thorneycroft had told me. It was what he had implied that mattered, the words behind the words. Using his terminology, it seemed he wasn't very certain of Welbeck's provenance.

But my first call, on my return to London, was on Mrs Bradshaw, who poured me a glass of Alsace wine. 'Just for a change,' she said. 'It's nothing but chardonnay and sauvignon these days.'

I told her about my prospective meeting with Paul Stacey and how the chance had come out of the blue.

'So there is a God.' Mrs Bradshaw was gleeful. 'Well, I know there is, but He sometimes doesn't pay attention. What are you going to do now?'

'I don't want to make him suspicious. I'll be masquerading as Jake's agent, so I'll have a bit of leeway. He'll expect some searching questions. The meeting will actually be in his offices in Slough, so I can have a look around. And I can legitimately ask him for his telephone number at home. From there we can get his home address and, bingo, you can serve your County court writ on him.'

The light on my answering machine was winking urgently when

I entered my flat. Before listening I delved into the refrigerator for a beer and searched in the freezer for something to eat. There was some pulau rice, the remains of a vegetable curry and a chicken masala. Ideal, especially since curry dishes seem, by some mysterious alchemy, to improve with keeping, even when frozen. Or is that an illusion because bachelors like me always consume curries after anaesthetizing their taste buds by drinking several pints of beer?

After a long swig at my bottle of Budvar, I played my messages. Laura's voice came first, slightly husky. 'Hi Chris. It's Laura. How about Tuesday? Don't worry, it's not another trip back to the sixties. It's Bruce Willis, dying hard for the umpteenth time, at the local fleapit. Shall we go? Call me.'

That was simple. I rang Laura and arranged to meet her on the following evening, at six o'clock on her insistence. 'I like the early show,' she said, 'then we've got the rest of the evening to play with.' Who could fault her planning?

The next caller was Toby, his tones peremptory as always when there was nobody to answer him back. 'Greenslade, hack and part-time private dick, here,' he began. 'Call me, please. I have some fascinating information about our noble friend.'

With a second bottle of beer by my side, I dialled Toby's number. Ten rings told me that he must be out and I was about to abort the call when the receiver was lifted. Toby was decidedly out of breath. I knew that he had as little regard for enforced exercise as he had for a bottle of corked wine. He enjoyed deriding my efforts to keep fit: my runs around Wimbledon Common, the exercise machine in my spare bedroom and my use of a bike around London. I guessed that there could only be one reason for his oxygen deficiency.

'Sorry, Toby,' I said. 'Is Isobel with you? Have I interrupted something?'

He tried to keep his voice steady. 'No, you lascivious young pup, you haven't and she's not. I've just been round to the off-licence, that's all.'

I knew he was lying because he always drove to the off-licence, even though it was only two streets away. 'You sound as if you've just walked up ten flights of stairs with a year's consumption of Aussie cabernet on your back. You must get into shape, Toby. Have you considered getting a personal trainer?' To forestall any abuse, I continued hurriedly, 'Tell me what you've found out about Welbeck.'

'Just for the record, my doctor gave me a clean bill of health the other day. Blood pressure a shade high but nothing to worry about.'

'Good. What about Welbeck?'

'Just a moment.' I heard the clink of a bottle and then a sigh from Toby. 'That's better. I had occasion to call old Rory Blackham the other day. Remember him? Got to the final of the Amateur a couple of times. He's helped me a bit with my book. Background on some of the Scottish courses. One of the good guys, drinks like a fish.'

'He's the one who married that supermarket heiress, isn't he?'

'That's him. He's never done a stroke of work but he was a fine golfer. And he was a Walker Cup selector.'

'And that's when he got to know Welbeck?'

'Yes and no. He'd known him for years because they'd played in amateur tournaments together and against each other in the Halford Hewitt, of course. Old Blackham was very amused at the thought of Welbeck losing his paintings. Tickled pink, in fact.'

'Welbeck doesn't seem to have many mates, does he?'

'No. Blackham said that he was an embarrassment as a

selector. He was more interested in how pretty the young men were than in the quality of their golf.'

'But where does that get us? We know Welbeck's a shirt-lifter. That doesn't make him a bad person.'

'I agree but apparently it made him a hopelessly biased selector. There was trouble with one of his protégés. Welbeck argued in favour of the lad's selection through thick and thin, even though he was really only a borderline case. Anyway, the rest of the selectors, including Rory Blackham, allowed themselves to be persuaded and the Welbeck protégé, called Gary I think, was pencilled on to the team sheet. Then he was accused of cheating, fortunately before the Walker Cup team was announced. Gary was playing in some event in the Midlands and his partner refused to sign his card.'

'But Welbeck stood up for him, I suppose.'

'Of course, and demanded a hearing to ensure fair play. The young man's honour and all that bullshit. Then all sorts of people came out of the treeline and declared that young Gary was a congenital cheat on the golf course. Even though he'd been told unofficially that he was in the team, the selectors had no option but to drop him.'

'The cup dashed from his lips. What an idiot,' I said. 'Then what? It was all hushed up?'

'Of course. That's how the Establishment works, you know that, Chris. And Welbeck resigned as a Walker Cup selector because of the pressure of work.'

'And what does that story, diverting as it is, tell us about Welbeck?'

'That his judgement is unsound, I suppose.'

While my frozen curry was defrosting in the microwave, I decided to ring the contact Andrew had provided at Browning's.

I had to undergo a cross-examination by a recorded voice before I made contact with a human being. I asked for Sonny Brew and was surprised when a woman took the call.

'Yeah. Sonny speaking. How can I help you?' It was a grainy voice, with a no-nonsense undertone typical of a New Yorker, but she sounded friendly.

I explained who I was and that Andrew Buccleuth had given me her name; she told me Mrs Buccleuth was a valued client and asked me to pass on her best wishes.

'So what can I do for you, Chris?'

'Sir Nicholas Welbeck. I believe you used to work with him. What did you think of him?'

'Oh, a sweet man. Very proper. He went over real well here. A good depth of knowledge about painting, especially twentieth century. He taught me a lot.'

'Look. I'm putting my cards on the table. Face up. I'm a consultant to a company here in London,' I lied, 'and they're thinking of doing a joint venture with Sir Nicholas. I can't tell you more than that except that a lot of money is involved. They're curious why he left Browning's. Someone told them he left under a cloud.'

'Hell, no, Chris. Mistakes are made in the art business, just like any other. It's possible that Sir Nicholas made one, or maybe he didn't. Some people said he got conned. Art is a huge market-place with big bucks at stake. Where you've got big money there're lots of con-men. Personally, I think he made an error but it was pardonable.'

'Tell me more.'

'Sure thing. It was no big deal. A dealer brought in a real nice landscape. It was eighteenth century and English but not by a big name. Naturally we asked old Nicky to take a look.'

I couldn't prevent my hoot of laughter at the idea of the

patrician and aloof Welbeck being called Nicky.

Sonny said, 'Hey, we didn't call him Nicky to his face. He's much too grand. Anyway, the painting wasn't of great interest, except for one thing. The lower left showed a group of four men and they were obviously playing an early form of golf. Now that made the work valuable. OK, so it goes into one of our auctions and we whip up some action. Articles in the press, quotes from Sir Nicholas, noted amateur golfer and consultant to Queen Elizabeth. You know the scene, Chris, I'll bet. So, it's showbiz time and, apart from the American collectors, we got some Japanese in on the act.

'So the painting is sold to a Californian collector for well into six figures. A great result for us and the dealer. But, about three months later, the buyer reappears. He's very unhappy because the golfers, he says, have been added later. He shouts fake and he shouts it loud – very loud.'

'So what happened?'

'We did tests, which were inconclusive. At least, our experts couldn't find anything wrong with the work. The paint seemed to be kosher for the period, the technique the same as the rest of the picture and so on. Of course you've got to be on your guard. It's amazing what an unscrupulous forger can achieve. They've been conning the so-called experts for centuries. You'll remember van Meegeren's exploits . . .'

'I remember Tom Keating's.'

'Well, yeah, but van Meegeren got away with it. But back to our golfers. The buyer insisted it was a forgery and he bad-mouthed us to everybody. There was only one way out. We gave him his money back and took possession of the painting.'

'So there was no particular blame attaching to Welbeck?'

'Not at all. But Nicky was upset by the publicity and he left us a few months later. He's *the* golf expert now, isn't he? A sweet guy. Is that OK? Have I told you what you wanted?'

'You have, Sonny. I'm very grateful. Who was the dealer, by the way, who brought that painting to Sir Nicholas?'

'I can't tell you off the top of my head. But someone here should know. When I get the name, I'll call you. Great to talk to you, Chris.'

The first mouthful of curry was on my fork when the telephone rang. I put the fork down. The caller was Jake, who insisted I told him why I wanted to meet Freeman and Stacey. He had arranged it for the following Monday, at their offices in Slough.

I told him about Mrs Bradshaw and the missing rent. Although her loss was nothing compared to his, he sympathized with my wish to get her her money. He happily joined with me in a rehearsal of our roles as client and business manager while my curry cooled on its plate.

# Chapter 19

As arranged, Jake and I met in the car park next to Paul Stacey's offices, which were housed in the sort of utilitarian concrete block which induces instant depression. I could hear an old Kinks number as I tapped on Jake's window. He jumped out, grinning amiably and jerked his thumb at the building. 'Doesn't look like Freeman's style. He used to have offices near Harrods.'

'He's getting in tune with the austere nineties, then. Remember, Jake, I'm your business adviser, so I'll ask most of the questions. It's Stacey I'm really after.'

'That's fine. The Freeman business is just piss under the bridge, as far as I'm concerned.'

The ground floor offices of R S Developments were far more salubrious than the outside of the building and the reception area was positively welcoming. Deep sofas, covered in a rich purple and green, were arrayed around three sides of the room, and a carved oak table, complete with an opulent display of flowers and a collection of up-market magazines, sat in the middle. A woman with platinum blonde hair piled high and a fixed smile was perched behind a desk against the far wall. Even from across the room I could see that her make-up was a major work of art – a two-hour job.

'Get the superstructure,' Jake hissed vulgarly in my ear as we advanced beyond the door. I could hardly have missed it –

her ample chest was not quite confined in a white cotton blouse designed for someone much smaller.

The woman smiled and said, 'You'll be Mr Stacey's visitors, I expect. I'll buzz him.'

I noticed that her telephone had six lines on it and wondered if Stacey had his own dedicated line. That would make it easier to tap into his conversations. Hang on, I told myself, this is real life, not a movie.

'He's ready for you, gentlemen.' The receptionist got up and led us to a door in the corner of the room. Her bottom wiggled under her tight skirt but the effect was spoiled by the red weals which the chair had imprinted on her thighs. Jake's grin left me in no doubt that he was enjoying the view.

As soon as we were through the door, a tall man, his long fair hair swept back from his brow, advanced on us. He was in his mid-thirties and was wearing a dark suit with a chalk-stripe, a blue shirt and a brightly patterned tie. I was willing to bet that he was wearing red braces under his jacket. I'd met similar men in their hundreds during my days in the City. This was obviously Charles Freeman. His greetings to Jake were effusive and he stressed how happy he was to meet Jake's, er, business manager.

'Is that the same thing as an agent?' he asked, with a sly look in my direction.

'Similar,' I replied. 'But as well as generating money for Jake, I make it my business to conserve it.'

'And make it grow, I trust,' said Paul Stacey with a smile, as he came from behind his desk and shook my hand.

Stacey was stocky and square-shouldered, with closely cropped dark hair. His eyes were a bit too close together and watchful behind his display of bonhomie. He looked like a well-fed ferret.

After the receptionist, whose name was Terri, had served us some tea, Freeman launched into his sales patter. R S Developments was a specialist in small-scale property deals and wanted a few outside investors to help their future expansion. He explained that they were in the residential property business. Sometimes the properties came to them as a result of repossessions by banks and building societies.

'Paul has great contacts in that area,' Freeman said with relish, 'and it's a foolproof way of turning a quick profit. We are able to buy at below the market price because the bank or whatever, wants its money back and the quicker the better. Then we tart up the property a bit and we bang it back on the market at the going rate.'

'So why do you need money from the likes of me?' Jake asked. 'Property isn't my favourite investment. Once bitten, twice shy. Eh, Charlie?'

'Nothing can go wrong the way we do it,' Stacey stepped in smoothly. 'It's all pretty quick. It's not like those complicated commercial deals that Charles used to be involved in. They take up too much time and your profit goes out of the window. That was behind the collapse of Charles's last venture and I know you suffered because of it. That's why Charles wants to bring you in – to make amends as it were.'

'What sort of investment are you looking for?' I asked.

Stacey looked questioningly at Freeman. 'What do you think, Charles? Something reasonably conservative to start with? Two hundred thou?' It was nicely rehearsed.

Freeman nodded in reply. 'Two or three hundred thousand, just to get your feet wet. How's that?'

'What's the return? And what are the guarantees?' Chris Ludlow, business manager, continued his Oscar-winning performance.

'We'll guarantee your client an annual return of twenty per cent. But it could be much greater,' Stacey said firmly. 'And the money will be safe because it will be secured against one of our properties.'

I looked at Jake who, as planned, said, 'I leave all this high-finance stuff to Chris. He's the expert.'

I told the two men that I'd think about the proposition and that it sounded interesting – as long as all the safety measures were in place. We exchanged cards, mine carrying the number of my temporary office at the Royal Dorset Club. I asked them if I could reach them out of normal office hours and they both wrote their home and mobile phone numbers on their cards.

With handshakes and smiles all round we prepared to leave the office. As Jake and I reached the front door, escorted by Freeman, I said, 'Charles, I'd like to look at one or two of your properties. Just to see what Jake's getting himself into. To get the feel of the market. How about it?'

'No trouble at all, Chris. A very good idea. I'll be happy to arrange it.'

Jake and I paused by his Mercedes and I noticed that there were two parking spaces designated for R S Developments. One was occupied by a large and sporty-looking BMW, the other by a Lexus.

'Look at the cars over there, Jake,' I said as I jotted down both registration numbers. 'They're doing very nicely for themselves, considering they're only in a small way of business.'

He smiled as he got into his car. 'I don't know how the bastards do it.'

'Neither do I, but I intend to find out.'

Freeman didn't waste any time. He called me on the following morning to ask me when I could spend a couple of hours looking at properties. We settled on the Wednesday of the following week.

Almost immediately my phone rang again. It was Helen to say that Mr and Mrs Kincaid were in her office and would I walk over and say hello. On the way over I wondered how the two women would get on together: Helen Raven, the capable and down-to-earth career woman and the flamboyant Amy who had taken advantage of an old man's susceptibilities and married into great wealth. I didn't imagine that they'd become bosom pals. But I was wide of the mark because the two women were chatting animatedly when I reached Helen's office. They had discovered a mutual interest in baseball and were discussing the merits of American teams which were simply names to me.

Kincaid pumped my hand heartily. 'Hi, Chris. We're off to see the stones at Avebury, and Stonehenge of course. Amy's interested in such things and I've got a few people in the antiques business to see. But, first off, we've arranged to play a few holes here. Mrs Raven couldn't have been more helpful.' He paused. 'You know of my interest in course design, Chris. I wondered if you'd show me what you're doing here in the way of renovation?'

We left Amy and Helen to their baseball and I led Kincaid back to my office. I explained the reasons for the changes Calvin and I had made and showed him some of the drawings. I used the Forgan niblick given to me by Jake to hold down the top of the drawings.

When I had finished he picked it up and examined it closely. 'It's an original,' I said. 'Jake Bowden gave it to me.'

'That was real nice of him but I'm afraid it's not an original. It's a very good copy. You can tell by the nicking where the shaft joins the hosel and by the fact that whoever made it didn't

149

bother to put a pin through the hosel.'

I was taken aback for a moment and wondered how Jake had acquired it, but Kincaid ploughed on, oblivious of my disappointment. 'The best fakes ever done were the Winton irons. They were over-sized niblicks and they fooled a helluva lot of people. They really looked the part. It was only when you put two of 'em together that you could tell. You could see that they'd been cast from the same mould and when you measured the name stampings on the back, they were identical. As you know, real hand-made clubs would show a variance.'

'But I suppose they've become valuable in their own right because they're such good fakes? Like Tom Keating's paintings?'

'There's some truth in that.' Kincaid sat down on one of the stools. 'Since we're on the subject of forgeries and fakes, Chris, I just heard that some very valuable diaries are up for grabs. You heard about 'em?'

I nodded. 'You think they're forgeries?'

'I *know* they're forgeries. They're tacky and the great Bob Jones couldn't possibly have had anything to do with them. I knew him well enough to be able to say that.'

'Those are my feelings too, Julius, but if you're objective you have to say that even the greatest men have secrets. What about William Gladstone and his unhealthy interest in prostitutes? Or President Kennedy with his penchant for nubile actresses? Gladstone was one of our great Prime Ministers and JFK was an inspiration for a whole generation, not just in your country but around the world. A weakness for women doesn't change any of that.'

'I know,' Kincaid said sadly. 'Nothing's immune from such foolishness. That's why I consider it a pity that it's assumed we have to know everything about our great men. Lord knows,

150

I understand any man's weakness for a beautiful woman. No doubt people look at Amy and ask themselves what an old fool like me is doing with such a lovely young lady.'

'Let them,' I said.

Kincaid smiled. 'As you know, Bob Jones had true integrity and it showed in everything he did. I'll bet my life, Chris, that those so-called Jones diaries are forgeries. And I'd be able to tell, I promise you. I know the Jones style and I'm very familiar with his handwriting. I've made a lifetime study of that great man and, I may be flattering myself, I think I know more about him than anyone around.'

'More than Sir Nicholas Welbeck?'

'Great God Almighty,' Kincaid spluttered. 'What's he got to do with this?'

I explained that the Welbeck imprimatur had been given to the diaries and that he had decreed them to be genuine.

'Well, well. That explains a lot.' Kincaid told me that he'd tried to contact Nick Adams but hadn't even got past the office receptionist.

'Adams wouldn't want anybody to rock the boat, would he?'

Kincaid nodded his agreement.

I had a thought: 'Would you like to take a look at the diaries?'

'I'd give my right arm.'

I promised to try and arrange it through Toby. I hoped that his editor would be willing to co-operate, that the opinion of an acknowledged expert on Bobby Jones would appeal to him.

There was a rap on the door and Amy walked in. She had changed into her golfing clothes: tight trousers in Black Watch tartan and a bright red cashmere sweater with a prominent Ralph Loren logo.

'Now, come on you two,' she said archly. 'Jules and I've got a date on the first tee. Let's go, hon.'

151

Kincaid got up and headed through the door. Their arms linked, the happy pair strolled away.

'I'll call you,' I shouted after them, my eyes on Amy's swaying backside. As if she knew, she waved an acknowledgement.

# Chapter 20

The Kincaids had based themselves in a grand hotel close to Hyde Park Corner and the windows of their suite overlooked the park. Toby and I arrived at five o'clock on the Friday evening to find that a full English tea had been laid out on one of the tables.

I was no great lover of the tea tradition, except after golf on a winter's afternoon, and Toby, I knew, was even less interested. He looked askance at the array of sandwiches and pastries and declined.

Kincaid, although impatient to see the extracts from the Jones diaries, glanced at his watch and said, 'No self-respecting journalist drinks tea at five o'clock, I'll bet. Amy, get room service on the phone, will you, hon? Toby, Scotch, beer, wine? What would you like?'

'A drop of champagne would revive me, Julius. I've had a very hard day at the office. A budget meeting.' I grinned. Toby had never been near a budget in his life.

When the champagne had been served, Toby delved into his briefcase and slapped a sheaf of papers on the table. 'Here's what you've been waiting for, Julius. Copies of extracts from the Bobby Jones diaries. There are some pages about his triumphs in nineteen-thirty and a little about how he conceived his course at Augusta, but it's mostly about his, er, domestic life.'

153

Kincaid took the papers and stood by the window. Rapidly, he skimmed through some of the pages and then read others in detail. He peered at the writing and turned the pages sideways and upside down.

After several minutes, Kincaid returned to the table, put the pages carefully down, pushed his glasses up his forehead and rubbed his eyes. He took a gulp from his glass.

'Hell, Toby, I don't get this. It sure looks like Bob Jones's writing.' He held up one of the pages. 'It slants to the right and it's a nice flowing hand. There's a good balance between the upper, middle and lower zones of the writing.' Kincaid pointed at 'h', 'a' and 'g'. 'That indicates a balanced personality by the way. And notice how the script goes in a straight line. I don't want to push the principles of graphology at you because they're highly questionable but that indicates honesty and reliability.'

'Julius used to employ a handwriting expert whenever he was choosing an important executive, didn't you, hon?'

Kincaid nodded and smiled. 'What I'm getting at, is that this looks like the Jones handwriting.'

'Looks?' I queried.

'Yeah, Chris, looks. Some of the passages could certainly have been written by Jones. Equally they could have been done by an intelligent journalist with a working knowledge of Jones's career and a copy of *Down The Fairway* and *Golf Is My Game* at his elbow.'

'Those were Jones's own books, were they, hon?'

'Yes. And he wrote them himself. None of that ghosted rubbish that the golf stars have done for them these days.'

'It all makes work for the working journalist to do,' Toby interrupted brightly.

'Yes, of course, Toby. I'm sorry,' Kincaid said. 'However,

there are other sequences that Bob Jones could never have written in a million years. There're references to someone called S and his assignations with her. And some damn near-the-knuckle accounts of what they got up to.'

'Sex, Julie, is that what you mean?' Amy cut in.

'Yes, Amy, sex and it's graphically described. And I don't believe a word of it. Jones wasn't capable of two-timing his wife. Mary was the one and only woman in his life, his one true love.' Kincaid, suddenly emotional, wiped his spectacles with a handkerchief. 'There's another reason why I'm questioning the authenticity of these diaries. The style. It's good and it mimics Jones very well, but there's something not quite right.'

'Something askew?' I hazarded.

'Yeah, that's a way of putting it. Can I keep these copies, Toby?'

Toby told him he could but when Kincaid asked if there were any chance of seeing the originals, said, 'Only if my editor is serious about buying them for the *News*.'

'And is he?'

'Doubtful. It's not really tabloid stuff. He knows his readers want the here and now. Who's bonking who on the set of *EastEnders*? Is Princess Di pregnant? That sort of thing. An amateur golfer from the thirties is as remote as the moon to them. One of the posh papers will pay good money for the story but not the *News*.'

'What about the provenance of the diaries? Are there any letters from relatives or friends stating that they are genuine? Have forensic tests been done? Is the paper and ink from the right period? Are the vendors offering opinions from handwriting experts?' Julius fired off his questions in Toby's direction.

I seized on his last question. 'Hang on, Julius, a few minutes ago you were casting doubts on the validity of handwriting analysis. So, why would that help?'

'It has its uses, but only as a part of more rigorous disciplines, let's say. The practitioners are trying to make it into a science, they call it holography back home. But if I ever found myself taking it seriously I used to remind myself of the fiasco of the Howard Hughes autobiography.'

'The very clever Mr Clifford Irving,' Toby murmured.

'You've got him,' Kincaid said. 'He wrote the whole damn thing himself and the handwriting experts said that it was "beyond human ability", I think that was the phrase, that a man could've done such a forgery.'

Toby laughed. 'He took a major publisher for a long ride, didn't he?'

'Sure did. McGraw-Hill, for Chrissakes.'

'To answer some of your queries,' Toby continued, 'I believe that Nick Adams has supplied independent scientific opinion which says the diaries are kosher. And of course he has the support of that most eminent authority, Sir Nicholas Welbeck.'

Toby's eyebrows and shoulders rose in sympathy as Kincaid groaned. 'But where were the diaries found? And who owns the copyright? Surely that's vested in Jones's family and they'd never agree to publication.'

'Apparently they were in the possession of the mysterious S, Jones's mistress. She has a letter from Jones, in which he makes a formal gift of them to her.'

'So she owns the copyright,' I concluded.

'On the face of it, yes. But who in God's name is she? I've never heard a goddam word said against Bob Jones in all this time,' he muttered sadly.

'How old would S be?' Toby interrupted. 'If she knew Jones

in the early thirties, she must be well into her seventies at the very least. Why wait so long to reveal all?'

'For money?' I offered.

'I guess,' Kincaid said. 'But this whole business doesn't stack up right for me. Look, Toby, I'm off to Scotland on a buying trip but I'll study this material in the meantime.'

We parted at the door of the suite. I sensed that Amy, as we shook hands, held on to mine a shade longer than was necessary. In the lift I asked Toby whether he thought she had a roving eye.

'She's hot to trot, dear boy. Preferably with a fit young Englishman whom she thinks can show her a good time between the sheets. Don't be tempted, Chris. It would only lead to tears.'

'My God, you've got a nerve to offer me advice.'

'Maybe. How about one last drink before we go our separate ways? I'm told the bar at Harvey Nichols has some nice scenery.'

A great deal of 'thank God it's Friday' euphoria was in the air and Toby was right about the scenery. One bottle of champagne led to a second and I saw the familiar signs of Toby settling in for what he called 'a proper drink'.

I was determined to get away as soon as we'd finished the second bottle, before I was totally unhinged. I tried hard to apply my fading faculties to the whole question of the art thefts, the death of Charlie Ito and the sudden appearance of the Bobby Jones diaries.

'Are they connected?' I asked Toby.

'Why should they be? How can you link a respected dealer like Ito, and nobody has spoken ill of him, and those thefts from Royal Dorset and the other clubs? You don't think Ito was some oriental arch-criminal, do you?'

'I don't know. I'm asking you. You're the seasoned journalist with the super-sensitive nose for a dirty story, not me.'

'You put it so eloquently, Chris. There's some logic in tying the theft of Welbeck's precious paintings to the burglaries at the golf clubs, don't you think?'

'Yes,' I said firmly. 'And Ito's death came before the Welbeck robbery which, in practical terms, knocks him out of the equation.'

'And the Jones diaries don't seem to tie in anywhere. They came out of the blue and, as far as I know, Nick Adams had no previous connections with Welbeck.'

'I wouldn't think they move in quite the same circles,' I said and Toby laughed at the thought of Sir Nicholas associating himself with bimbos and the tabloid press.

'He obviously picked Welbeck because of his reputation in that field.'

'Sure, but I'd trust old Julius's opinion ahead of Welbeck's any day.'

'Well, I don't know,' Toby mused. 'Kincaid's judgement may be flawed in this case because, to him, Jones is an icon, as he is to many Americans.'

'And Brits.'

'Old Julie can't cope with the idea of his idol being anything but pure as driven snow. I never quite bought that almost-saintly Southern gentleman mythology that grew up around him. The thought of his committing adultery makes him, for me, a bit more human. I'm all in favour of a bit on the side.'

Two women, who were sharing a bottle of white wine at a nearby table stopped in mid-conversation to glare at Toby. He acknowledged their distaste and, with a smile and a slight bow, apologized and offered to make amends with some champagne. It had the desired effect. Lindy and Emma joined us and Toby ordered another bottle. They were thirty-somethings who worked in a nearby advertising agency. It was soon established that they were both divorced and met in the bar every Friday night.

At Toby's suggestion we went for dinner at one of his clubs, an establishment in Kensington which was run, badly, by a former England cricketer. The clientele was a mixture of sporting has-beens and minor celebrities and the inevitable throng of hangers-on that such people attract. I don't know why I went, particularly since I knew the food was pretentious, over-priced and execrable. However, I didn't want to leave an old friend in the lurch – and I could tell from Toby's not-so-covert looks at Emma's breasts that he fancied some close combat with her. In the normal way of things I would have fancied the same sort of engagement with Lindy, a lively, dark-haired woman with a lean and curvy body and knowing green eyes.

My reservations, still in place despite the volume of wine I'd drunk, were prompted by my thoughts of Laura. There was, as yet, no real commitment on either side but . . . When the two women suggested that we went on to a great club they knew in Chelsea, I decided to make my excuses and leave, as the tabloid press puts it.

'Sorry, Lindy, sorry Emma,' I muttered. 'I'm on a plane to, er, Caracas in the morning. Must go. Talk to you when I get back, Toby.' I staggered off to the lavatory and then up the stairs to the pavement. I was lucky enough to get a taxi almost immediately. As usual, I was amazed at Toby's stamina; he seemed to have the strength of ten, but then he rarely saw a new day before eleven o'clock.

# Chapter 21

The following Wednesday Laura and I took the Docklands Light Railway to a street not far from Canary Wharf. During the journey I explained that what had started out as an apparently simple task to retrieve some back rent for my neighbour had become more complex. It was obvious that Stacey and Freeman had designed an ambitious scheme to relieve people like Jake Bowden of their money.

I had arranged to meet Charles Freeman outside one of the properties acquired by R S Developments. Despite myself I was impressed. The grime of decades had been removed from the sturdy old warehouse block and the conversions to dwellings for the aspiring professional classes had been completed with some panache.

'Some friends of mine bought an apartment near here,' Laura said. 'They love the flat and hate the area.'

'And their investment has dropped in value?'

'Like a stone.'

The BMW I'd seen in Slough screeched to a halt outside the building and Charles Freeman jumped out. He was in a no-parking zone but he propped a 'Doctor on call' sign inside the windscreen.

He didn't notice Laura's glare because he was busy flashing his smile at her. 'Lovely to meet you, Laura. You work for Chris?'

'No.'

'What line are you in?'

'Photography.'

'Oh, yes. I can only just manage one of those idiot-proof compact cameras myself.' He could see that his attempts to charm Laura were falling on stony ground. 'Let's go into the building.'

He fiddled about with various locks and then we went into the ground floor, which had a sizeable integral garage, a ten-metre swimming pool and a gymnasium. There were three more floors, Freeman explained, and an enclosed roof garden. The next floor had four bedrooms, all with their own bathroom. The furniture and the decorations would, in estate agent's jargon, have been described as opulent. The floor above contained a huge bedroom suite, a games room with a full-size snooker table ('they put special girders in to take the weight,' Freeman said smugly), a bar and a music-and-television room.

Laura inspected the equipment and murmured, 'State of the art'.

The top floor was given over to an open-plan living room with more music and television equipment. The dining room was at one end with a long galley-style kitchen in one corner; there were enough serious appliances and gadgets to service a restaurant.

'Let's go outside,' Freeman said. He led us on to a terrace and then up an iron staircase to a roof garden enclosed by glass. A myriad of small trees, shrubs, plants and bright flowers were scattered over the considerable area.

'Take a seat,' Freeman said. 'It's a bit warm, isn't it?' He pressed a switch by the door and the roof panels slid back to expose us to fresh air. The smooth sod – you'd have thought he'd done all the work himself.

'Tell us about this place,' I said.

'Sure. It belonged to a guy in the video business. Very big-time, lots of disposable income. He paid well over a million for the place in the late eighties and I gather he then spent another half mill on it. Then his company hit some rough water and the property market headed south, especially properties like this. He wanted out. At one stage he had this place on the market for nearly two mill.' Freeman smiled in his patronizing way. 'No chance, of course.'

Laura got up, stretched and produced a miniature camera from her shoulder bag. She began to take photographs of some of the flowers.

'So what did you pay for it and what's it worth?' I asked, assuming the mantle of Jake's business manager.

'The owner was desperate, so we picked it up, furniture and fittings included, for less than a million pounds. We've since had it valued at a million and a half. And we have several other properties, mostly smaller than this but one or two that are similar, where we've pulled off the same trick.'

'That's pretty smart of you,' I said encouragingly. What a prick he was.

'We try hard and we *are* experts in the field,' Freeman said, with a quick smirk. 'That's why your client should get involved. The rewards can be considerable.'

'You already owe him, Charles,' I said sharply.

'Indeed and we'll make up for that other unfortunate, er, blip.' He looked quickly at his watch. 'I can show you another property nearby. I don't want to hurry you but I know our other partner wants to meet you and he should be arriving at any moment.'

I stared at Freeman for a moment as I digested his comment. 'Your other partner?' I said weakly. 'Who's that?'

'David Reynolds. He's a well-known solicitor.' Freeman went out and peered over the edge of the building. 'I can see his car. We'll go down and I'll introduce you.'

On the way down the stairs I muttered in Laura's ear to keep her camera handy. If Reynolds attacked me it would be nice to have the documentary evidence.

He was propped against the wing of his Mercedes as he waited for us. He straightened up as Freeman greeted him. In his light grey double-breasted suit he looked even bigger than I remembered.

'This is Mr Ludlow,' Freeman said. 'He's a business manager for a number of golfers.'

'I know who he is,' Reynolds said as he advanced towards me. 'If he's a business manager then I'm Mary Poppins.' He stopped about two feet away. He was breathing hard as he tried to contain his anger. His eyes were bright and I wondered if he was going to get his retaliation in at once.

'I don't believe in coincidences,' Reynolds continued, 'so I guessed it must be you as soon as I heard your name. I told you to piss off out of it last time we met and I meant it.'

'What the hell is the problem here, David?' In his anxiety Freeman's voice hit a higher pitch than usual.

'The problem is this arsehole. How the fuck did you and Stacey get conned by him?' He reached out for the lapels of my jacket and I took a step back out of range. I had no wish to be on the wrong end of a Glasgow kiss from someone his size. I heard the click and whirr of Laura's camera.

Reynolds turned on her and she took a full-face picture of him as he snarled, 'Who's the tart with the snot-ring?'

I knew that we'd reached the point of no return and I took a step towards him. In a no-holds-barred rough-and-tumble he was too powerful for me but I reckoned I could inflict some damage on him before my lights went out.

The tart with the snot-ring saved the day. Laura's privileged-class accent sounded more languid than ever. 'Come on, Chris. Don't waste your energy. Mr Reynolds doesn't know any better, poor lamb. He's probably only used to female companions he's paid for.'

She put her camera back in her bag, took me by the hand and walked me away from Reynolds and the awestruck Freeman.

'You won't be able to hide behind her skirts next time,' Reynolds shouted after me. 'I'll come looking for you, slag.'

Laura pointed out that she was wearing jeans. It broke the tension for me and I managed a laugh. 'I'm sorry about that,' I said. 'I was hardly Sir Galahad, was I?'

'No need. You don't have to go all macho to impress me. Save it for when it counts.' She squeezed my hand. 'My God, what a frightful bunch. That Freeman creature is a real slimeball. I wouldn't trust him with a penny piece. As for Reynolds, he's seriously unpleasant. Chris, promise me you won't get into a fight with him, OK? They're obviously up to something. It sticks out a mile and Reynolds thinks you're on to him. I'm sure that's why he reacted so aggressively.'

'You're right, Laura. That property, despite all the plush fittings and the gimmicks, isn't worth a million and a half pounds. There's a scam on the go but I can't see what it is yet.'

'One of my old boyfriends is a surveyor in the City. Shall I ask him to take a look and give us an opinion?'

'OK. Good idea.'

# Chapter 22

On the day after my brief but lively encounter with Reynolds, the celebrated public-relations consultant, Nick Adams, popped up on the *Today* programme. His voice was a bizarre mingling of Essex-boy-made-good and mid-Atlantic and, as I listened to him, I wondered whether he knew the obstreperous lawyer. They would have made a great partnership.

The interviewer's first question was simple enough, since he merely asked Adams why there was such interest in the diaries of a golfer who'd retired from active competition ten years before the start of World War Two. 'It's all very remote, isn't it, Mr Adams?'

'Not really, John, because Bobby Jones was the superstar of his day. He was Palmer, Nicklaus and Ballesteros all rolled into one, John. He was the real, twenty-carat gold item.'

'Yes, so I understand. He achieved what Bernard Darwin called the "Impregnable Quadrilateral" in 1930. But why have these diaries caused such a fuss?'

'Because in them, John, a great sportsman opens up his heart. Jones was special in every way and so are his diaries.'

'Mr Adams, I'm told that you've sold the diaries for a huge amount of money to a book publisher and a newspaper. Is that right?'

'Yes. The parties concerned approached me with a preemptive offer. It's a nice little package deal, yes.'

'A package deal worth nearly a million pounds, or so I'm told.'

'Well, John, I really can't discuss the finances. It wouldn't be right.'

'No. But there must be a very compelling reason for hard-headed businessmen to pay a large sum of money for the diaries of a long-dead golfer. That leads me to assume that there is some unusual material involved, some scandalous material perhaps. The sort of thing you wouldn't anticipate from a man like Jones who was renowned as a gentleman.'

'There're some very revealing, er, revelations, John. I think you'll enjoy reading them.'

'And there we must leave it. Thank you, Mr Adams.'


As soon as I reached my office, I called the Kincaids' hotel. The telephone rang half a dozen times before it was picked up. Amy sounded half asleep. I asked for her husband.

'He's still in Bonnie Scotland, Chris, but he'll be back at the weekend. Is there anything I can help you with?'

'A number where I can reach him?'

'Hold on. He's at the Old Course Hotel in St Andrews.'

'Fine. I'm surprised you're not with him.'

'Oh, Chris, I've got so much shopping to do and London is the place to do it. But my evenings are pretty free. Why don't I buy you dinner? How about tonight? Or tomorrow would be fine. Just the two of us.'

I remembered Toby's strictures about Amy and I knew that, for once, he was probably right. 'I'd love to, Amy, but I'm speaking at a golf-club dinner tonight and I'm at the theatre with a girlfriend tomorrow. I'm sorry.'

'Well, if you change your mind. It would be nice to have a

real good chat to someone near my own age,' she said wistfully. 'I love Julie, as you know, but . . . I'll tell him you're going to call him, Chris.'

Visitors to St Andrews tend to be unashamedly sentimental about the Old Course and Kincaid was no exception when I talked to him that evening. 'I just love that course, Chris. I felt I was walking with history. All those great men who've played their hearts out there, for glory, I truly believe, not just for money. But, my God, the bunkers. I think I was in every single one.'

I made some sympathetic noises and then asked him whether he'd heard the news about Nick Adams's sale of the Jones diaries.

'I heard him on air this very morning. What's with that accent of his? I never heard anything like that before.'

I laughed and asked him the burning question: did he think the diaries were genuine?

'I still need to look at the originals but, if I had to hold up my hand and swear on the Good Book, I'd say they're forgeries.'

'Why?'

'Because there're some oddities of language that I don't think Jones, even when writing presumably for his own purposes, would've perpetrated. He wasn't a great stylist but he used the language well.'

'Any examples?'

'Lots of little things. He talks about his win in the British Open at Hoylake and he writes that he was in fantastic form. That's the sort of modern hyperbole that Jones wouldn't have used. He'd have said something like "I was at the top of my game." And, anyway, he wasn't in great form at Hoylake. Even though he won, he struggled at times and readily admitted it.

And you know my views already about the kiss-and-tell aspects of the diaries. There was no way Jones would've written such salacious comments.'

'Your old friend, Welbeck, has played an important role in getting those diaries accepted as the genuine article. You hinted the other day that you weren't entirely happy with his judgements. Maybe it's time now to be more specific.'

'Maybe, but I don't . . .'

'Will you talk with me and Toby? Give us some hard evidence?'

There was a pause while Kincaid considered my request. Then he said, 'OK, Chris. I'll be back in London a bit earlier than planned. Why don't we repeat our engagement of last week. Champagne at the hotel at, say, six o'clock tomorrow evening. With Toby, of course. I know Amy will be pleased to see you again.' Not half, I thought.

I told Toby about the arrangement and he agreed to be there. 'Excellent, young Chris. We may yet get a big story out of all this.'

'In any event we can have some fun at Harvey Nick's afterwards, eh?'

'No. It was all too much for me. Emma made me feel my age. A sweet girl but a bed too far for me.'

As an afterthought, I read out Paul Stacey's home telephone number and asked if one of the *News*'s journalists would be able to find an address to go with it.

'No problem,' Toby said. 'Those boys'll get his inside leg measurement if you want it.'

When we met the Kincaids again, Amy's attentiveness towards her husband struck a false note for a moment. But then I realized it was a genuine expression of her affection for the old man and I upbraided myself for being cynical.

As soon as the champagne glasses had been filled, Kincaid went to a desk drawer and pulled out a folder. He rummaged inside and then held up a one-dollar bill.

'Item one,' he said. 'A dollar bill, signed by Bobby Jones and dated nineteen-thirty and signed also by the President of the day, Herbert Hoover. It was amongst a batch of memorabilia I bought from Welbeck some years back.' Kincaid delved into the file once more. 'There's a letter here from the Chamber of Commerce in Atlanta, Georgia, saying that the dollar bill was auctioned by Jones at a lunch to raise money for out-of-work people in the city. So, there's your provenance, right?'

Toby and I nodded. 'Wrong,' Kincaid said. He sipped at his champagne. 'There's no record of his having been at such a lunch and, in fact, on the date of the lunch as stated in the letter, Jones was playing in the Inverness Invitational Four-ball Tournament in Ohio.'

'But the signatures could still be genuine,' I objected.

'No, they're forgeries. The Jones signature isn't bad but the Hoover one is way off.'

'A mistake?' Toby said doubtfully. 'Some of these forgeries get passed on from generation to generation, don't they?'

'Yes, but an expert like Welbeck,' and Kincaid emphasized the word expert with bitter relish, 'should know better. I don't have the next item here to show you because it's back home in my little museum. Another purchase from Sir Nicholas. It's the driver which Walter Hagen used when he won the British Open at Muirfield in twenty-nine. He had it made specially so that he could hit the ball low through the wind and, boy, was it windy and cold that year. The Haig wrote that Muirfield is located in the Arctic Circle part of Scotland. The driver had a funny kind of head, like a mallet, and the face was set with around eight degrees of loft.'

'And it's a fake?' I asked.

'Yeah. Another good one but the loft is all wrong. It's over ten degrees.'

'Any supporting documents?'

'Oh, sure. A note scrawled apparently in Hagen's hand that he gave the driver to his caddie. Skip Daniels, his name was. Hell, he'd already given his prize money to Skip. The princely sum of seventy-five pounds, which would've kept the old boy drunk for a year or more. Why should he bother to give him a club as well? It wouldn't have meant a thing to a caddie in those days. No, the whole thing is a nonsense.'

'Tell them about that medal, Julie,' said Amy. 'That's a fraud, too, isn't it?'

'Sure is, hon. Amy's referring to the medal that Ky Laffoon was given when he won the nineteen thirty-eight Cleveland Open. Another purchase from Welbeck. It's real nice but it's also a fake because Laffoon had all his trophies, and his golf clubs by the way, buried with him when he died.'

'And the family respected his wishes?' Toby asked.

'They did and I've checked that out with his sons.'

'As a matter of interest, Julius,' I said, 'why on earth did he do that?'

'Who knows? But he was eccentric and that's putting it mildly. After one tournament he tied his putter to the rear fender of the car and dragged it all the way to the next venue to teach it a lesson.'

We all laughed at the image and Toby said, 'I know how he felt.' He nodded his assent to another glass of wine. 'What you're telling us loud and clear is that Sir Nicholas, for all his reputation and his royal connections, is a crook.'

Kincaid considered the remark for several seconds. 'A crook? Well, not proven. Yet. But let's say that he sometimes appears a little less than scrupulous.'

'In that case, perhaps we should twist his tail a little,' Toby mused. 'And that goes for the obnoxious Adams too. I'll kick off with a piece in the *News* about the diaries. I'll say that they're forgeries and that a well-respected American expert says so.'

'Be careful, Toby,' Kincaid said doubtfully. 'Your libel laws can be very severe.'

'You don't have to sorry about that. The *News* will take up the cudgels if necessary. I'm going to challenge Adams to come forward with the original material and let you authenticate it.'

'He won't rise to it,' I said. 'He's already got an expert opinion from Welbeck. You'll find a writ for libel winging its way to your office.'

'Good,' Toby said. 'That's the sort of thing that newspapers thrive on.'

On Monday afternoon Toby telephoned to tell me that the challenge he'd promised to lay down for Nick Adams would be in the *News* on the following day. He also gave me an address for Paul Stacey; it was in west London, not all that far from my own home. That evening I was able to pass it on to Mrs Bradshaw, who was delighted at the prospect of at last beginning County court proceedings against Stacey.

As soon as the *Daily News* dropped through my letter box on the next day, I seized upon it eagerly. Amid the morass of football news and racing tips, Toby's story had been given reasonable prominence and a big headline which read: 'Jones diaries a fraud, says American golf expert.'

The report went on to say that Julius Kincaid, a leading

173

collector who was renowned internationally for his knowledge of golfing antiques and memorabilia and who had known Bobby Jones well, considered the great golfer's diaries to be forgeries. 'Kincaid, an immensely wealthy man and a long-time devotee of golf, takes an impartial view of the whole matter. Unlike Nick Adams, who is said to have sold publishing rights in the diaries for a cool million pounds. Adams, so-called publicity consultant to Page Three bimbos and purveyor of sleazy kiss-and-tell sagas to the rough end of the tabloid press, has no interest in objective truth. His interest is only in money, at whatever cost to a great man's reputation.

'The *Daily News*, in its fearless quest for truth, challenges Adams to submit the original Bobby Jones diaries to the scrutiny of an expert on the subject. Mr Julius Kincaid has put his vast knowledge at the disposal of this newspaper and is ready and willing to analyse the material and to give his verdict.'

I called Toby at around midday to find out whether there'd been any reaction to his article.

'The editor doesn't know which way to turn,' Toby said gleefully. 'He loathes Adams and would like to see him well and truly shafted. But he's bought quite a bit of sleaze from him in the past and now wonders if he's cut himself off from an important source. They deserve each other. My editor will probably slither away from the horns of his dilemma though – to mix the images a bit.'

'You usually do.'

'Thanks. And Adams has served the paper with a writ for libel.'

'That was predictable, wasn't it?'

'Yes, but what the editor had forgotten was that our proprietor also has a business relationship with Adams.'

'What sort of relationship?'

'His youngest daughter is trying to make it in television. She's done kids' shows and slots on those ghastly holiday programmes. And, guess what, she's a client of Nick Adams's.'

'It's a funny old world,' I said helplessly. 'So Adams is not about to accept your challenge? He won't get involved in your unflagging search for the truth?'

'No chance,' growled Toby.

'What's the next move?'

'I'll pay him a visit – doorstep him as we say in the trade. I'm going to ask him why he's so reluctant to let the diaries be examined.'

'I think I'd better come with you in that case.'

'I'm certain you should. It might get bumpy.'

# Chapter 23

'There's an awful lot of money in sleaze,' Toby said thoughtfully as we arrived at Adams's offices in a street only a few yards away from Kensington Square. His building mirrored the style of many of those in the celebrated square. It was an eighteenth-century house of stately proportions on five floors. A discreet brass plate on the wall carried the legend, Adams & Associates.'

'I wonder who the associates are?' I said.

'Bent journalists, drugs dealers, showbiz wannabes and Eurotrash,' Toby replied succinctly.

'You haven't entirely taken to Nick Adams then?'

Toby had established that Adams, when in his London office, left for lunch at a quarter to one on the dot. One of his favourite restaurants was Launceston Place, which was less than half a mile away, but he rarely walked to it. A cream stretched Cadillac with darkened windows for extra privacy was parked outside the front door. It could only belong to Adams.

At a quarter to one precisely the impressive front doors swung inwards and Adams appeared. There was nothing distinctive about the man. He was of middling height, wore a dark suit with a sober tie and was well groomed. He must have been in his mid-forties and his smooth, unlined face was very pale, almost waxy; he looked as if he spent all his life indoors.

As Adams walked down the few stairs below his front door,

Toby's photographer, Karl, took a few pictures of him. The front door of the Cadillac swung open and a lanky black man, clad in a suit the same colour of cream as the car, got out. He was closer to seven feet than six in height and had an array of gold rings on his fingers. I could see a gold bracelet on one wrist. There was scar tissue around both eyes. Maybe he'd been a basketball player; I hoped he hadn't been a fighter.

'OK,' said the chauffeur, as he swung the back door of the car open and exposed its cavernous interior, 'let the boss through.'

But Toby didn't. With Karl popping away with his Nikon, he put his considerable bulk directly between Adams and his car. 'Mr Adams, can you give me a quote about the Bobby Jones diaries, please?'

'I can. But where are you from? Who do you represent?' Adams's vowel sounds really were quite remarkably peculiar and I found myself leaning closer to him to register every inflexion.

Toby waved his press pass and plonked it back in his pocket. 'I'm from *Golf World*, Mr Adams,' he lied glibly. He produced a tape recorder. 'We'd like a quote. Are they genuine?'

'They certainly are and the public will be able to see for themselves when they're published early next year.'

'So, Sir Nicholas Welbeck is right and Julius Kincaid is wrong.'

'I've never heard of this guy Kincaid. Which crack in the wall did he crawl out of? What I do know is that Sir Nicholas is the top authority on the subject and that's all I need to know.'

'Kincaid was a close friend of Bobby Jones,' Toby persisted. 'He says the style is all wrong in those diaries. They couldn't possibly have come from his pen.'

Adams looked ostentatiously at his watch. It was a gold

Rolex, wouldn't you know. 'I'm already late, friend,' he said, 'and I've given you enough of my time.'

Toby still didn't move and Adams made as if to push past him. But Toby stood firm and said, 'The buzz is that you and Welbeck are in cahoots to make a lot of money out of a forgery. What d'you say to that, Mr Adams?'

Adams stood back and to one side. 'Andy.' He flicked his fingers in the direction of his chauffeur. 'Move this tub of blubber from out of way, will you?'

Andy moved swiftly. He grabbed Toby by the right arm, twisted it sharply behind his back and then hurled him across the pavement at Karl. The diminutive photographer took the full force of Toby's sixteen or more stones and they both went down in a tangle of arms, legs and cameras. I noticed that Toby kept a firm hold on his tape recorder.

'Was that necessary?' I tried my fearless look on Andy.

He didn't reply but his long right arm snaked out and grabbed hold of my shoulder. Christ, another man with bloody great hands. His grip was fierce. 'Look, man,' he began, but his words tailed off to a grunt as I swung my right foot and kicked him with all the force I could muster under the left knee. That was effective; he let go of my shoulder and grabbed me by the throat. I knew that he was capable of squeezing the breath out of me in a matter of seconds. I grabbed his wrist with my left hand and then pivoted towards him, my other arm rigid and the fingers outstretched. He half-ducked away but I caught him partly on the bridge of the nose and partly in the left eye.

'You bastard,' he screamed and I lashed out and kicked him again under his left knee. This time, he let go of me completely and I was able to duck close to him. I chopped him smack on his Adam's apple with the edge of my hand, just as my brother Max had taught me. Down went Andy on the pavement, fighting for breath, his hands scrabbling at his throat.

The whole incident had taken a matter of seconds and only two passers-by, on the other side of the street, stopped to see the fun.

When I looked at Adams, he had produced a mobile telephone from his pocket and was about to dial – the police, I assumed, but maybe some reinforcements. I walked towards him and he began to back away.

'Don't bother to call for help,' I said. 'We're on our way. Your minder started the rough stuff, not us. I'd suggest he goes back to night school for a refresher course.'

I couldn't resist patting Adams on the cheek, hard. Just as they do in the mafia movies.

Toby was brushing down his jacket when I turned towards him, and Karl was looking regretfully at one of his shirtsleeves which had been ripped as Toby's weight knocked him to the ground.

'Put it down to expenses,' Toby said, as he urged us away from the incident and towards Kensington High Street. 'Is your camera OK, Karl? That's the important thing.'

'Oh yeah, the pictures are safe, Toby. That's the important thing,' Karl said sarcastically. 'The fact that you've been using me as a trampoline doesn't matter at all.' He grinned quickly. 'Christ, I didn't realize golf was such an exciting game. I thought it was just blokes in check trousers bashing a little white ball around a field. As for bleedin' James Bond over there . . . Where did you learn those nasty little tricks?'

'Here and there,' I said diffidently, though with a silent thank you to my father who'd encouraged me and Max to learn self-defence.

'He has a brother called Max who not only has an alarmingly brilliant mind but is also a tearaway,' said Toby telepathically.

'Did you get any good pictures?'

'I fired off a few frames of Chris and the black geezer doing the tango. Trouble is, I had to reach around Toby here and just blast away one-handed. God knows what I got. Should be something usable. And I got some good shots of Chris saying ta-ta to that Adams bloke.'

'Excellent,' Toby said. 'This calls for a good lunch, I think.'

'Launceston Place?' I suggested.

'I think not. There's a little French place I know on the other side of the High Street.'

'You realize that Adams will put two and two together and identify you, Toby, and then me, don't you?'

'I'll make it easy for him. The story, with pictures, will be in the *News* tomorrow. The freedom of the press must not be threatened by bully-boy tactics.'

'Jesus,' said Karl, 'he even writes his own headlines.'

Over a long and enjoyable lunch, Toby and I came to the conclusion that we needed to know more about Welbeck's activities and his character. He was one of the central figures in the controversy about the Jones diaries and, in Toby's opinion, could probably shed some light on the other alarums and excursions which had afflicted the golf antiques scene.

'I'd simply like to know more about the way Welbeck operates,' Toby said pensively. 'How does he make his money? Who does he do the big deals with? Is he as successful as he looks? His life-style is that of a very rich man.'

'He must have inherited money along with his title,' I said.

'I don't know, though I assume so. The boys in the office will have the press cuttings. We can look at the accounts for his business. We can even try to look at his personal finances, though that'll be a bit more difficult. Does he have any

181

significant investments, here or abroad? Does he own that house in Chelsea? Does he have property elsewhere? We don't know all that much about him, do we?'

'Since you put it that way, no,' I agreed. The waitress placed the list of desserts in front of me and, in view of my earlier exertions, I had no intention of resisting something sweet and sticky. *Tarte aux pommes Normande* with fresh cream got my vote and Toby, who had ordered a *creme brûlée*, insisted on our accompanying the dishes with large glasses of Barsac.

By this time Karl had tottered off in search of a taxi. He promised to have the photographs on Toby's desk by five o'clock.

'Why don't we interview Welbeck?' I said, the seed of an idea beginning to germinate in my mind. 'We can simply ask him all the questions about his background. OK, he won't give us all the answers but his evasions and half-truths will be revealing in themselves.'

'I don't think the old pseud would agree to my doing a profile of him,' Toby said.

'Not you. Laura Stocker.' It had suddenly come to me that an interview in a glossy magazine, accompanied by lots of flattering photographs of Welbeck and his possessions, would be a lure he would be incapable of resisting. It was well within Laura's compass to pretend that she'd been commissioned to do the piece by one of the prestigious monthly publications that pandered to their readers' dreams of a luxurious life.

Toby gave the suggestion a few moments' thought and said, 'Laura's not an experienced journalist. She'll cock it up.'

'No, she won't. She's very bright and you and I will brief her thoroughly. She's also young and pretty and terribly nice. She's from the same background as Welbeck and she'll flatter the old bugger. He'll love it.'

'You've got a point.'

'The important thing is that because she's young and inexperienced, she'll be able to ask all sorts of leading questions and get away with them. He'll be able to patronize her. He'll love that and she'll get away with blue murder.'

Toby laughed. 'Do you know, Chris, I think you've got something. In fact, it has the makings of a brilliant idea. Let's arrange it. But we'd better tell your girlfriend to be non-committal about which magazine is going to take the article. Otherwise, Welbeck might ring up the editor – he's bound to know them all – and then she'll be in the mire.'

'Laura will know someone who knows Welbeck, I'll bet you. She'll get an introduction and he'll take the bait.'

# Chapter 24

The *News* did Toby proud on the following day. Having already received a writ from Adams, they were now prepared to go after him whole hog, never mind the proprietor's connection. Toby had three-quarters of a page, including a photograph of Adams, poised self-consciously outside his office. There was also a picture of Andy, with his hand seemingly around my throat and his other arm raised threateningly. Since my back was to the camera, I couldn't be recognized as the object of his aggression. That was just as well because, although my mother was emphatically not numbered among the readers of the *Daily News*, someone would have told her about the photograph and it would have confirmed all her fears about the violent and wicked city in which her eldest son lived. She would then have assailed me with a remorseless series of questions about the incident and entreaties to behave myself.

As he had promised, Toby had penned a thunderous indictment of Adams's cowardly attack on a member of the press who was merely trying to go about his business in a thorough and impartial way. I had to smile at the picture Toby drew of himself – St Toby, sturdy seeker-after-truth. Sometimes I think he even convinces himself. He went on to emphasize how Adams had refused to meet his challenge to allow Julius Kincaid to authenticate the Jones diaries and that this was the

185

action of a man with something to hide.

However, Toby's final paragraph took the controversy to a new level. 'Your correspondent cannot help but wonder,' he wrote, 'how a man like Adams, a purveyor of trashy tales to the down-market tabloids and a publicity-monger for wannabes on the sleazier shores of showbiz, has become involved in a gentlemanly sport like golf. It is even more incongruous that he should have any connection, however remote, with a man like Bobby Jones who had the divine spark of genius allied to the chivalry and humility of a great champion.

'In recent months, in a spate of robberies, golfing treasures of incalculable value have disappeared. A well-known Japanese dealer in golf antiques, Charlie Ito, has been murdered. Diaries of dubious origin have been offered in the market-place by a dealer in sleaze who, when challenged by the *News*, has reacted by serving a writ on this newspaper.

'I ask myself whether this is coincidence. Or has some syndicate, organized by ruthless criminals, moved in on what it sees as a new and lucrative market? Whatever happens, the *News* will keep asking the right questions until we have the right answers.'

Within minutes of arriving in my office, Helen Raven came through the door brandishing a copy of the *News*. 'What were you doing taking on a thug like that?'

So much for being unrecognizable. She responded to the surprise she saw in my face. 'It's the shape of your head, Chris. It's unmistakable. Anyway, I guessed that if Toby was in trouble you'd be on hand.' She gave me a more thorough once-over. 'You seem to have come through unscathed. How's the bruiser?'

'I, er, dissuaded him from making too much of the incident.'

186

'Well done. And Toby got his story. I hope he pays you danger money.'

'Some chance,' I said, as my telephone rang.

It was Laura. Helen blew me a kiss and left the office.

Laura told me that she'd had no trouble in finding someone who knew Welbeck. One of her uncles was on the Sotheby's board of directors and he'd already written to Welbeck to ask him to grant her an interview. 'Uncle Rob, my ma's brother, he's very sweet. He's a publisher and he used Welbeck to edit a series about the great twentieth-century painters. So, he can't refuse me really, especially as Uncle Rob said the article would help my career along.'

'Sounds great. When d'you think you'll get to meet him?'

'Sometime next week, if he's free. Meanwhile, Chris, I've been talking to my surveyor friend.'

'Giles? Was that his name?' I laughed dismissively.

'Do I detect an acid quality in your voice? He's been very helpful.'

'Perhaps he's hoping to make a comeback.'

'We had a fling and it was nice while it lasted. Now we're good friends. It can be done, Chris,' she said severely.

The gist of Giles's comments was that, like us, he couldn't quite rumble what the boys at R S Developments were doing. In his view the property was still only worth around a million pounds, so their valuation was wrong. In the mid-eighties, he could have understood an investment in such a property because a healthy profit could have been made in a matter of weeks. But no longer.

'On the contrary, in fact,' Laura said. 'Giles wants to look at some of the other places that R S have got. He'll run his rule over them, so to speak. Can you fax the addresses to him?'

\* \* \*

187

Some days before, Jake Bowden had asked me to caddie for him on the coming Sunday. A new golf club was being opened near Canterbury by one of Jake's friends, a multi-millionaire who'd made his money from garden centres. Mad on golf, he had built, with the help of a large investment from a Japanese bank, his own golf complex. No expense had been spared and Jake was to be attached to the club as its touring professional.

When he first called, I had been evasive, since I fancied a quiet day with Laura: a laze in bed with the papers, a late breakfast, a few drinks at lunchtime and perhaps a movie in the afternoon. Or more bed.

I was hoping that Jake had found a replacement for me but he called me later that day to confirm the arrangements.

He sensed my reluctance and said, 'Look, Chris, it's an easy day for you. You turn up for lunch, and it'll be a bloody good one by the way, and then we do our stuff. They've flown a top Japanese golfer over and Nick Spencer and Tony Swan are making up the numbers, old son.'

I laughed at the idea of Spencer and Swan, both winners of majors and stalwarts of the European Ryder Cup team, making up the numbers. 'The owners have really pushed the boat out, haven't they? Those two won't have left them much change from a hundred grand.'

'Normally, yes,' Jake replied, 'but they each designed a course and so they're playing the exhibition match as part of the deal. By the way, I told the guv'nor that your caddying fee is a monkey. OK? In cash, of course.'

My resistance began to weaken. A day out in Kent and five hundred pounds at the end of it was not to be spurned. I told Jake I'd be there.

'Oh, Chris, bring old Toby with you, can you? A few of the press boys have promised to give us a plug but I told the guv'nor

188

you'd bring him. I knew he wouldn't be covering the Scandinavian Open.'

That was true. Toby had a profound antipathy to the northern parts of Europe and confined his trips to what he regarded as the more civilized areas: Paris, Monte Carlo, Cannes, Madrid, Rome and Salzburg found their way into his itinerary, but not many other places. I promised to try and persuade him to make the trip. I knew he'd enjoy the lunch – it was the golf that might put him off.

When Jake had said that no expense had been spared he wasn't exaggerating. The two courses at the Great Stour Golf and Country Club were both of championship standard. The clubhouse was a huge edifice, with acres of glass between soaring pillars clad in wood. The interior had marble floors, extravagant decorations and a vast amount of space in which to relax. There were three bars, a restaurant and a brasserie, a swimming pool and a fitness room.

Even Toby was impressed. 'My God,' he said, as he headed towards the first bar he saw, 'this must have cost millions.'

A marquee had been erected outside to cope with the large number invited to the opening and a horde of waiters and waitresses tried to keep up with the demand for champagne. The lunch was a lavish affair and included Dublin Bay prawns, several varieties of smoked salmon, caviar ('the real thing' said Toby approvingly) and a selection of cold meats including succulent slices of rare roast beef. Toby was impressed with the wines, too, especially a 1982 claret.

Mercifully, the speeches of welcome were short and many of the guests, especially Toby, were reassured to be told that refreshment booths had been stationed around the course. I slipped away to change into my caddie's gear: cords, golf shirt, short-sleeved sweater and trainers, plus a bib with Jake Bowden's name on the back and the crest of the new club on the front.

Jake was teamed with Tony Swan against Nick Spencer and the Japanese golfer, whose name was unpronounceable. 'Call me, Joe,' he said, but that was the extent of his English. Our Japanese wasn't very good either.

There was a side-stake of £25,000, provided by the owners, for the winners of the four-ball better-ball match. Jake hadn't mentioned that but it meant that all the players were trying hard, especially Jake. Fortunately, his partner, Tony Swan, was in majestic form and Jake hardly came into the match during the first twelve holes, by which time he and Swan were two holes in the lead. Spencer reduced the deficit at the long thirteenth with an eagle but Jake chipped into the hole for a birdie at the very difficult fifteenth for a win. He secured the match at the next hole, a par five, with an eagle when he holed out from a greenside bunker.

Theatrically, Spencer held his head in his hands. 'You are a fookin' horrible bastard,' he said in his flat Midlands accent. 'We knew we'd have fookin' trouble with you. Didn't we, Joe?' He shook hands with his Japanese partner. 'Twenty-five big ones down the drain, eh, mate?' Joe nodded and smiled politely.

'Come on,' Tony Swan said, 'we'll play the last two holes for a hundred quid each. OK?'

Both were halved and Swan good-humouredly conceded a putt of four feet on the last hole to ensure the result.

As we walked towards the changing room, Jake said, 'Well, I owe you a bonus for that. Ten per cent?'

'That's very generous,' I said. I knew that my fee of £500 was already waiting for me in the manager's office.

Jake patted me on the back. 'We're a good team, my old

son. Now, you are going to carry my bag at the Open, aren't you?' I nodded. 'And the week before at the Scottish Open?'

'Doubtful, Jake, there's so much on.'

'Think about it. I'll even try and bribe you with another antique club. Another Forgan, maybe.'

'Ah, Jake.' I paused because it's difficult to tell someone that a present you've received isn't what it seems. 'That niblick you gave me. I don't know where you got it but I'm afraid it's not right.'

'How d'you mean?'

'It's a fake.'

'Shit. Are you sure?'

'You've heard me talk about Julius Kincaid? He took one look and called it. He knows his stuff, Jake.'

'I can't believe it. Of course, I handle replicas as well as the real thing. I must've mixed them up. Never mind, Chris, I'll find you a real good one.'

'Where do you get the replicas made?'

'A bloke I know called Ted Merton. He's got a place down near Camber Sands on the coast. East of Rye. He uses a hut on what used to be an Army camp. It's a God-forsaken place. Ted's brilliant. He doesn't just make replicas. He restores old clubs as well. You can't see the join.' Jake winked at me.

'Will you give me the address?'

'Sure. I'll write it down for you now.' I was curious about Ted Merton. I decided I'd take a look at what he did.

Having collected Toby from one of the bars, where he was regaling a noisy group of revellers with the reason why the European team couldn't possibly win the next Ryder Cup, I told him that we were going to take a slight detour on our journey back to London. I almost gave in to his grumbles about the consequent delay and the price we would pay when we joined the heavy Sunday traffic on the M25; but I hardened my resolve, thrust a road map in Toby's hands and told him to get me on the road to Rye.

It didn't take as long as Toby had predicted and, after asking for directions a couple of times, we arrived at the address that Jake had given me for Ted Merton. A sagging fence of concrete posts with rusted barbed wire still marked the perimeter of the old Army camp. Four lines of battered wooden huts spread out from what had once been the barrack square. Many of the windows were broken and roofs were open to the elements. A faded sign by the gates told us that this was the Camber Sands Workers' Cooperative. I drove the Porsche slowly on to the square and we got out. Beyond the far fence there was an expanse of dun-coloured scrubland; a van lay abandoned on its side and there were other piles of scrap and rubbish dotted about.

Toby shivered slightly, although the evening was mild. 'Watch out for the mad axeman,' he muttered.

I pointed at one of the huts. 'That's what I wanted to look at.' The wooden door had been painted yellow and there were sturdy bars protecting the windows, which were all intact. A sign by the door read 'Ted Merton, antiques restorer.'

'Terrific,' Toby said. 'Now you've seen it let's get back to London.'

The door had an iron plate across its centre and a staunch padlock. There was no way in. I stepped back and looked at the roof but there weren't any skylights to open. Since all the windows were barred I was reduced to peering through one of them. All I could see was a workbench, tools neatly racked on the wall above it and a desk to one side. I thought I could smell glue but it was faint enough to be illusory. The door on the

192

adjoining hut sagged open and I gave it a shove and looked inside. There were signs of a former occupant; a tattered sleeping bag lay in one corner and an upended plastic crate held a chipped mug with its handle missing. I looked hard at the wall which divided the two huts, tapped it and leaned against it. It was surprisingly sturdy. Not only would it be difficult to break into Merton's hut but it would be obvious that someone had done so. Anyway, what was I hoping to find? That was what Toby asked me impatiently when I went back outside.

'I don't know,' I admitted. 'Merton is the bloke that Jake gets his replica clubs from. Says he's a craftsman. I was just curious.'

'And I'm curious to see how long it'll take us to get back to civilization. This place gives me the creeps.'

The answer was over two hours and we arrived back in west London shortly before ten o'clock. I agreed to drop Toby at his house in Fulham and happily fell in with his suggestion that we had a couple of pints at one of the local pubs. At closing time we were both hungry and headed for a nearby Indian restaurant. It was busy and by the time we'd finished our meal it was nearly one o'clock.

Toby lived in a quiet street of small terraced houses and his house was situated on the end of the row. But it wasn't at all quiet as we drove around the corner towards his home. There was a fire-engine outside Toby's house, its warning lights flashing, and I could see the back end of another one parked in the side street. A police car, its blue light winking, was double-parked alongside the fire-engine. I was lucky enough to see a gap among the parked cars and I reversed the Porsche into it.

Toby was out of the car with understandable speed and he broke into a trot towards his house. As we got nearer we could see the hoses snaking indoors from the fire-engines.

'Great God Almighty,' gasped Toby. 'What about my wine? And that sodding manuscript?' As usual he had his priorities right. His main concern was for two cases of Gevrey-Chambertin that he'd recently been given; his book on famous British clubhouses came in second place.

Toby positively galloped up the short path to his front door but was prevented from entering by one of the firemen. 'You can't go in there, sir,' he said, his arms up like a policeman directing traffic.

'I'm the owner,' Toby said curtly.

'Nevertheless, it's not been declared safe yet.'

'What happened?'

'It's not as bad as it seems. You were lucky, sir. The fire started in the kitchen and we got there before it spread too far.'

'Someone spotted it then?' I asked.

'Yes, a bloke on his way home. He got caught short and stopped for a pee against the garden wall. He saw flames through the window and called nine-nine-nine. Drunk as a lord he was but he probably saved your house.'

'Where is he?' Toby said. 'I must thank him.'

'Wouldn't stay, sir. Wouldn't even give his name and address.'

'That's a pity. I'd like to have thanked him in person. Have you any idea what caused it?'

'It looks as if it was started deliberately, I'm afraid. The glass in your kitchen door was broken and it seems that a bundle of rags was set on fire and thrown inside. But don't quote me. There'll have to be a proper investigation.'

'Are you sure?' Toby said. 'I don't understand. Why would anybody . . .?'

'The police will deal with all that,' the fireman said firmly. 'Here's Sergeant Bartram.'

There wasn't much we could tell the policeman or that he

could tell us, but it took us nearly an hour to establish that. The firemen collected their equipment and declared that there was no further danger of fire. I offered to help Toby clear up the mess in the kitchen but he said he'd got a better idea. He led the way into the sitting room and poured us both a brandy.

'It's unnerving, isn't it?' he said. I nodded sympathetically. 'I was bloody lucky. I could've been upstairs asleep. God knows what would've happened.' I nodded again.

'Who would do such a thing?'

I nearly suggested that it could have been one of the millions of *Daily News* readers but it wasn't the time for that brand of humour. 'Has anyone got it in for you?' I asked. 'Any nasty disputes on the go? You're not late with your alimony payments, I hope?'

'No, even though those women are bleeding me dry. Could it be Welbeck, do you think?'

'No. It's not his scene. But . . .'

'Nick Adams?'

'One of his thugs, maybe. You've hit him where it hurts and he's taking his revenge.'

'He's a bloody idiot,' Toby said. 'If it is him, this only confirms what we suspect, that the Jones diaries are fakes.'

'Not necessarily. Adams is a piece of low-life who isn't used to being messed around. So he hits back. Did you mention him to Bartram?'

'It didn't occur to me.' Toby drained his brandy, poured himself another and offered me the bottle. I took a small tot.

'I'll talk to Inspector Rattray,' Toby said.

'Rattray? The man who had the temerity to feel your collar?'

'I don't hold that against him,' Toby said huffily. 'Anyone

can make a mistake. Though how he could've suspected me . . .
Anyway, I won't mind talking to him about that hooligan,
Adams.'

# Chapter 25

Toby rang me the next afternoon and, once again, I pressed him to let me help him put his kitchen back into some kind of order.

'No, no,' he said. 'Isobel is already hard at it. She sees it as a great opportunity for a total redesign of that part of my home. God help me and my bank account. The insurance money won't cover even a small part of what she has in mind.'

'Well, you didn't ring me about interior design. Did you talk to Rattray?'

Toby had done so, at length. He had aired his suspicions about the diaries and his theories about who had caused the fire. Rattray had been noncommittal.

'He's like a bloody sponge,' Toby complained. 'I threw all sort of ideas at him and he absorbed them and that was it. But he did give me one piece of information – about Charlie Ito.'

'He's made progress on his murder?'

'Nothing to speak of. But he's been making inquiries about Charlie in the Far East, in Hong Kong and Singapore and Japan and it appears that old Charlie had some very dodgy associates. For a start, he'd done time for fraud and he's suspected of being involved with a bunch of crooks who handle stolen antiques and so on.'

'The yakuza by any chance?'

'Yes. The yakuza. What d'you know about them?'

'Not a lot but they're the Japanese version of the mafia, aren't they?'

'And just as powerful. Rattray said the yakuza generate annual income well in excess of ten billion dollars. They're into everything, just like their Italian counterparts. Drugs, brothels, gambling, extortion and they launder their money in all the usual ways. They even own a few golf clubs.'

'Not a great investment these days. I suppose they're well connected in business and politics?'

'Absolutely. Anyway, Ito was apparently a member of one of the biggest yakuza organizations.'

'That doesn't say a lot for Sir Nicholas Welbeck, does it?'

'Guilt by association? I made that point to Rattray but he was very stand-offish. He still seems to regard Welbeck as a pillar of the establishment.'

'He has an immaculate public persona,' I said regretfully. 'But we'll see what Laura can find out. She's interviewing him on Thursday.'

'And we've got to rehearse her, haven't we?'

'Don't worry, Toby. I'll deal with it.'

'Yeah, I bet you will.'

Not that Laura needed much in the way of coaching or rehearsal. She came round to my flat that evening with a couple of pages of questions already prepared. Apart from anything she might uncover which would be of interest to Toby and me, she said confidently that she was treating the interview as the real thing. 'I'll sell it to one of the glossies, whatever happens to Welbeck.'

Laura had to leave early the next morning and I went to the front door to wave her off. My car was parked near the front gate and was mostly hidden by Laura's little sports car. As she reached it she stopped suddenly, as if puzzled, and then waved urgently at me.

I padded down the steps and across the driveway. Laura merely pointed at my Porsche. It had been comprehensively trashed. Three of the tyres had been slashed and the lights, the windscreen and the side-windows were shattered. Crude scratches had been gouged down both sides of the body and the paintwork on the bonnet was cracked and blistered.

'Oh, Chris.' Laura was almost in tears – she was even more upset than me. 'Who could've done this? What's that stuff on the bonnet? Acid?'

'Brake fluid probably. That'll lift the paint off.'

'We didn't hear a thing, did we?'

I shrugged and made an effort to control my anger. The nearby main road would have helped to cloak any noise and the bastards who did the damage would have used padded hammers to smash the glass. I had always scorned the idea of having a car alarm; they were unreliable and were heard, it seemed to me, by everyone but the car owner. Anyway, you could bet the people who'd done over my car would've known how to immobilize an alarm.

'Local vandals?' Laura, her arm on my shoulder in sympathy, asked quietly.

'Maybe.' I didn't want to frighten her by suggesting anything more sinister.

'Or is it Adams? Toby thinks he tried to burn his house down, so trashing your car would be a comparatively minor reprisal.' Laura obviously wasn't concerned about frightening me.

'Adams doesn't have my address though I suppose he could get it easily enough. I wonder if it's got something to do with those bent lawyers, Reynolds and Stacey. I should think that

Mrs B's writ has been served on Stacey now and he's realized that I was the one who uncovered his address.'

'Are they that vicious?'

'I wouldn't put anything past those two.'

'You'll report this to the police, won't you, Chris?'

I promised to do so but only because I'd need a crime number to put on my insurance claim. I had no intention of passing on to the police my theories about who had planned the damage to my car. But I did let Toby know about it and he had no doubt that Adams was the man to blame. My money, however, was on Reynolds and I was in the mood to tell him what I suspected.

I rang his office and spoke to Tania who told me that her boss was due in the office at eleven o'clock. 'But he won't see you without an appointment,' she warned.

That wasn't necessary. I'd be waiting for him.

At several minutes past eleven I spotted Reynolds crossing the road towards his office building and ducked quickly into the gap between the inner and outer doors. As he entered I stepped in front of him. I saw a distinct look of unease flicker in his eyes and then it was covered by his habitual arrogant stare.

'Out of my way, slag.' Such a gent. He hunched his shoulder and prepared to shove past me.

I didn't move. 'Did you trash my car yourself or employ some other hooligan to do it?'

'Trash your car? What're you on about? I've got better things to do.'

'Like set up property scams? That sort of thing?'

'Get out of my way, shithead, or you'll lose worse than that sodding Porsche of yours.'

I let him go. My suspicions had been confirmed. One day soon it would be my turn. With luck.

# Chapter 26

Laura had agreed that, on the evening following her meeting with Welbeck, she would come to my flat to talk Toby and me through the interview. We were sceptical of her chances of uncovering anything of importance but, as Toby said, it was a good excuse for a meal and a few drinks. I had prepared all the ingredients for a stir-fry meal and Toby arrived by taxi, with a bottle of champagne and two bottles of claret. He doesn't like to go short.

'I'm looking forward to Laura's debriefing,' he said with a leer.

I didn't bother to reply just then because the doorbell rang and I went to let Laura in. She gave me a smacking kiss on the lips and said, 'Christ, I'm exhausted. I couldn't stop Welbeck talking. He's very full of himself, isn't he? He dropped enough names to fill the Albert Hall.'

'So it went well?' Toby said eagerly.

'Give me a glass of that fizz,' Laura replied, 'and I shall tell all.' She opened a plastic briefcase. 'I have the Welbeck tapes in here and also a selection of photos.'

'The Welbeck Tapes,' Toby said with relish. 'There's a certain ring to that, don't you think? I smell a big story and a lucrative one for all concerned.'

'I don't know about that,' Laura replied. 'I didn't get any

earth-shattering information from him, I'm afraid. In fact, I had a distinct feeling that he'd been through this kind of interview several dozen times. His replies were well-practised and he had many an apt quote at the ready.' She flicked through her notes. 'Let's see. "The object of art is to give life shape." That's one from Jean Anouilh. I looked it up afterwards. "Abstract art? A product of the untalented, sold by the unprincipled to the utterly bewildered." That, believe it or not, was written by Al Capp, the cartoonist.'

'And he was spot on, in my opinion,' Toby said.

Laura described Welbeck's house, a classic Georgian building in Chelsea. It was like entering a superior art and antiques centre. Each room was stuffed with elaborate furniture and every horizontal surface covered with *objets d'art*; the walls were hung with a variety of art that looked extremely valuable, although Laura confessed that her knowledge of painting was limited.

'Did you ask him about Van der Neer and the other works that were nicked?' I said.

'Yes, and he said that the Van der Neer was the only one that he really cared about. Despite the fact that they also took works by Thomas Hodge and Francis Powell Hopkins and a well-known piece by Charles Lees.'

'Presumably not worth bothering about in comparison with the Van der Neer?' Toby said.

'That's right. That's exactly what Welbeck said.'

'Which confirms what everyone has been saying, that the paintings were stolen to order,' I said. 'But with the accent on the Van der Neer. What was it worth?'

'He was cagey. He just muttered that it was worth hundreds of thousands of pounds.'

'Half a million was the estimate I heard,' Toby said.

'"The work was beyond price to me, my dear. I was distraught."' Laura did a passable imitation of Welbeck's mellifluous tones. 'That's what the old poseur said. He went all solemn and sincere. He really laid it on with a trowel. There were times when I didn't know whether to scream with laughter or throw up.'

Jamie Tilden had been present for most of the interview, except when answering the telephone or making coffee for her and Welbeck. She had asked about Charlie Ito but had learned nothing. Welbeck had described him simply as a fringe operator, an unimportant dealer who, nevertheless, had quite good contacts in the Far East.

'You can say that again,' Toby growled.

Laura had not taken to Tilden, whom she described as a charmless toy-boy.

'What about the diaries? Did you tackle him about their authenticity?'

'Yes and he got very high-falutin',' Laura laughed. 'He wittered on about his high standing in the world of golf and his integrity. He said that the diaries were unquestionably the work of Bobby Jones. The handwriting experts had confirmed this but "my textual analysis, my dear" was the clincher. So there.'

It was clear that our stratagem hadn't taken us very far and Toby agreed to listen to the tapes to see if he could pick out anything of interest. Before I went into the kitchen to do the stir-fry, Laura showed us the photographs she had taken. Welbeck certainly lived in sumptuous surroundings – that is, if you wanted to live in an art gallery-cum-antiques shop. He wore his usual charming, if patronizing, smile. Tilden had edged his way into several of the pictures.

Laura saved the most interesting photographs to the end. They showed several pages of a diary and had been shot from different angles: head on, from the side and even over Welbeck's shoulder. We could see his long, beautifully manicured fingers in most of the pictures.

'How did you get these?' I asked.

'I went through the usual boring business of getting him to describe his typical working day and working week. "A life in the day of" sort of thing. Of course, he was eager to let me know how important he is, how many top-notch people he knows and so on. I was wide-eyed with wonder and admiration. I egged him on and took a few shots of him and the odious Jamie supposedly sorting out his appointments and work schedule. And then I thought it would be interesting for you two to have a look inside his diary.'

'How did you persuade him?'

'I simply suggested that a few snaps of him and Jamie going through his diary and assessing his commitments would be fun. But I took close-ups of the pages instead.'

'Clever girl,' said Toby, 'but does it tell us anything?'

Laura looked immensely pleased with herself. 'Take a look. They're bloody good pics.'

I had a magnifying glass which went with a two-volume set of the *Compact Oxford English Dictionary*. We laid out the six photographs on the table and focused a lamp on them. Apart from the appointments for each day there were several names at the top of each page; they were obviously reminders to Welbeck of people he had to contact. Harry Goodison cropped up twice, as did Nick Adams's.

Toby and I went carefully through the names but we could see nothing that struck us as interesting. I handed the magnifying glass to Toby and left to get on with the cooking.

A few minutes later Toby wandered into the kitchen with one of the photographs in his left hand. His right hand had a firm grip on his glass of wine. 'Steeple A P,' he said.

'Eh?' I stirred the vegetables vigorously, admiring their colours. Red, yellow and green.

'Steeple A P,' he repeated. 'It means something to me but I know not what. It crops up three times.'

'It's probably a firm. Steeple Something & partners.' I juggled the vegetables into a dish and put them in the oven.

'I hope there's a meat dish to go with all those noodles and vegetables,' Toby said plaintively.

'Lemon chicken with mushrooms and king prawns in oyster sauce.'

'Oh, excellent. I'll send Laura in to help you serve up. Steeple A P,' he muttered, as he left the kitchen. 'I swear I've heard that somewhere.'

When we had demolished the main course and the cheese was on the table, accompanied by another bottle of claret, Toby declared that he'd also been doing some research on Welbeck or, rather, that 'one of the boys in the office' had done some digging for him.

It transpired that Welbeck was not as sound financially as the casual observer of his life-style would have imagined. His house in Chelsea, although its value was approaching £750,000, was mortgaged up to the hilt. So was his apartment in Biarritz.

'That was left to him by his father,' Toby said. 'But that was about the only tangible asset he did leave and it was outweighed by the debts. Welbeck inherited a title but it carried a lot of negative equity with it. Apparently his dear old dad was a colourful character. He liked to gamble and he liked the ladies.'

'Unlike his son,' added Laura.

'Not the ladies, perhaps,' Toby said, 'but he has inherited

his father's penchant for a flutter. According to my colleague at the *News* he's blown away a lot of money in the futures market. As you know better than me, Chris, there are huge rewards if you get it right . . .'

'And potential disaster, if you don't.'

'And he didn't. He's also a name at Lloyd's.'

I groaned. 'Don't tell me. He joined some dodgy syndicates and now he owes hundreds of thousands.'

'Correct. The result of all this is that Welbeck's assets lag way behind his liabilities. In effect, he's insolvent.'

Toby's colleague had also managed to collate some of his trips abroad over the last eighteen months. Welbeck had visited Brazil, Thailand, Hong Kong, the Philippines, the Bahamas and South Africa.

'All on business, of course,' Toby said. 'And he goes first class, with Tilden, and they stay in the very best hotels.'

'How did you find all this out?' Laura asked.

'Don't ask,' Toby replied. 'But I think my colleague has an invaluable contact inside one of the credit agencies.'

'What about his company accounts?' I said. 'They ought to tell us something.'

'Unfortunately he's set up several companies and his money is switched hither and thither between them. It's a financial labyrinth and impossible to work out what he's up to.'

'But do they look like prosperous businesses?'

'There's quite a lot of income sloshing about, especially from what are loosely described as consultancy fees . . .'

'From people like Adams, I suppose,' I said.

'And maybe from Charlie Ito. But Welbeck's expenses are huge. So it's difficult to see whether his companies are solvent.'

'Welbeck's in the financial mire right up to his neck,' Laura said decisively. 'He's also trapped by his style of living and by his puffed-up conceit. He really does consider himself to be one of the elite in British society. What a pathetic delusion.'

# Chapter 27

The more I thought about Laura's brutal summary of Welbeck's character and his financial situation the more accurate I thought it. His self-assertive pose as the doyen of the golfing art market had irritated me soon after I'd met him at the Royal Dorset Golf Club; his subsequent posturings as a man of integrity had put me on my guard even more. Men of integrity don't declare it; they allow others to make their own judgements.

I cast my mind back to the various people with whom I'd discussed Welbeck and his career. Not a single one had given him a whole-hearted endorsement. Neville Thorneycroft had told me about the Matisse and hinted that Welbeck might have acted improperly. And Sonny Brew at Browning's in New York hadn't exactly given Welbeck a clean bill of health over the eighteenth-century picture which might have been a forgery. Neither of them had actually accused Welbeck of being a crook – in fact they'd taken care to defend him. But they would because he was one of their own, a member of a relatively exclusive tribe whose living depended on the public's belief in its knowledge of paintings.

I recalled the picture dealer whose opinion had been quoted by Toby: 'Half the pictures on the market at any one time are wrong-'uns.' I bet he hadn't been very popular amongst his colleagues.

I was reminded that Sonny Brew had promised to track down the name of the dealer who'd brought the dodgy painting to Welbeck when he was at Browning's. After lunch I called her. She was as helpful as before and told me that, yes, she had been given the name by one of her colleagues. She asked me to hold. She knew she'd written it down somewhere. I heard the shuffle of papers and the occasional muttered curse.

'Here we are, Chris,' she said, after a minute or so. 'He was called Baron de Murat. Hey, that must be French or Belgian maybe. Anyway, he was the guy.'

I thanked her and she told me to be sure to call in and say hello when I was next in New York.

The dealer who'd been involved in the Matisse affair when Welbeck was at Sotheby's was called Piet Mulder. In his other guise as Baron de Murat, the dealer had connived with Welbeck to unload another highly questionable work, this time on Browning's. Since I'm no believer in coincidences, I decided that Welbeck and Mulder were up to their necks in a conspiracy.

Later in the day I contacted Toby and told him what I'd found out and he expressed his delight that 'the pompous git' might be as crooked as he was patronizing. He had also discovered something.

'Steeple A P. It's Steeple Ashton Priory,' he said triumphantly. 'I knew it was somewhere in the old retrieval system.'

'Well done. So, Welbeck's trying to buy something off them, d'you think, or do a valuation?'

'Nothing like that, I think. It's one of those havens for drop-outs. Drunks, junkies, anyone who's been damaged by society . . .'

'Do I detect a sneer in your voice, Toby?'

'No, you do not, I assure you. Better that they're getting some advice and some square meals than cluttering up the pavements. Apparently the whole place is funded by some millionaire philanthropist. Benny Hutt, he's called.'

Toby rapidly sketched Hutt's background. He had founded a remarkably successful computer software company and had sold it for well over a hundred million pounds about five years before. He already owned Steeple Ashton Priory which included several hundred acres of land. One of his daughters had become hooked on drugs and, despite undergoing the best treatment that money could buy, she couldn't kick the habit. That had concentrated her father's mind and he had decided that her failure was his failure. He took her and a number of other addicts into his own personal care.

'His methods aren't popular with the social workers and the tame psychiatrists,' Toby continued. 'In fact he won't have any truck with them or other grisly manifestations of the Nanny State. Hutt emphasizes individual and collective responsibility. If his clients don't accept the rules of his community he kicks them out. His theory, and it seems to work, is that these addicts are at odds with themselves and with society but they actually crave acceptance. By working at Steeple Ashton and accepting its philosophy they can, by a gradual process, rediscover their dignity and claim their place in his community.'

'In *his* community,' I said. 'What about the outside world? What happens when they quit the security of Steeple Ashton and tackle the real world again?'

According to Toby, many of the inmates had made a successful return to society but they were not forced out and some stayed on for years at the priory. They included Hutt's daughter. There were nearly a hundred in residence.

'How does he fund it all?'

'From his own resources but he also gets contributions from other rich individuals. And he puts all his charges to work.

Apparently, the place is virtually self-sufficient. They grow much of their own food and they even make their own wine. A glass a day for anyone who wants it, except the alcoholics of course.'

'A bit short of your quota, Toby.'

He grunted. 'And they manufacture quite a range of goods for the outside world. Toys, clothing, furniture, shoes. They have a printing shop and, of course, they undertake computer programming.'

'So what was Steeple A P doing in Welbeck's diary?'

'I don't know. Sure as hell Welbeck won't be throwing money in Hutt's direction. Maybe Hutt is a collector. Anyway, I think we should go there and try to find out.'

During the next few days Toby went away to cover one of his favourite tournaments, the Côte d'Azur Open, and I caught up on some of my own work at the Royal Dorset Club. I followed Jake's progress down in Cannes and he finished in the top thirty. Not bad. It augured well for the Open Championship. It wasn't until the middle of the following week that I spoke to Toby again. He rang me late one evening and asked me whether I'd seen the evening paper. I hadn't.

'Well, when tomorrow's paper arrives you'll find that our friend Welbeck is about to pull another rabbit out of the hat.'

'Another unknown Matisse?'

'Not quite. He's called a press conference for midday tomorrow to announce his acquisition of a significant collection of historic golf clubs and balls. That's all he'd say. All will be revealed tomorrow. I've had a call from Julius Kincaid and he and Amy will be there. So will all the other major collectors or their representatives. Can you make it?'

212

I decided I could and promised to be at Franklin's Hotel in Chelsea just before midday.

Franklin's was a small and exclusive hotel in a stately building a couple of hundred yards from Sloane Square. The room where the press conference was to take place was already quite full when Toby and I went in. There were probably around fifty people and two middle-aged waitresses in black skirts and white blouses were distributing glasses of wine. Amy Kincaid waved to us from the far side of the room and indicated that she'd reserved a couple of chairs for us near the front. Her husband smiled benignly in our direction.

Amy waved even more enthusiastically at us and Toby and I eased our way to the front row to take our seats. 'Hello, you guys,' she said, 'isn't this exciting?'

A long table faced the room with four chairs behind it: one for Welbeck and one, presumably, for his assistant. The treasures which were to be revealed at the press conference had been stacked on the table and covered by a cloth; two security men stood guard.

Just as I was wondering who the other participants were to be, a side door opened and Welbeck walked in, followed by Harry Goodison. The two men offered a distinct contrast: Welbeck immaculately groomed in a beautifully cut pinstriped suit; Goodison in a baggy brown suit, the top button of his shirt undone, his tie awry and his hair in wild disarray. Jamie Tilden followed them in, as smoothly presentable as his master, and then Jonathan Wright, who looked mighty pleased with himself.

Welbeck rose to his feet, held up his hands for silence and told us how pleased he was to see us. Golf had been a passion for most of his life and he had been lucky enough to have acquired some knowledge of the history of golf, its equipment

213

and its art. He had been even more fortunate to have seen at close quarters some of the great golfing treasures. All collectors, he went on, have their dreams; most of them dream of unearthing something thought to be lost for ever or of finding a hitherto unknown collection of antiques or paintings which is of great historical value.

Like the actor he was, Welbeck held his pause a shade longer than was natural and then continued. 'I once had the great good fortune to find an unknown Matisse and it was one of the most exciting moments of my life. And my delight was compounded when Her Majesty the Queen did me the signal honour of adding it to her collection. So, it can happen. No doubt you have read of the recent discovery of a painting by Turner. The crucial factor in its identification was the artist's fingerprints in the paint. A wonderful story. And then there was the Poussin which was attributed, by Sotheby's of all people – I'm glad I don't work for them any more – to a minor painter and valued at around fifteen thousand pounds. Now it's estimated to be worth eight million. These are the events which make the art and antiques market so romantic and so exhilarating.'

Welbeck paused once again and Toby muttered 'Get on with it man.'

'We've all heard tales of amazing collections, hoarded for generations by mysteriously elusive families,' Welbeck continued. 'And we dream of uncovering them. Some of you will know of golf's first serious collector, Mr Falconer, who was said to have hundreds of clubs as early as seventeen-ninety. His collection has never been uncovered. Now, I haven't found that but I have found one of the finest hoards of golf artefacts ever seen. The physical evidence lies under that cloth. A treasure trove, ladies and gentlemen.'

Welbeck nodded at Wright and Tilden, who moved to

214

opposite ends of the table and whipped off the cloth. The audience craned forward, eager to see the treasures. There were over twenty golf clubs laid out on the table and a dozen or more balls, both featheries and smooth guttas. Several people stood up to get a better view and Welbeck said, 'Please remain seated everyone. You'll have a chance to look at the collection. But, as you all know, the items must not be touched.'

He seized a glass of water, drank deeply and continued. 'This is an astonishing array of treasures of great historical significance.' Welbeck reverently picked up a wooden club. 'This is a long-nosed wood used by Willie Park when he won the first Open Championship at Prestwick in eighteen-sixty.' He gently replaced the wood and plucked another from the table. 'Here's another driver which belonged to Old Tom Morris. He used it when he won the Open in eighteen-sixty-seven which was his last victory. This baffing spoon was the property of his son, Young Tom.'

On he went, listing the treasures: the putter used by John Ball, the first amateur to win the Open; a driver, a spoon and a baffy made by Hugh Philp in 1830 and presented to William IV on his accession to the throne; a niblick which belonged to Horace Rawlins, the first winner of the US Open. Then Welbeck held up what he called the jewel in the crown.

'This is an iron with a medium loft. You can see its square toe. It was a multi-purpose club with which the golfer could play out of sand or out of bad lies. It's extremely rare and probably dates from the eighteenth century. It has a shaft made from alder, not the usual hickory. I know of only a couple of dozen clubs of similar style and antiquity.'

On the other side of Amy, I saw Kincaid lean forward and push earnestly at his glasses. 'If that's genuine,' he muttered, 'it's worth a king's ransom.'

215

Welbeck told us that there was a full list of the clubs in the press release which would be handed to us on the way out. 'I was also fortunate enough to acquire eight feathery balls, which are in mint condition. Four of them are by Allan Robertson and the others by John Gourlay of Musselburgh and by Thomas Alexander.'

'There won't be much change out of a hundred and fifty thousand dollars for those balls alone,' I heard Kincaid whisper to Amy. 'If they're genuine, that is,' he added automatically.

'Finally,' Welbeck said, 'half a dozen smooth gutta balls, two of which are painted red. You see, ladies and gentlemen, there were golf fanatics even in those days who wouldn't forsake their game of golf even when snow lay on the ground.' He was rewarded with a few laughs. 'They are all in excellent condition.'

There was a concerted buzz of conversation as Welbeck paused and Kincaid leaned across his wife and said, 'Chris, Toby, he's got well over a million bucks of antiques on that table, maybe nearer two million. I just can't believe it.'

'Bearing in mind what we all know about him,' I said, 'what do you think, Julius? Can we believe it? Are they kosher?'

'Hell, I'd have to take a real close look. Some of those things are tough to copy but it's amazing what a clever faker can do. It's all in the provenance. What's Welbeck got to back up his story? That's what I want to know.'

Right on cue Welbeck, prompted by Wright, spoke again, his urbane voice pitched just strongly enough to quell the noise from his audience. 'My colleague has asked me to reassure you about the provenance of these articles. It is, as I'm sure you would expect, impeccable.' He smiled briefly. 'One last thing. The clubs and balls will be auctioned during the week of the Open Championship at Royal St George's. It's a fitting venue in my view, a traditional course where those great champions whose clubs we see before us would have felt thoroughly at home. My good friend, Harry Goodison, will be handling the sale. In conclusion, I'd like to thank you all for coming here today.'

As Welbeck moved towards the door, Kincaid stood up and said loudly, 'Do you mind if I ask a question, Sir Nicholas?'

Welbeck turned, looked pointedly down his nose at the American and said, 'Ah, Mr Kincaid. What a pleasure to see such an avid collector at our little gathering. Please, ask away.'

'Will you please tell us more about the provenance? You kinda passed lightly over something which is real important. OK, we can establish that they're from the period you claim they're from, that's easy. We can look at the materials and the way they've been manufactured and apply some science, but how do we know that they actually belonged to Park and Old Tom Morris and the others? Do you have documentation?'

'It's good to see that our transatlantic cousins retain such a firm hold on reality, isn't it?' Welbeck said disdainfully and was rewarded with a few scraps of laughter. 'Of course, Mr Kincaid is right. I can assure him that there is documentation to support the integrity of all the items.'

'From the players themselves, attesting that they really owned the clubs?' Kincaid persisted.

'Not in every case,' Welbeck admitted, 'but I have examined the clubs and the balls very carefully and they are genuine. We also have the word of the family who inherited the collection that everything is as it seems.'

'Their word?' Kincaid made no attempt to hide his astonishment. 'Their word? What the hell kinda provenance is that? Without real back-up those are just nice examples of antique clubs. A good collection but nothing special.'

'Mr Kincaid is, as usual, a victim of his own scepticism,'

Welbeck retorted. 'I am happy, and so are the other experts I've consulted, with the clubs. They are genuine treasures. I would stake my reputation on that.'

'That could be a very dodgy bet,' Toby murmured.

Marshalled by Welbeck, the four men began to move towards the door. The security men started to wrap up the clubs and place them in a metal trunk.

But Kincaid was not giving up. He advanced on Welbeck, with Amy in his wake. Wright barred his way and, although his arms were folded, he looked militant. I followed Kincaid in case civilities were not maintained – not that I thought Wright would get heavy in front of nearly fifty journalists and potential customers.

Before anyone could speak, however, Harry Goodison loomed over us and, with a conciliatory smile, invited us all into the ante-room 'to continue our discussion'. Toby was close behind me as we joined Welbeck and Tilden, who were clinking glasses of champagne. Toby stepped forward eagerly – raised his eyebrows hopefully in Tilden's direction – without effect.

Although his equanimity seemed undisturbed, Welbeck went on the attack at once. 'Julius, it's a shame that you couldn't restrain yourself from making those ridiculous assertions. At my press conference. Not terribly good form, even for an American.'

'Good form doesn't come into it, Sir Nicholas,' Kincaid replied. 'The truth does.'

'The truth is that those artefacts represent a wonderful addition to the history of golf.'

'Only if they're genuine,' Kincaid replied.

'What possible grounds have you for doubting it?' Wright asked, his voice hard but emotionless. 'Sir Nicholas is an expert of world renown. Where does that leave you?'

'Gentlemen, gentlemen,' Goodison began but was overridden by Kincaid's next remark.

'I don't have any particular axe to grind,' he said, 'and if the items are right I'll be in the bidding with the best of 'em. But this game isn't like a court of law where a man is innocent till proven guilty. The onus is on you to show that the goods for sale are genuine. By the way, where'd you get the stuff?'

'A very old-established Scottish family who've been associated with golf for generations,' Tilden said.

'Oh yeah, who?' Amy spoke for the first time. 'Julie will know 'em. He goes all over Scotland looking for his golf things.'

'We are not at liberty to say,' was Tilden's predictable reply. 'It's a confidential matter and the family wish to remain anonymous.'

'I'm not surprised,' Kincaid said sharply. 'They'd be off my guest list if I was a Scot and I found out they'd sold part of my golfing heritage. Why, in God's name, didn't they offer it all to the R & A, for their golf museum? They'd have come up with a reasonable price, surely.'

I watched Welbeck finger his Royal St George's Club tie and then smooth his hair quickly. He was either irritable or nervous, or maybe both.

'This is getting us nowhere,' Wright began but Welbeck interrupted.

'No, Julius can have an answer. The family in question is impoverished and it's their privilege to dispose of their collection in any way they wish. They asked me to help them and that is exactly what I'm doing.'

'You seem to be involved in quite a lot of controversy these days, Sir Nicholas,' Kincaid stated quietly.

'What's that supposed to mean?' Wright's tone was harsher.

'One of your associates, Charlie Ito, ended up dead. Your

house was burgled. And you authenticated the Bobby Jones diaries which, from my analysis, look like forgeries. Now you've suddenly uncovered all these treasures. My, you are a busy fellow.'

Welbeck's hand went to his tie again. He shook his head and turned away from Kincaid and the rest of us. 'Jonathan, would you see our guests out,' he said. Wright walked over to the door and opened it.

'Well, we're obviously not going to get a drink here,' Toby said and he led the way out. We straggled along behind him. Wright said nothing but his malicious glare in the direction of the Kincaids spoke volumes.

# Chapter 28

The telephone roused me from a doze on Saturday morning. To my surprise it was Toby and his message was brief: he was on his way over at once. Just stay there. Before I could question him he rang off.

When he arrived I was in the bathroom and Laura was making bacon sandwiches and coffee. Toby walked in as I was drying myself.

'Good God, Toby. What's got you out of bed so early?' It was just after ten o'clock. The lack of response to my light-hearted remark and a closer look at Toby's face told me that something serious was up. I led him through to the bedroom.

'Julius rang this morning. Amy has gone missing. He's in a terrible state.'

'Gone missing? She's left him?'

'Not voluntarily. She went for a stroll in the park. Apparently she does so most mornings, if it's fine. That was the last he saw of her.'

'He's told the police?'

'No. He wants to talk to us. There's a note, apparently.'

'A ransom demand?' Toby shrugged. 'Look, Toby, this is a matter for the boys in blue. Kidnapping is serious. We're not competent to help. They'll want a lot of money from poor old

Julius and then, when they've got it, you know what happens, don't you?'

'Victim found dead.'

I nodded. 'So this is one for Scotland Yard.'

'We can at least talk to him first. He's an old man. He's in a terrible state. We have to give him our support.'

When we arrived at Kincaid's suite, it seemed to me that he was reasonably composed. But his face was grey and looked as if it had suddenly sagged.

He sketched out what had happened. It added very little to what Toby had already told me. Then he said, 'The note's on the table. I've tried to hold it by the edges just in case I have to call in the police. They might find something. A fingerprint, maybe.'

'You should call the police now,' I said gently.

'Read the note,' he replied. 'Then we can talk it through.'

The kidnapper had used a ball-point pen to print a few words on a piece of lined paper. The message read: 'Kincaid, if you behave yourself your wife will be returned unharmed. No police or else. Look for her at the Open.'

His head propped on his hand, Kincaid was sitting on the edge of an armchair. 'It's real obvious where that note came from,' he said forlornly.

'Where?' I asked.

'Welbeck. And the message is plain too. Keep your nose out of my business, he's saying, or take the consequences. There's no other person has reason to do this to me. It's Welbeck. Do you agree, Chris?'

'Yes and no. He's involved, that's for sure. But he may not be the prime mover.'

'Agreed,' Toby said. 'Welbeck wouldn't condone a kidnapping. He's too soft. He's devious and doesn't mind a bit

222

of fakery if it brings the money rolling in, but I doubt he's got the guts for violence.'

'Somebody has,' Kincaid said, his voice suddenly strong. 'And it's Amy who'll suffer . . . Who could've done such a thing?' His voice tailed off again.

In an effort partly to concentrate our minds and partly to encourage Kincaid to think positively, Toby and I went through the sequence of events. It had begun with the successive robberies at three golf clubs; the removal of valuable paintings from Welbeck's own home; the sudden appearance in a blaze of publicity of the hitherto unknown Bobby Jones diaries; their authentication by Welbeck and Kincaid's doubts about their integrity; and, finally, Welbeck's miraculous discovery of a hoard of valuable antique clubs and balls. Tactfully, we didn't mention the deaths of the Royal Dorset steward and of Charlie Ito.

Kincaid remained in his chair, his eyes listless. It seemed that he was already grieving for Amy. But he didn't avert his mind from stern reality. 'And one man beaten to death and another tortured and killed,' he said. 'So we've got fraud, murder and kidnapping. That doesn't give me much hope for Amy.'

'The Ito murder may well be a coincidence and have no connection with the other incidents. And the killing of the steward wasn't a deliberate act,' I said gently.

'But we have to assume that one or more of Welbeck's associates, if not Welbeck himself, has taken Amy,' Toby said.

'Who's your money on?' Kincaid asked.

'Nick Adams perhaps. We know he'll use any means to get his own way.' I reminded Kincaid of our contretemps with Adams and the subsequent attempt to burn down Toby's house. 'Maybe it's Wright,' I continued. 'He's the same stamp as Adams. Nasty, with a potential for violence.'

'How do I get Amy back?' Kincaid gulped at his coffee, which must have been stone-cold. He looked old and frail as he struggled to control his despair.

Toby patted him on the shoulder. 'Chris and I will put our thinking caps on. We'll find her.'

'We must call the police,' I stated firmly.

'No, Chris,' Kincaid said. 'Remember the note. I've got to keep clear of the police. Amy's all I've got . . . I'm an old man and she's made me very happy.' He looked up and smiled suddenly. 'Hell, we're all men of the world and I know that Amy has her followers, let's say. But she's the soul of discretion – she pays me that compliment – and I know she loves me as much as I love her. So I won't run the slightest risk of anything bad happening to her.'

There was silence for a moment as Toby and I digested Kincaid's remarks. I was glad that I hadn't accepted Amy's invitation to dinner. The American was shrewd and remarkably frank. He also possessed the integrity to which Welbeck merely laid claim.

'What if we go to Inspector Rattray and tell him everything we know about Welbeck and his friends?' I said. 'That might flush them out of the woodwork and Amy along with them.'

'That's far too dangerous,' Kincaid said, alarm in his eyes. 'Your bobbies are probably like our big city cops, the LAPD or the New York guys. They won't be subtle. No, Chris, I'll put my trust in you and Toby. You're my best shot. And I'll give you all the help you need. Money's no object.'

The thought of the elderly Kincaid being closely involved with our efforts to find his wife disturbed me. He would inhibit me, that was certain. I wandered over to the window and gazed over the park, while I considered how to get him out of the way. Japan might be the answer.

'Julius,' I said, 'I promise you Toby and I won't involve the police without your permission. But, quite honestly, I'd rather you were out of the firing line. You know the important collectors in Japan, don't you?' He nodded. 'Despite what I said before, I'm willing to bet that Charlie Ito's murder ties in with Welbeck and his various frauds. So, why don't you do some detective work?'

'I don't really want to leave Amy . . . but I see your point. If you think I can help.' Kincaid's words petered out for a moment. Then he continued, 'There's a whole bunch of people I can talk to out there. I'll call them. Maybe I can find out just how close Ito and Welbeck were. If they were in bed together—'

'What an unedifying thought,' Toby said, a look of disgust on his face.

Kincaid smiled a wan smile. 'If I can show that Welbeck had close links to Ito and therefore to a criminal organization—'

'Then we might tie him or his associates to Ito's murder,' said Toby.

'I'll have to move fast,' Kincaid's voice trailed off, his thoughts again on the dangers afflicting his wife.

'You might find it more effective to take a trip to Japan,' I suggested. 'Make some calls first and then hop on a plane.'

'I don't really want to leave London.'

'You'll be more use to us and to Amy in Japan,' Toby stated. He was clearly as keen as I was to get Kincaid out of the way.

'First stop for me is Steeple Ashton Priory,' I said briskly, as if Kincaid's Japanese trip was agreed. 'We need to know why Welbeck's been in contact with them. How about a trip there today, Toby?'

'I'm busy today, dear boy. Off to Lord's. But thereafter I'll be at your disposal. Why don't you take the delicious Laura.

225

Make sure she's got a camera with her. What's your story, by the way? You can't just turn up and wander about for no good reason.'

'I'm an acquaintance of Welbeck's. I'm looking for suppliers of this and that and could I have a look at what they do? I'll ring them up and say that I've got to be in the area today. Sorry it's short notice.'

'Fine,' said Toby. 'There's one thing that really bugs me about this business. Where does Harry Goodison fit into the scheme of things?'

'I agree,' Kincaid said. 'He seems like a nice guy. What's he doing with the likes of Wright and that Tilden fellow?'

'You're closer to Harry than anyone, Toby,' I said. 'Why don't you try and find out more about what he's up to?'

'We tried that, if you recall, and we got the brush-off.'

'Yes.' I thought for a moment. 'Jonathan Wright got rid of us. He seems to have a lot of influence, doesn't he?'

The voice at the end of the line at Steeple Ashton Priory was both languid and frosty, but thawed ever so slightly when I mentioned the name of Sir Nicholas Welbeck and my wish to look at some of the products they made with a view to supplying them to a mail-order customer of mine. I would be bringing my assistant, I said. The kick Laura gave my leg was gentler than I expected.

She was happy enough to accompany me on the unexpected visit and I was grateful for another pair of eyes. Her sharp intelligence would be useful.

The priory was to the north-west of Salisbury in lovely rolling countryside. It was about half a mile outside the village, a huddle of stone cottages along a zig-zag main street, with a post office, a store and a small pub on a corner. We asked directions at the store and I got the feeling that the middle-aged man behind the counter only just stopped himself from spitting on the floor in response. With ill grace, however, he gave me directions.

The entrance to the priory was set well back from the road and a crescent-shaped patch of grass, sheltered by oak trees, lay in front of it. It was a cool day, with rain in the air, but at least a dozen people were sitting or lolling on the grass. A couple of battered vans were parked and more people were huddled in the back of them.

We drew up by the iron gates and I pressed a button on a security panel. I announced myself and, after a minute or so, a slender man in jeans and a Status Quo T-shirt came out of the stone lodge on the other side of the gates and let us through.

Laura rolled down her window and asked the gate-keeper what the people on the grass were waiting for.

'They're waiting to be let in. Some have been there for weeks. Mr Hutt only takes a few at a time and mostly on recommendation from friends and from former clients. So that lot have to prove they really want to join us.'

'By hanging around until they get the nod?'

'That's it. Off you go. Straight up the drive, please.'

The driveway, flanked by graceful birch trees, was nearly half a mile in length and finished at a stone archway. Beyond, there was a sprawling manor-house, built from mellow stone. Its elegant pointed windows, steep roofs and corner turrets gave it a melodramatic look and I guessed that it had been built by some Victorian bigwig. A plaque by the huge double doors told us that it had been commissioned by Sir Arthur Trentham, a shipbuilder, in 1835.

We pushed through the doors into a high-ceilinged hall with oak-panelled walls. Our footsteps echoed on the marble as we walked into the centre of the room. We paused. Solid-looking sofas and armchairs were scattered about and a broad wooden staircase led upwards for several feet before branching away in two directions. A woman, clad like the gate-keeper in jeans and a T-shirt, appeared from a door to the right of the stairs. She was tall and very thin, her greying hair scraped back away from her face. I was beginning to wonder if Benny Hutt bothered to feed his charges.

'How do you do, Mr Ludlow? I'm Barbara Durrant.' It was the woman I'd spoken to earlier in the day. I shook her hand which was like grasping a few small but knobbly twigs. She smiled at Laura and I noticed how yellow her teeth were. 'The workshops are all out at the back. I'll show you round. Mr Hutt would like you to have a cup of tea with him later. Since you know Sir Nicholas.' Christ, I hoped Hutt hadn't called him to check me out.

The workshops were at the back of the house in what had once been the stables. Other outhouses had been pressed into service and a few wooden huts had been constructed to augment them. There was nothing amateurish about the equipment and organization of the various work areas, although there wasn't much action except what looked like a bit of routine maintenance. Barbara Durrant explained that work stopped at one o'clock on Saturday and began again on Monday morning.

A coachhouse had been converted into a showroom and Barbara, as she asked us to address her, showed us the full range of the Steeple Ashton products. Laura and I displayed our acting talents once more; I assumed the role of a retailer and asked questions about delivery dates and discounts, while Laura tackled the subject of the raw materials used in the workshops. Were they environmentally sound? Was the wood used in the furniture from sustainable resources? We were pretty good.

Naturally, Barbara had an impeccable environmental stance and made capital of the fact that the priory was, as near as practicable, a self-sufficient community. As we left the showroom, she pointed at the roofs of the various buildings. 'There are the solar panels that provide much of the heat we need and we're experimenting with wind and water generators. We even use clockwork radios. Of course, you can't have clockwork television, not that we encourage our clients to watch it. But since many of them enjoy it so much . . .' She shrugged.

As we approached the back door of the house, Barbara gestured towards another doorway and said, 'That's where your friend, Sir Nicholas, has his work done. Specialist stuff, as you can imagine.'

'Specialist?' Laura queried.

'Yes. Mostly picture restoration. Some *objets d'art.* And odds and ends for the golf market. Not an area I'm interested in, actually.'

'It's quite a growing market,' I said quickly. 'Can we have a look inside?'

'Only if Pat says so, I'm afraid.'

'Pat?'

'It's his domain. Nobody enters without his say-so. Mr Hutt gives him a pretty free rein because his work is valuable in terms of the income it brings in for our community.'

'From Sir Nicholas?'

'Yes. Pat was in a bad way when he came here a few years ago. In fact, Sir Nicholas introduced him.'

'What was wrong?'

'We don't discuss our clients' problems, Mr Ludlow.'

'Quite,' I said. 'I'm sorry.' I tried to peer through the window

229

but couldn't see anything. 'Pat is obviously a very talented man.'

'I'm told he can turn his hand to anything,' Barbara replied. 'A very skilful painter. Mr Hutt has some of his work in his study. I'll take you there for tea.'

# Chapter 29

Benny Hutt looked as if he was just the right side of fifty, a man of medium height neatly dressed in faded jeans and a short-sleeved cotton shirt. He had closely cut grey hair and a few days' growth of stubble on his face. Half-moon spectacles sat on the end of his nose but he removed them as he rose from behind his desk to greet us. His study, large and rectangular, was made more impressive by the oak-panelled walls and the curved windows on two sides. They overlooked a wide stretch of lawn enclosed by high hedges.

Hutt saw me glance outside and said, 'One of my indulgences. I like the privacy.' He waved us towards a table which had part of an ornate china tea service on its top. My eyes were caught by the paintings which were arrayed on the walls.

Again, Hutt interpreted my look and said, 'Interesting, aren't they? There's a Gauguin, a Braque and a Miró. The Picasso you'd recognize, of course. And the Hockney. Then there's the Turner and the Constable. My apologies, since you're friends of Sir Nicholas you'd undoubtedly know them all.' He smiled and began to pour the tea. 'Only one is genuine. The rest are copies. Brilliant copies, in my opinion.'

'They were done by Pat, I suppose,' Laura said.

'Oh yes. He's unrivalled. That's why Sir Nicholas sends so much work his way.'

231

'They've known each other a long time, of course,' I said, trying to imply that I knew much more about Pat than I really did.

'So I believe,' Hutt replied. 'I don't inquire too closely into a client's past, though they all have counselling sessions. It's the present and the future of these people that matters. Sir Nicholas sent Pat here. He had a severe mental breakdown. He's an alcoholic. I sometimes wonder whether he'll ever be able to leave. Meanwhile, Sir Nicholas keeps him busy with restoration work and other projects. A shade too busy, I sometimes feel.' Hutt shrugged. 'I suppose it's good therapy.'

I'd already decided that Pat must be Patrick Moloney, the man of whom Neville Thorneycroft, the ex-Sotheby's man, had spoken. Patrick Moloney, alias Piet Mulder, alias the Baron de Murat. Several things were clicking into place and I decided the only way to progress was by asking a leading question.

'Sir Nicholas has spoken so often about Pat Moloney. Could I meet him?'

Hutt studied me through his sharp brown eyes. He smiled fleetingly; good humour seemed to be close to the surface. 'We don't use clients' surnames here. Why are you so interested in him, Mr Ludlow?'

'I've heard a lot about him and I have a customer who'd be interested in his work.' I gestured at the paintings. 'Genuine fakes, we could call them.'

'Pat's got enough on his plate,' Hutt said, and popped half a biscuit into his mouth. 'And he's not terribly good with outsiders. I'm not sure that Sir Nicholas would like it either. He's an important contributor to our funds and pays us a generous stipend to look after Pat, as long as he has first call on his skills.'

I'll bet he can afford to be generous, I thought.

'I'd love to have a look around his workshop,' Laura said. 'Photography's my hobby but I'm keen on most of the visual arts. Do you think Pat would mind?'

Hutt paused and I thought that he suspected we were not exactly what we claimed to be. 'Well, it's my workshop, not Pat's and it's certainly not Sir Nicholas's, though I sometimes wonder . . . So why not?' He smiled broadly at Laura, rather like an indulgent uncle. It's amazing what the gentle touch can achieve.

It was no wonder that I hadn't been able to see into the interior of Moloney's workshop, since the window which took up most of the wall opposite the door was covered by a blind. Hutt released it and we then saw all the accoutrements of the painter-cum-picture restorer: racks of brushes, tubes and pots of paint, bottles of turpentine, knives and razor blades, pots of varnish and glue, several palettes, and canvases of various sizes stacked against a wall. There were components for frames of all shapes and sizes, and a pile of old and presumably worthless paintings piled in a corner. I assumed that Pat would re-use them. On a wide shelf I saw an array of pens, many of which looked like collectors' pieces, and inkpots of different hues. A bottle of olive oil, some eggs, a loaf of bread, some flour and a jar of honey lay incongruously amid the clutter. In another corner there stood a contraption that looked like a baker's oven and, against one of the walls, there was a bookcase full of tomes on the major painters and their techniques.

'This is it,' Hutt said. 'Not terribly romantic, is it?'

I looked up as a figure appeared in the doorway. It was Barbara, who asked for a few moments of Hutt's time. As he went outside to talk to her I took a close look at the papers which were strewn across the top of a pine table. There was a yellow folder with a thick sheaf of typewritten material inside.

Stuffed in the back of the folder were several invoices from a firm of paper manufacturers in Somerset. I scribbled their telephone number on a scrap of paper. I heard Hutt concluding his conversation and Laura hissed a warning as, in desperation, I grabbed several sheets from the middle of the manuscript, folded them roughly and shoved them into my trouser pocket. When he walked back into the workshop I pretended to be studying a canvas on which the outlines of some figures were lightly sketched.

Laura looked over my shoulder. 'It looks as if Pat's going to do a Degas,' she said to Hutt.

'That wouldn't tax him, I can assure you,' he replied. He told us that, regretfully, he would have to leave us in order to greet a new client. I wondered if it was one of those forlorn creatures waiting by the front gates.

As we parted outside the workshop I asked Hutt again if I could meet Pat to discuss some projects. I promised to clear the ground first with Welbeck. He shrugged and asked me to call him. 'My people can do what they like, within reason, as long as they abide by the rules of my community. Self-discipline and self-respect are the watchwords here. Of course, we need money and if you can enable one of them to earn more for the common good, that's fine by me.' I would have been glad to help Hutt and made a mental commitment to do so when the Welbeck affair was over.

'Would some more publicity help?' I asked. 'I could bring a friend of mine down from the *Daily News*.'

'By all means. Anything like that is of great value. The donations come rattling in after a sympathetic piece in the press.'

'Is Hutt on the level?' Laura asked as soon as we'd turned out of the gates of the priory. 'I can't quite make him out.'

'You mean he doesn't play the role of the wild-eyed idealist or the saintly father-figure.'

'Far from it. He seems a very cool and pragmatic character. A businessman who happens to be running an unusual venture with a bunch of drop-outs. He's got something, hasn't he?'

'Sure has. A touch of charisma and bags of determination. And what did you think of the artistic Mr Moloney?'

'Hutt was very up-front about the copying he does, wasn't he?'

'But does he realize that Welbeck is passing off Moloney's fakes as the real thing?' I said. 'I'm assuming that the Matisse that is now in the Queen's collection was forged by Moloney and that he doctored the golf painting that caused all that trouble at Browning's. I wonder just how many other little coups he and Welbeck have pulled off. And, if Hutt knows, does he care?'

'He might just turn a blind eye but I don't think he'd be in on the scam,' she said and I agreed with her.

By now we had reached a fast road and Laura wound up her car to well past the speed limit. 'What about those bits of paper you pinched?' she yelled at me over the noise of the engine and the stereo which was belting out some Wagner.

I felt about in my trouser pocket and fished out the crumpled sheets of paper. The first page began:

'After the pressures of the match at Royal St George's, it was a great relief to relax. We won easily, as in most years, but I found foursome play especially testing, mainly because of the responsibilities you feel towards your partner.

'In contrast the *Golf Illustrated* Gold Vase at Sunningdale was a delight, nothing serious about the competition. My golf not good in the morning but when S appeared after lunch, divinely beautiful in a grey and red dress, my game reached a higher plane. A sixty-eight in the afternoon won the competition for me.

'We dined with friends at the Ritz this evening, including Lord Lurgan, who made a great fuss of S. She came to my room just after midnight and . . .'

I read on in growing disbelief as the writer described his passionate couplings with the anonymous S.

'Come on, Chris,' Laura said impatiently. 'What's it all about?'

'Listen to this.' I read out some of the action scenes and she giggled.

'Yum, yum,' she said, 'we'll try that as soon as we get home.'

'You see the implications, don't you?'

'Yes. But I believe that form of love-making is banned in Catholic countries.'

'Laura, this is a part of the so-called Bobby Jones diaries. I've no idea when he played in the *Golf Illustrated* Golf Vase but that match he refers to could be the Walker Cup. He played several times in that. It could've been nineteen-thirty if it was Royal St George's,' I mused.

'I'll stop the car,' Laura said sarcastically. 'I'm sure I've got a copy of the *Golfer's Handbook* somewhere. Anyway, what does it matter? Julius has said all along that the diaries were forgeries. I'm assuming, as you undoubtedly are, that our friend Pat not only forges paintings but turns his hand to diaries, too.'

'Yes, but we've got to prove it.'

'All you have to do is match your pages to the material that Ashton has put up for sale and you've done it. Game, set and match to Chris Ludlow, the Marlowe of the golfing scene.'

'That isn't proof, Laura. We've got to get Moloney to admit he did the forgeries and that he did them under instructions from Welbeck. He'll probably swear blind that Welbeck simply lent him a transcript of the diaries.'

'If he does, you and Toby'll have to beat a confession out of him. I'll help.'

'You're a bloodthirsty young woman, aren't you?'

'Not really, but I bet you can sort Moloney out. If he's an alcoholic and as unstable as Hutt suggested . . .'

'There is a problem, Laura.'

'Amy Kincaid?'

'Yes, we've got to find her before I do anything about this. Otherwise, she might be killed.'

'But that won't stop you trying to find out what's going on in the meantime, will it?'

'No. But I must be careful. Just imagine if someone tells Welbeck that we've been sniffing around. He might put two and two together and then it's curtains for Amy.'

'It's a risk we have to take. Why should anyone at Steeple Ashton say anything about us? Hutt won't. It's obvious he doesn't even like Welbeck. He's happy to use his money and his influence but that's it. His commitment, above everything, is to his people at the priory.'

I hoped to God she was right.

# Chapter 30

On Monday morning, I received a call from Kincaid in Tokyo – he'd arrived earlier that day. 'I'm on the case, Chris, and I'll contact you at regular intervals.' His voice had a desperately cheerful tone which he was unable to sustain when I told him that I had no news of Amy. I tried to be as upbeat as possible but the American probably sensed an undercurrent of doubt in me. Our lack of progress made me feel inadequate.

Toby was indulging himself at the Monte Carlo Open that weekend and I eventually tracked him down on the Monday afternoon. He was at home and claimed that he'd been struck down with food poisoning.

'A dodgy oyster at lunch yesterday,' he groaned. Enormous quantities of free champagne was my diagnosis. 'But I've got to be up and about tomorrow,' Toby continued. 'I had a call from Harry Goodison. He wants to talk to us both. It sounded urgent, so I arranged lunch in a pub near Salisbury. Harry was insistent that we didn't meet in his office.'

'He doesn't want Wright to know he's seeing us, I assume.'

I gave Toby an account of our visit to Steeple Ashton Priory and told him how vital it was that we went back there and talked to Moloney.

'You'll have to pretend to be a journalist,' I said. 'Can you manage that?'

'I will ignore that comment,' Toby said, somehow mustering a dignified tone. 'Is your car back from the garage yet? If so, I'll cast aside my dislike of Teutonic bone-shakers and travel with you.'

As it happened, my old Porsche was ready for collection and it was a real treat to sit behind the wheel again. Despite the heavy traffic, I enjoyed the journey down to Salisbury and Toby directed me to a pub not far from Wilton House.

Harry Goodison was waiting for us, his pint glass like a toy in his hand. With his disordered clothing and unruly hair, he looked every inch the unworldly academic rather than a sharp auctioneer. Although his smile was as warm as I remembered, he didn't seem at ease. There was a wary look in his eyes. Whenever a customer came through the door he quickly checked him over.

He ordered some sandwiches for us and we carried our drinks to a table in the corner. We chatted inconsequentially for a few minutes and, in answer to Goodison's inquiry, I told him that I would be carrying Jake's bag at the Open.

'I'm going to try and be there every day,' Goodison said. 'It's a long time since I've had a chance to watch the pros. Let's hope Sandwich gives them a real test.'

'It will, especially if the wind blows,' Toby responded. Then, with a smile in Goodison's direction, he said, 'Come on, Harry, what's on your mind. I can't ever remember you being on edge but that's how you seem today.'

'That's putting it mildly,' Goodison said sombrely. 'The trouble is, I don't know whether you can help me.'

Once he got into his stride, Goodison went at a gallop. There was little he told us that we hadn't known or surmised. His firm had become very closely allied with Welbeck. They were the principal auctioneers in the golf market, even though they were much smaller than businesses like Sotheby's and Christie's. Modesty forbade Goodison from saying that his standing as an expert on golfing memorabilia had done much to make his firm a force in the market. It had seemed natural and mutually profitable to forge close links with Welbeck and so it had proved. They had enjoyed great successes over the years.

Goodison paused and I took the opportunity to buy another round of drinks. On my return I prompted him gently: 'But now you have some doubts about Welbeck?'

'There've been several over the years,' he replied, 'but nothing terribly serious. There are always antiques knocking about that have questionable provenance. Everyone knows it. Sometimes you turn a blind eye and sometimes not. I know Kincaid has some grouses about stuff he's bought from Welbeck and I have great respect for his opinions. Kincaid's very sound.

'I have serious reservations about these latest discoveries of Welbeck's. The clubs and the balls. I've never had a satisfactory explanation of how they came his way. At first he wouldn't even tell me the name of the family who owned them. And Kincaid was right to pursue the crucial point of the clubs' provenance. If you're hoping to sell Old Tom Morris's driver for tens of thousands of pounds, you've got to provide the proof.'

'But Welbeck has the documentation to support his claims, hasn't he?' I asked.

'Yes. Letters and other documents were found in the Scott-Browns' attic somewhere in Scotland.'

'Somewhere in Scotland? Wasn't he more specific?' Toby asked. 'Have you seen these papers?'

Goodison nodded his head and told us that they looked the part. Archibald Scott-Brown had put together the bulk of the collection; the letters, from the famous golfers whose clubs he'd acquired, were addressed to him. There was even a photograph of Old Tom Morris holding the driver which he used in the 1867 Open Championship; on its reverse there was a note to Scott-Brown in which Old Tom confirmed his gift.

'So, could they be genuine?' Toby asked.

Goodison shook his head and I said, 'Or are the letters forgeries like the Bobby Jones diaries?'

'That's what I suspect,' Goodison stated sadly. 'I don't believe in so many rabbits coming out of the same hat. Not in the antiques business. And Welbeck's got involved with some dubious people. It's not my style, Toby, you know that.'

Toby nodded sympathetically. 'Dubious people like Nick Adams.'

'Exactly. And Charlie Ito. You know that Welbeck did a hell of a lot of business with him. God knows what they were unloading on the Japanese. I shudder to think.'

'You'll have to pull the rug from under them,' I said. 'Talk to that policeman, Inspector Rattray.'

'No. I'm not ready to do it yet. Jonathan's been working flat out on this auction. I can't imagine what he'd do if I cast doubts on its integrity at this late date.'

'*He* works for *you*, Harry, doesn't he?'

'In theory, but he's in a very strong position. He's Welbeck's protégé. I had to take him into the firm. If the chairman of the firm had to decide between the two of us . . . well, I'm not sure it'd be me.'

I looked hard at Goodison, an essentially decent man who found himself in dire trouble, and then at Toby. He nodded imperceptibly and I spoke directly to the auctioneer. 'I don't think you have any option, Harry. If you have doubts about those clubs you should shout fake now. Toby and I, and Julius

Kincaid of course, think that Welbeck is up to his eyebrows in fraud. You've rightly pointed the finger at Adams and Charlie Ito, and Welbeck is no better than either of them. I think we'll be able to prove that those Jones diaries are forgeries, maybe within a few days. And, as you said, God knows what Welbeck and Ito have been foisting on the Far East market.'

'There have been some nasty rumours,' Goodison said. 'Not just fakes and forgeries, but stolen stuff ending up in the hands of collectors in Japan and Singapore.'

'Like the gear that was nicked from Royal Dorset and the other clubs?' Toby asked. 'Do you think Welbeck had anything to do with that? That he and Ito shipped it out?'

'No, I don't,' Goodison stated firmly. 'That really wouldn't be Welbeck's scene at all.'

'Nor murder?' I said. 'When thieves fall out, mayhem usually follows.'

'No, he's incapable of such a thing,' asserted Goodison. 'Welbeck is vain and greedy and one of the great snobs of our time but he's not capable of violence. You've only got to look at him – he's a softie.'

'So what are you going to do?' I asked him. 'Let him get away with his frauds and subterfuges, or stop him?'

Goodison sighed. 'Let's talk again in a few days,' he suggested. 'I've got a lot to think about and maybe, by then, you'll have made headway on the Jones diaries. I'll call you and Toby before the weekend. How's that?'

It was the following morning, when I had settled down to work in my office at the Royal Dorset Golf Club, that I remembered the paper manufacturer whose invoices I'd seen on Moloney's desk. I dialled the number I'd noted and told the receptionist I was looking for small quantities of high-quality paper. She put me through to the firm's sales manager, Mr Rowley, and I said I'd seen a fine example of his company's work at Steeple Ashton Priory and needed something similar.

'Hang on a minute, Mr Ludlow, that rings a bell,' he said, a pleasing West-country roll to his voice. 'What have we here? Ah.' There was a pause and I heard him hitting some keys on his machine.

'Here we are. That'll be Mr Moloney's order.'

'Ah, Pat Moloney. Not Mr Hutt?'

'No. I don't know Mr Hutt; we dealt only with Mr Moloney.'

'A tricky order, I imagine?' I ventured.

'Yes, it was. It's coming back to me. He gave us a very exacting specification for a small run of paper.'

'It sounds as if I've come to the right place. The paper I saw at the priory was very impressive.'

'Yes,' Rowley said enthusiastically. 'Mr Moloney was very precise. He even made us look back in our records to check the whitener we used before the war. We had to get hold of Hughie Carey. He retired years ago. He's one of the few left who knows the ins-and-outs of pre-war manufacture.'

'It was an interesting job for you, then?'

'Oh yes. It cost Moloney a small fortune but old Hughie was as happy as a sandboy to be back at work for a few days. Now what would you like us to do for you?'

In the face of such enthusiasm, I felt mean at my deception in telling him I'd ring him in a few days to arrange to discuss my order.

The helpful Mr Rowley had established that Moloney had been meticulous enough to procure paper that was apparently manufactured when Bobby Jones was supposedly writing his diaries. Since Moloney had made all the arrangements it was probably safe to assume that Benny Hutt was not involved in the scam. If so, I was relieved because it would make my task and Toby's much easier. We had less than a week to go before Goodison's auction on the Monday before the Open Championship.

# Chapter 31

As I turned the Porsche into my usual space by the front gate, I looked forward to sitting down quietly and getting my thoughts in order about Welbeck and his various misdemeanours. However, I found a note under my door summoning me to Mrs Bradshaw's apartment, 'as soon as possible for a small celebration'.

A bottle of champagne was waiting in a silver ice-bucket in my neighbour's sitting room and she asked me to do the honours. As soon as our glasses were filled, she said, 'Here's to us and down with snotty little fraudsters.'

We drank to that with relish, whereupon Mrs Bradshaw waved an official-looking letter at me and said, 'Judgement has been entered in my favour in the County court and I will receive my money within seven days. Mr Stacey has got his just deserts, thanks to you. We'll go out and celebrate. Dinner's on me. Bring Laura.'

When I returned to my own flat it struck me that I might well be the target of some retaliation from the Reynolds/Stacey combo. I checked that my car hadn't been tampered with and then told myself not to be so pathetic.

However, with thoughts of the two bent lawyers in my mind, I contacted Laura to ask her whether her surveyor friend, Giles, had discovered any more interesting facts about their activities in the property market. Her answering machine was on and I asked her to call me if she had any news.

Fifteen minutes later Laura returned my call. 'Giles has indeed got some info, darling, and he's suggested we meet for a drink. He's free this evening.'

We agreed to meet at a pub near Hammersmith Bridge and, when I arrived on my bike, Giles and Laura were already outside. A cheerful, heavily built man of around my age, Giles went inside and bought me a pint.

It was a calm sunny evening. We leaned on a wall and looked out over the river, rippling smoothly below. Occasionally an oarsman went by in a skiff. The buzz of conversation from the drinkers was a counter-point to the peaceful scene.

Giles and I discovered that we had friends in common in the City. Then he said, 'I think I see what Reynolds and Stacey are up to. The best illustration is that property in the Docklands and they've got two more nearby.'

Giles said that the Docklands property scene had been subject to so many fluctuations that it had become difficult to put an accurate value on anything. The amount of fast and dubious money that had gone in and out of there had muddied the waters even further. Giles knew that the house we'd seen had dropped dramatically in value and its owner had wanted to get rid of it quickly to cut his losses. As Charles Freeman had told us openly, R S Developments had bought the place for less than a million pounds but had managed to have it valued at one and a half.

'Where does that get them?' Laura asked.

'It gets them a mortgage from their bank at a higher figure. As I said, the market is so volatile that the bank would've taken their valuation on trust.'

'So they're half a million or so ahead,' I said, 'until they have to pay the loan back.'

'Yes, and they've pulled off the same trick on five other properties. But this is where it gets interesting. Three of the properties are in areas where values are relatively easy to establish and yet they've still managed to obtain a mortgage which is three to four hundred thousand above the market value.'

'OK,' said Laura, 'but I still don't see what they've achieved except a whacking great burden of debt that they'll have to clear one day.'

Giles held up his hand to indicate that all would be revealed and I asked him how he'd uncovered the information. He tapped his nose and said that every trade had its tricks.

'How do you reckon that R S Developments have masterminded these exaggerated valuations?' I asked.

'Through a bent surveyor,' he said simply.

'But what are they up to?' Laura asked plaintively. 'They've got six properties, all on mortgages and all over-valued. What's the scam?'

I was wondering about that, too, and Giles told us. By his reckoning, Reynolds, Stacey and Freeman had spent just over five million on their property portfolios and they had advances of around eight and a half million from various banks and finance companies. That put them three and a half million pounds ahead of the game.

'I can do the arithmetic, Giles,' I said testily, 'but where's the pay-off?'

'They're planning to do a runner,' he said.

It was that simple.

'Along with all the money they've raised from gullible investors,' I said and explained how Freeman and Stacey had tried to persuade Jake to put several hundred thousand pounds into their scheme.

'That's it,' Giles nodded. 'They've probably suckered another

249

million or two out of various people. I don't think those boys will be around for much longer. They'll be planning to put their feet up in some sunny clime where there's no extradition treaty with dear old Blighty and spend their lives slamming into the pina coladas. Would anyone like another drink?'

When I told Helen Raven about the Reynolds scheme, she expressed not the slightest surprise. I assumed that she had experienced far more elaborate conspiracies during her career in the police force.

'What should I do?' I asked simply.

'What do you want to do?'

'Shop the bastards.'

'It's only white-collar crime,' Helen said teasingly. 'Why're you doing your avenging angel act?' I reminded her about Mrs Bradshaw's battle to make Stacey pay his arrears of rent. 'But they'll only do time in an open prison or even get away with a couple of hundred hours of community service.'

'Reynolds and Stacey will be struck off the list of solicitors. That'll be a start.'

Helen could see I was serious. 'OK,' she sighed. 'This is what we'll do. I have a friend in SO6 . . .'

'What's that?'

'A branch of the Metropolitan Police which deals with company fraud. Give me all their addresses. I'll call her now. She's a bright woman. In fact, she's wasted in the police force.'

For a moment I was tempted to ask her advice about Amy's disappearance but I knew what her answer would be: go to the police. And she would have been right. I realized that I was becoming more and more apprehensive about Amy's fate, especially when I listened to Kincaid's message on my office answering-machine. He was making progress, he said, how was I doing? Bloody badly was the answer. Nevertheless, I had to let the action play itself out for a little longer. I was hoping that Harry Goodison would supply the impetus we needed.

Just before lunchtime a call came through from Goodison. I had just grabbed a bag of practice balls and a couple of my wedges and was about to walk over to the practice ground. I was trying to improve my short game, to put into practice some of the techniques I'd learned from watching Jake.

Goodison seemed to be in a hurry. 'Hi, Chris,' he said. 'Can we meet? I thought about what you said and you're right. It can't go on like this, especially now I've found out more about Welbeck and Ito's activities.'

'Like what?'

'I can't talk now. Come and see me, will you? You and Toby? Can you make it later today?'

I promised to get to his office in Salisbury by the late afternoon. Toby had forgone the chance to cover the Scottish Open, traditionally held in the week preceding the Open, and I tracked him down before he went to lunch. He told me that Kincaid had also called him to say that he was making lots of progress. He said he'd catch a train to Salisbury.

'Do you think Harry's ready to tell us everything he knows about Welbeck?' Toby asked as he settled with a grunt into the passenger seat of my Porsche.

'Yes and he's got something of interest to tell about Ito. But I hope to God he can give us a line on Amy. By the way, have you organized our visit to Steeple Ashton yet?'

'I have, dear boy. It's tomorrow.'

I parked outside Goodison's offices and the name of the old

cinema seemed to show up even more boldly on the façade.

The receptionist looked up from her magazine as we approached her desk and smiled vaguely. We asked for Harry Goodison and she told us that he'd already left the office.

I checked my watch. It wasn't yet half past five. 'We had an appointment with him,' I said, letting my irritation show.

'I'm sorry, Mr Ludlow. Mr Goodison was called away suddenly after lunch. Would you be kind enough to go to his house?'

The receptionist gave us Goodison's address and explained that it was very close to the cathedral. 'It's the next street along from Edward Heath's house,' she said helpfully.

'That's useful to know,' Toby muttered, 'for when Ted invites me to dinner.'

# Chapter 32

'The old boy lives alone,' Toby said.

'Well, he's happy with his music and his sailing, I suppose.'

'Not Ted Heath – Harry.'

'I'm sorry, I thought . . .'

'Harry's wife died some years ago. No children. He put all his energies into his work after that.'

'At least he's taking some time off to see the Open this year.'

'Yes,' Toby said, 'that'll be good for him. I'll look after him, get him a pass for the clubhouse and so on.'

Goodison's home was very close to the cathedral precinct, in a street of compact and handsome Georgian houses. I parked and, just as Toby opened his door, a car surged around the corner. He just had time to pull the door shut before it was ripped off its hinges. With a muttered curse, Toby finally got out.

We headed towards the far end of the street, where the car had come to a halt behind an ambulance. Its hazard lights were flashing. We looked at each other and by common consent began to walk faster.

The ambulance was outside Goodison's house. A police car was also there and a small knot of people stood on the pavement. Some of them were tourists and one had a camera at the ready.

253

Perhaps he thought the excitement was laid on by the English Tourist Board.

Toby shouldered his way through the onlookers and up to the house. A uniformed policeman stood just inside the door. With his chin thrust out, arms akimbo and weight nicely balanced, he made it clear that nobody was going to get past him.

'What's the problem here, officer?' Toby said in his fruitiest and most commanding tone.

'An accident, sir. Can I help you?'

'I'm a close friend of Mr Goodison and I'd like to get inside to see him.'

'Can't be done, sir.'

'Who's in charge?' Toby persisted.

'Inspector Rattray.'

'Please tell him that Greenslade of the *News* wishes to speak to him.'

The policeman was far from impressed to hear that Toby was a journalist. But, with a warning to us to stay outside, he retreated a few yards into the hallway and had a short conversation with someone we couldn't see.

'You can't go in yet, sir,' the policeman said. 'The body's about to be brought out.'

'Body?' I said, suddenly aghast. 'Is Harry Goodison dead?'

'You'll have to talk to the Inspector, sir,' the policeman said stolidly.

As he finished, two ambulance men manoeuvred a stretcher down the hall and through the door. It was on wheels, which was just as well in view of Goodison's size and weight. All that now remained of him was a still shape under a blanket. Toby's face was nearly as grey as the dusty pavement.

Rattray appeared in the doorway and beckoned us inside.

We followed him into the sitting room. 'You two have an uncanny knack of being in the wrong place at the wrong time,' he said sourly. 'I seem to remember that Goodison was one of your golfing chums. What was your connection apart from that?'

'Friend,' Toby muttered.

'Well, I'm afraid he's dead,' Rattray said, his tone softer. 'Murdered, and in a most violent way, poor man.'

'How, er, did it happen?' Toby asked.

'This is off the record, Mr Greenslade, and I do mean that. Mr Goodison was attacked with a bronze statuette. Of Harry Vardon, so the police doctor told me. He was battered to death. His face was unrecognizable.'

'Oh God.' Toby sat down heavily in an armchair. 'Poor Harry. What a way to end up.'

'What was the purpose of your visit, sir?' Rattray directed his question to me, since Toby was sitting with his head in his hands. I felt an almost overwhelming desire to tell Rattray the full story, but didn't feel I could speak until Amy's safety was assured. They'd killed Goodison – I didn't want Amy to be next.

'It was business. About an important auction next week. Harry was keen to get some publicity in the *News*.'

'He'll get plenty now, the poor devil,' Rattray observed. 'What do you know of his associates? Were there any disputes going on?'

'Not that I know of.'

'What about Ito?'

'What about him?'

'Goodison knew him well presumably since Ito was a big-time dealer in the golf market.' Rattray spoke with exaggerated patience. 'Ito's dead and now Goodison has copped it.'

'Are you suggesting that Harry Goodison was murdered in revenge for Ito?' I asked.

'If you've got a better theory, let's hear it,' Rattray said knowingly.

'First of all, Goodison wouldn't have got involved in a killing.'

'OK. But Ito's men weren't to know that and someone else might have put Goodison on the spot.' Rattray suddenly tired of the speculation and said, 'The deaths are linked, that's certain.'

He went on to tell us how Goodison's death had been discovered. A neighbour heard some shouting and other odd noises from his house sometime in the early afternoon but had thought little of it. Later, however, he had heard Goodison's dog barking continuously in the back garden and that was unusual. He had looked out of a back window and seen the spaniel scratching at the windows and whimpering. The garden gate, which led to a side-road, had been left open. The neighbour had become worried at that stage and had hopped over the garden wall to see what the problem was. He had looked through the french windows and seen Goodison's body stretched out on the floor of his study. He had called the police.

'So we assume the killer made his exit stage left through the garden gate,' said Toby, whose face had recovered its normal lively colour.

'Yes, and nobody noticed a damn thing,' Rattray said bitterly.

'I wonder if Goodison's receptionist knows why he left in such a hurry?' I asked.

'I doubt it,' Rattray replied, 'but be sure that we'll be asking her.'

'Has anything been stolen?' I asked.

'We don't know,' Rattray replied, 'but this doesn't look like

256

an opportunist burglary, does it? An opportunist murder, yes. By the way, gentlemen, I'm sorry to touch on this but can you tell me about Mr Goodison's sexual orientation. I mean, he was middle-aged and lived alone . . .'

'And so you are wondering,' Toby finished the sentence for him.

'We have to ask these questions.'

'I know, but the answer is that Harry was happily married for twenty-odd years until his wife died of cancer.'

'By the way, Inspector,' I said, 'Harry's assistant, Jonathan Wright, should be able to help you with regard to whether anything's been stolen – and other matters, I expect.' I hoped that Rattray would read a lot more into the remark than it deserved.

In view of our visit to Steeple Ashton Priory on the following day, we elected to stay the night in a Salisbury hotel. Toby was very much subdued, the weight of Goodison's murder hanging heavily on him, and, after an unappetizing dinner in the hotel's restaurant, we went to our rooms. It was an unexpectedly sober evening for Toby and he can rarely have retired to bed so early.

At breakfast the next morning he grumbled that he'd never had such a sleepless night. 'I heard the cathedral clock strike every quarter,' he claimed.

I didn't tell him that I'd slept like a baby, though my dreams had been shot through with distorted images of menace and undefined danger. I could remember that Laura and I were being chased but I didn't know why or who was doing the chasing. I made a mental note to have a look at one of Freud's books, or maybe it ought to be one of Krafft-Ebing's.

# Chapter 33

We presented ourselves at Steeple Ashton Priory at just after
ten o'clock. There were still numbers of supplicants outside
the gates and I recognized the two clapped-out vehicles which
had been parked there on my last visit. Hutt really made his
clients work for their salvation. The same gate-keeper sent us
on our way along the drive and Barbara was in the hallway to
greet us. She told us that Mr Hutt was ready for us.

Benny Hutt served us strong coffee in some beautiful china
cups and Toby made the appropriate admiring comments about
the priory and about Hutt's collection of paintings.

Before Toby got into his interviewing stride I asked Hutt if
he would allow me to talk to Pat Moloney.

'You're very keen to meet him, aren't you?' he said. 'Remind
me why?'

'Business,' I replied firmly. 'I could put quite a lot of copying
and restoration work his way. It'll pay well and I recall your
saying any extra money is welcome. That's why I've brought
Toby to see you, if you remember. The power of the press.'
Toby looked pleased and I knew I'd made my point: that there's
no such thing as a free interview.

He nodded and called Barbara in. 'Take Mr Ludlow to see
Pat, would you, Barbara? Tell him he's a friend of Sir Nicholas.'

She knocked peremptorily on the door of Moloney's

workshop and walked straight in without waiting for a reply. Moloney was lolling in the only easy chair in the room and gazing at a half-finished canvas on his easel. His moon face was enlivened by bright hazel eyes and heavy jowls drooped over the collar of his shirt. What remained of his hair was drawn back into a ponytail. His trousers and a bedraggled sweater were an indeterminate shade of brown and spotted with drops of paint.

'Now I've told you before, Barbara, not to burst in on me like that. I might be in the middle of a creative conference with myself or, even better, I could be asleep and having a nice erotic dream.' He grinned up at me. 'And who's this?'

'Mr Ludlow. A friend of Sir Nicholas,' Barbara said frostily and left the workshop.

'She thinks I fancy her,' Moloney laughed. 'What would I do with that bag of bones, I ask you? I'd rather have the erotic dream. So you know Welbeck, eh?' He had the merest suggestion of an Irish accent and I guessed that he could turn it on when he wished. I nodded and he continued, 'I can offer you some instant coffee but I expect you've been supping the boss's Colombian. It'd taste like weasel-piss after that.'

I decided that a subtle approach would be wasted on Moloney and, anyway, I wasn't sure that subtlety was within my compass any more. Too much rested on my ability to solve the problems associated with Welbeck: Amy Kincaid's survival above all.

'Do you still use your *noms de plume*?' I asked. 'Or maybe that should be *noms de pinceau*?'

'That's an erudite approach but I don't know what the hell you're on about,' he replied. He got up from his chair and ambled over to take a closer look at his canvas.

'Piet Mulder, the Baron de Murat. Surely you remember those characters? They came in handy when you and Welbeck discovered the Matisse that's now owned by the Queen. And when you passed off that dodgy painting of some golfers to Browning's in New York.'

Moloney had his back to me and made no comment. I padded over to him and stood within a couple of feet of him. 'Come on, Pat,' I said quietly. 'Nobody cares if the artistic establishment has its tail twisted occasionally. After all, it's accepted that hoaxes are part of the game. But now you've got yourself involved in a very nasty business and I want your help to sort it out.'

He edged away from me. 'You've got the wrong man, Mr Ludlow. You see, I don't remember what went on years ago. That would've been the drinking years. Days of wine and poses, you might say.' He laughed at his own joke.

'It's no laughing matter, Pat,' I said quietly. 'Fakery and fraud is one thing but robbery, murder and kidnapping are entirely different. That's what your friend Welbeck and his associates have been about.'

Moloney swallowed audibly and tried a weak smile on me. His self-confidence must have been fragile at best and it was ebbing away. 'What the hell are you on about, man?'

I told him about the various robberies, the death of the steward at the Royal Dorset Golf Club, the murder of Charlie Ito and Amy Kincaid's sudden disappearance. 'And you're part and parcel of the whole vicious business,' I ended emphatically.

The colour had left Moloney's face apart from vivid patches on each cheek. He gulped again. 'No, no,' he whispered, 'maybe I helped Welbeck out with the Matisse but I didn't know what he was up to. He was a clever old thing to sell it to the Queen now, wasn't he just? I wonder how much he got?' The thought seemed to revive him.

261

'And you added the golfers to what was a pretty average eighteenth-century painting, I assume.'

Moloney ignored my question. He wandered over to the table and picked up a knife. It looked sharp and very business-like. I tensed and looked around for something to use in self-defence. A wooden chair was within reach. That would do for a start. But he put the knife down and leaned against the table.

'My memory's not very good,' he stated. 'Especially if it's going to cause me any pain. That's why I'm in here. I'm an alcoholic, Mr Ludlow, and if I didn't have the help and support of the people here, especially Benny, I'd be back on the booze within hours and a complete bum within a week. So, I don't want to know about the past. The past to me was drinking until I passed out and then waking up in my own vomit and filth and not being able to remember where I was.' Moloney looked nervously at me and I could see that sweat had broken out on his forehead. 'So don't ask me to relive all that.'

I had the feeling that Moloney had made that speech more than once. I was moved by his sentiments but didn't let it show. Moloney had the means to provide some of the critical parts of the puzzle. I already had many of the pieces in place but his knowledge would allow me to complete the picture.

There was little point in holding anything in reserve and I emphasized that all the evidence showed that Welbeck was guilty of fraud on the grand scale. The police had evidence that he'd had close links with Charlie Ito who, in turn, was a member of the Japanese criminal fraternity, the yakusa. Julius Kincaid was convinced that the latest batch of golfing treasures acquired by Welbeck were fakes, just as were the Bobby Jones diaries. Finally I told Pat that he could look forward to being a leading player in a murder inquiry before he was much older.

'Charlie Ito and Harry Goodison,' I said. 'They got in the way. The police will pull in everybody with the slightest connection with Welbeck.'

Moloney had no resistance left. He went over to his chair and sagged into it. 'I couldn't face all that shit,' he muttered.

'So help me and maybe I can help you.' He looked up expectantly. 'Maybe we can keep the cops away from you.'

I had no idea how I would achieve that half-promise but I hoped that Benny Hutt would be a vigorous ally.

'How did you get on to the diaries?' Moloney asked. I explained that Kincaid had expressed his immediate doubts and that I'd found a transcript of the diaries in his workshop.

'Barbara told me I'd had visitors but I paid no attention.'

'I tracked down the paper-maker too,' I explained. 'He told me how meticulous you'd been about the formula.'

'Yeah, I'm a real pro. You can be sure of that,' he said bitterly. He paused and then seemed to gather strength as he talked about the techniques he'd used.

'I aged the paper a bit just to show that it'd been around for a few decades. But the ink worried me.' He pointed to one of the shelves. 'You see those bits and pieces – olive oil, eggs, flour and so on.' I nodded; I'd noticed them on my previous visit. 'You can do a lot with those. They give you a fluid that looks like faded ink. But Welbeck told me not to bother, to use ordinary ink and thin it out a bit. I was a bit worried in case somebody did a chloride test . . .'

'What's that?'

'You can measure the evaporation of chloride and establish roughly when the ink was used. But Welbeck told me not to worry. He said that as long as I did a really good job on the forgery, his authentication would carry the day. I remember him saying, "They're damned gullible, Patrick, my dear. They'll be eager to believe me, so don't give it another thought." So I didn't. I got on with the job.'

'You make it sound easy.'

'It is. Once you can forge a few words, you can forge a page and then twenty pages and then a book. It's a matter of confidence. You just let it flow. What you don't want to be is too painstaking because an expert can pick out the little hesitations, the tremors. I practised for about a week and then I was away.'

Moloney went over to a cupboard, unlocked it and scrabbled amongst a stack of papers. He thrust half a dozen sheets into my hands. 'Here are some of my early efforts at the Jones hand. Not bad, eh?'

I didn't know whether they were good or bad but I asked if I could keep them and Moloney shrugged in agreement. 'Who wrote the diaries for you?' I asked.

'I don't know. All I know is that Welbeck had the idea and brought Adams in to do all the hype with the newspapers and the television people.'

'How about those letters that Welbeck has to give provenance to the stuff he's selling at auction next week? I suppose you did those, too?'

Moloney nodded. 'A bit of a rush job but much easier than the Jones diaries. Welbeck brought me the right sort of paper – end-papers cut from books printed during the correct period. It's an old trick and a good one. He provided samples of the handwriting, of course. Old Tom Morris, Willie Park, John Ball and the rest. And off I went.'

Moloney walked over to the cupboard and reappeared with a piece of yellowed paper, one of its edges curled. He sat down at the table. 'Have you got any old clubs knocking around?' he asked. I told him about the niblick that Jake had given me and

264

that it had supposedly been made at the turn of the century.

He asked me for the name of my great-grandfather and, since I didn't know it, said he'd call him William. Moloney sat silently for a minute or so, a pot of ink and an old pen with a steel nib in front of him. Then he began to write. Soon afterwards he handed me a note addressed to William Ludlow Esquire. It certified that Harry Vardon had given William Ludlow the gift of a niblick, used in the Open Championship at Prestwick that year, 'as a token of his friendship and great respect'. The note was dated August 1898.

'There you are,' Moloney said. 'Vardon won the Open in eighteen ninety-eight, as you probably know. That's a bloody good version of his writing and signature. Instant provenance for you. You can knock out your old niblick to some sucker for a few grand. The punter will be happy as Larry and so will you and nobody'll be any the wiser.'

Carefully I folded the piece of paper and put it in my pocket. It would amuse Julius Kincaid.

Moloney's enthusiasm for his subject had completely overtaken his apprehension at being dragged into an inquiry into large-scale fraud, robbery and murder; even his complexion was back to normal. Now was the time to drain the last drops of information from him.

'What about the clubs that go with the letters you've done. Are they genuine?'

'Yes. Welbeck would've acquired genuine old clubs from somewhere. He wouldn't cut any corners. It's not worth it. It's attaching the club to a famous name that counts. But I wouldn't think that eighteenth-century square-nosed iron is genuine.'

'Why do you say that?'

'Just a hunch. Maybe they used an old tool, a billhook or something like that, that had been lying around for a century

265

or two and made the clubhead that way.'

'Who does Welbeck use?'

'I don't know his name but it's some bloke on the south coast. And he makes the feathery balls for Welbeck, too. He's got some fellow in the Midlands who fakes medals and statuettes.' I knew where I could find Welbeck's club-maker; the whereabouts of the metal-worker was irrelevant.

Taxed again with my questions about the authenticity of the Matisse, Moloney admitted that he'd forged it and that he'd added the golfers to the picture that caused all the hullabaloo at Browning's.

'How many pictures have you faked for Welbeck?' I asked.

'A few dozen.'

'You should be rich. Where did all the money go?'

'Champagne. High-priced tarts. Expensive presents for the tarts. Hotel suites at hundreds of pounds a day. Gambling. I'm an alcoholic with a love of gambling. Now that's a licence to burn money. It was great while it lasted, I'll say that. Until the booze really got me.'

There was a pause while Moloney contemplated his past. I said how ironic it was that Welbeck's own treasures, his Van der Neer and the other golf paintings, had been stolen.

Moloney laughed loudly. 'That's rich.' He looked at my face which clearly showed my bewilderment. 'No, you're not joking, are you?' he said. 'Chris, that Van der Neer that was pinched from the old bugger's house was a copy. I know because I copied it. He sold the original to a Japanese collector years ago. As usual he was short of the readies. And the other pictures, by Hodge and Hopkins and Charles Lees, were copies too. He'd sold those on to the same collector, for much more cash than he'd ever have got here.'

'And now he's got his hands on the insurance money as

well. It's a profitable scam, isn't it?'

'That's it. You've got there. Welbeck is a complete bloody fake. Even his burglaries are faked. I expect he fakes his orgasms, too.'

'But Welbeck looks after you, I assume. He pays the going rate to Hutt for your bed and board.'

'And a bit more for the work I do for him.'

'Who gets the extra money?'

'Sir Nicholas assures me that there's an account in Jersey, in my name, which is doing very nicely. But it's irrelevant.' I looked questioningly at him. 'Irrelevant because I'll never leave this place. I wouldn't dare . . .'

'What wouldn't you dare, Pat?' Hutt asked from the doorway, as he ushered Toby inside.

'I can't see myself ever leaving the priory,' Moloney said.

'The doors are open,' Hutt said. 'You'll leave us when you feel the time is right. When you can live your own life again.'

'From what Pat's just told me, I'd suggest he stays at the priory for a while longer,' I said and explained what he'd told me about Welbeck's various conspiracies. Hutt listened intently, little sign of emotion on his face. No doubt he'd heard much nastier stories from his clients. Apart from a couple of questions, he heard me out. I began to apologize for deceiving him.

Hutt interrupted me. 'Chris, I knew you weren't in the retail business. At first I thought you might be doing some research for one of those shit-stirring TV programmes. Or maybe that you were from some shady government agency. So, I'm not annoyed.' He turned to Toby. 'However, I will be irritated if I don't get my article in the *News*. What are the chances?'

'Well, I'll have to talk to my features editor, Benny. I'll do my best.'

'That's all I ask.'

'So we've got that old bugger Welbeck where we want him, have we, Chris?' Toby said, changing the subject.

'Yes and no,' I said. 'We know what he's up to but I can't openly use what Pat told me because I've promised not to implicate him.'

'That's excellent,' Hutt murmured as Toby groaned his disappointment. 'The psychiatric reports alone . . .'

'Yeah, I'm a real nutter,' 'Moloney said cheerfully.

'We'll have to nail Welbeck some other way,' I said firmly.

# Chapter 34

For the first half of our journey back to London, Toby berated me for offering promises to Moloney that I had no conceivable means of keeping.

'You'll have to shop him, Chris. It's the only way. Then we're out of the wood.'

'I gave him my word and that's the end of it,' I said sharply. 'Moloney's sick. God knows if he'd survive a trial, but jail would be the end of him.'

'That's not your usual hard-nosed style, is it?'

'No. I loathe the likes of Welbeck and Reynolds and Stacey but there's not a lot of real harm in Moloney. And what a talent he's got. What he's told us is great evidence to have in reserve but we'll have to use other means to pin Welbeck to the wall.'

'I'm surprised at you, Chris.'

'I'm thinking about Amy Kincaid. Her safety comes first. So far we haven't got a clue where she is. Secondly, I'm thinking of your future, Toby.'

'What on earth d'you mean?'

'Steeple Ashton Priory is what I mean. You never know, you might need their help one day.'

Toby treated my remark with lofty contempt and we discussed the Welbeck situation in desultory fashion for several more miles. We also speculated about the golfer we would be best advised to put our money on in next week's Open Championship. But our minds were on Harry Goodison and Amy and the evil bastards surrounding Welbeck.

'Why don't we tell Rattray what we know,' Toby said. 'He could pull Welbeck in for some harsh questioning.'

'Not a good idea. Welbeck would have a sharp lawyer over there pronto and in no time at all he'd be released. What could Rattray offer as evidence? The ramblings of a broken-down old drunk, that's all. Welbeck could argue that it's his generosity that's keeping Moloney on the straight and narrow and that it's made him bitter and twisted. Anyway, Amy is the priority. We must make sure we don't do anything which might threaten her life.'

'So what do we do?'

'Put some pressure on the weakest link in the chain.'

'Welbeck? Wright? Tilden?'

'Tilden, for sure,' I said. 'He's flaky. We need to put some surveillance on him. What about that photographer of yours, Karl?'

'What about Laura? She's got all the gear, the long-range lenses and so on. And she already knows what we're about.'

'I'll ask her.'

My answering machine was blinking but my first action on returning home was to ring Welbeck's house. I recognized Tilden's voice and cut the connection without speaking. I had assumed he wouldn't be far from his master – not with such an important auction in the offing.

My next call was to Laura who fell in eagerly with my suggestion that she should try a bit of low-key surveillance, but absolutely refused the idea of my accompanying her. I'd get in the way, she said, and I'd be conspicuous. She and her long-range lens was all that was needed. She began to talk in a mid-Atlantic accent and attempted some B-movie dialogue.

I interrupted her hastily. 'You're not V I Warshawski. Just trail Tilden when he leaves Welbeck's house. Make a note of what he does and who with. Look out for anything unusual and get as many shots of him and his friends as you can.'

'It's done, man,' Laura said, chewing some invisible gum. 'I'll stay closer'n a flea on a dog's neck.'

'Laura, don't get carried away; if there's a problem, get the hell out. Please. I'll be here in the flat.'

'Don't worry. I'll be heavily disguised in my trilby and trench coat. Suspenders underneath, of course.'

Somehow, I didn't think she was taking this very seriously. 'Ring me,' I said but she'd already put down her phone.

The message on my machine was from Julius Kincaid who had left me a number in Nagoya which, he said, was over 150 miles west of Tokyo. He picked up his phone on the first ring and immediately asked about Amy.

'We're working hard on it, Julius,' I replied inadequately. 'I think we'll crack the problem in the next day or so.'

'OK, Chris, I won't press you. No point. You know what I'm going through. I've made some progress here. In fact, I've got enough rope to hang Welbeck. I've got one more fella to see. That's tomorrow night. Then I'll get on a flight to London. I'll be back on Sunday night and I'll be at the auction.'

'Are you going to tell me what you've found out?'

'Too complicated, Chris, my boy. But you'll love it. You'll find Amy, won't you?'

'We'll find Amy,' I assured him. Alive, I hoped.

There was no answer from Toby's telephone and I left a message that things were beginning to warm up and that I would have to contact him early on the following morning. He wouldn't like the idea.

I spent the next two or three hours trying to remain calm. I kept telling myself that Laura was sensible, street-wise in the best sense; then I berated myself for suggesting that she became involved so directly. I should have insisted on going with her. I tried to read but my eyes kept straying to the telephone. I even went out of the front door to scan the road for Laura's car. Finally I went into the spare room and did a few sets on my exercise equipment.

I was in the shower when the phone rang. It was Laura and I thanked God for that as I stood, water dripping off me on to the carpet, and listened to her excited words.

'Chris, you'll never believe this. I followed Tilden and some other guy. They were obviously having a furious row. They went back to Tilden's place . . .'

'What was he like – the other guy?'

'Slim, just short of your height, curly fair hair, smartly dressed, a real smoothie . . .'

'Sounds like Jonathan Wright.'

'OK. So off they go to Holland Park and I'm tucked in a couple of cars away, just as they do it on the telly. And when they get back they're still having this bloody great argument. I'm double-parked opposite, going click-click-click with one of the cameras . . .'

'Double-parked? Christ, did they see you?'

'They were much too busy, darling. Anyway, then I got lucky and nipped into a space right opposite Tilden's flat. Doubly lucky because it's in the basement. And you should see the pictures I got. Wow.'

'When will I see them?'

'In an hour at most. They're dynamite.'

'Great. Tell me about them.'

'No. A picture's worth a thousand words. See you in a few minutes, lover. Get some fizz ready. *Ciao*.'

As good as her word, Laura was knocking on my front door within the hour. I was sorry that she wasn't wearing a trilby hat and, since she had on a pair of jeans, I assumed she hadn't bothered with the suspenders either.

'Are you all right?' I asked foolishly, because she clearly was very all right.

'All right?' she grabbed my head and kissed me. 'I loved every minute of it. It's the most fun I've ever had with my clothes on.'

Laura followed me into the kitchen and, while I ripped the cork out of a bottle of champagne, she opened a large brown envelope and deposited several sheets of contact prints on the table. The photographs showed a sequence of events over a period of less than an hour. I recognized the front door of Welbeck's house as Tilden closed it on his way out; the first close-up confirmed that Tilden's companion was Wright, looking bitterly angry; then the body language showed that the two men were in the middle of a fierce argument. My money would have been on Wright every time. He looked furious but the photographs nevertheless conveyed that he had his rage under control. In comparison, Tilden seemed on the edge of hysteria.

The two men were still arguing when they got out of the their car and then there were shots of them disappearing down some steps into a basement area.

'Now,' Laura said, smacking her lips, 'these are the juicy ones. It's kiss-and-make-up time, folks.'

Laura had two sheets of prints but the first few shots showed Tilden with his head in his hands. Then Wright came into view, put his arm around him, pulled his hands away from his face and dried his tears with a handkerchief. From there the two men clutched each other and the photographs showed a succession of passionate embraces, lips and bodies glued together. Fortunately, they kept shifting position and both men were easily identifiable.

'Christ, these are clear, Laura,' I said suspiciously. 'And you got these from the car?'

'It's amazing what a long-focus lens and high-speed film can achieve in the hands of a professional, isn't it?' she said pertly. 'Added to the fact that our two lover-boys were so obsessed with each other that they didn't bother to check whether they were being indiscreet. They left the blinds up for a while. What a pity that they remembered to pull them down before they pulled down their trousers. I'd love to have got them on film in flagrante.'

'What you might call a full exposure. You're a fantastic woman.'

'I know. I got you what you wanted, didn't I? Now there's something I want from you. I think the boys turned me on, Chris.'

'You're disgusting,' I murmured, as I followed her into the bedroom.

'You bet,' she agreed.

# Chapter 35

Despite protests from Laura, whose usual Saturday morning ritual centred around many cups of coffee and a thorough perusal of several newspapers, I'd set the alarm for seven o'clock. I put the kettle on, jumped in the shower, dressed and set about persuading Laura out of bed.

At half past seven I took a perverse pleasure in telephoning Toby, thinking that he might have left on his answering machine as protection. To my surprise he picked up the receiver almost immediately and sounded alert, if grumpy. I gave him a rapid summary of what I intended to do.

'I want to corner Tilden and ask him some leading questions. But not until later. He'll be expected at work so we don't want to jump the gun and arouse Wright and co's suspicions. But we've got to keep an eye on him.'

'We?'

'You and me, Toby.'

'Chris, there's no point in our playing at private eyes. We won't be much good at it. Let's take advantage of the Kincaid millions. Money's no problem, he said. Remember? I'll get a reliable man to do the surveillance for us, OK?'

'Fine. But I'll have to hold the fort until your man is in place. I'm off to watch Tilden's flat and you're going to keep me company.'

There was quite a long pause, a few grunts and then Toby said sourly, 'Very well then, I'll get there as soon as I can, even though it's the middle of the night.'

Laura went off to print enlarged copies of the more intimate shots of Tilden and Wright; I hoped they would be the means to force Tilden to tell everything he knew about Amy's whereabouts and Welbeck's activities. I prayed that he would be fully in the picture.

I parked my car about a hundred yards from Tilden's flat, on the opposite side of the road. I opened the car's bonnet and pretended to look for a fault, hoping that no passer-by would offer assistance.

The only event of any interest was Wright's departure from Tilden's flat. He strode briskly towards the main road, without looking to his left or his right. It was a reasonable assumption that his boyfriend was still inside the flat.

Time drags by on leaden feet when you are waiting for something to happen. I kept glancing at my watch but the hands didn't seem to be moving. After ten minutes of nervous inaction a taxi rumbled along the road, stopped by the Porsche and Toby got out.

'Anything happening?'

'No,' I replied just as I spotted Tilden emerge from the steps to his basement flat.

Toby and I took cover behind one of the many trees which contributed to the street's considerable charms and watched our quarry ease himself into the confines of a Corrado VR6. He revved the engine as he manoeuvred his way out of the small parking space and then roared off towards the main road. Tilden was wearing a smart grey suit and a tie, and I assumed that he must be on his way to work rather than the local supermarket.

When he was safely past I slammed shut the bonnet of the car and we jumped inside. The traffic was already starting to thicken and it wasn't difficult to keep Tilden in sight, especially since he was a compulsive lane-changer. We followed the boy-racer south from Notting Hill Gate and then through the Kensington streets. It was obvious that he was heading for Chelsea but we followed him all the way and watched him safely inside Welbeck's house.

Toby had remembered his mobile phone, which he regarded as one of the more offensive manifestations of modern times, along with personal stereos, vegetarianism, camcorders, feminists, social workers and youth in general. But a mobile phone had its uses as he admitted while he contacted his private detective. Mr Bostock promised to be in place near Welbeck's house within minutes and so he was.

On the way back to my apartment I emphasized the importance of wringing the truth out of Tilden. 'It's now Saturday,' I said in summary. 'The auction's on Monday at midday. We've still no clue where Amy's being held. We've got to get our skates on.'

'And our fingers out. And our gloves off,' Toby said with apparent enjoyment. 'Well, your gloves had better come off. I'll do the cerebral stuff.'

Toby's price for being ripped untimely from his slumber was a plate of bacon and eggs. I was busy cooking it when Laura arrived.

'I've got some super close-ups of the two lovers,' she said. 'We won't have to beat Tilden into submission, more's the pity. These snaps should do the trick.'

Toby called his office. From the kitchen we heard the occasional rumble of his voice and long intervals of silence as he listened to his respondent. He glowered at us when he returned.

'What's up?' Laura and I asked in unison.

'That was my lick-spittle lout of an editor. He reminded me that I'm supposed to be employed as the golf correspondent of the *News*. Notwithstanding the fact that I'm chasing a very big story he requires me to be at my desk today since there is important work to be done. If I don't do it, my employment is in grave danger of termination. Odious toad.'

'We can't let that happen,' Laura said cheerfully. 'That would be a tragedy for the world of sporting literature, wouldn't it?'

'The members of the Fourth Estate have pressures that other mortals know little of,' he said solemnly. 'You're aware that the Open Golf Championship begins on the links of Royal St George's next Thursday. On Monday the *News* will publish an eight-page supplement about the prestigious event and I have to add my uniquely stylish patina to the whole endeavour.'

'He means he's up against a deadline,' I translated for Laura.

'Nearly beyond it, but who's counting? You can contact me at the office. I shall fly to your side when required.'

Laura had to print up some photographs of a polo match for one of the glossies and I decided to spend my time in writing my monthly report on the progress of the work at the Royal Dorset Golf Club. It was already two weeks late and I wanted to have it ready for Calvin Blair when we met again at the Open. Nothing much could happen until Tilden got on the move again.

I made myself some pasta for lunch and watched half an hour of the Scottish Open on television. Jake was lying in the top thirty with about six holes to play. It was good preparation for the test that would await him next week at Sandwich.

All my notes were laid out on the desk in my spare bedroom and, after putting one of Bruckner's symphonies on the stereo,

I settled down to write my report. I felt virtuous because it was a rare experience for me to be doing that kind of work on a Saturday. My normal routine would be either caddying in a tournament or playing golf with some friends.

Hardly had I typed more than a couple of sentences when the buzzer on the main door of the building sounded. I picked up the entry-phone – there was a delivery for Mr Ludlow. I let the man through the outside door and then glanced at him through my own door's spyhole. He was a tall man, clad in a motor-cyclist's black-leather gear and helmet. He carried a brown envelope.

As I pulled open the door I had a sudden heart-lurching premonition. It was his hands. Big hands. A micro-second too late I tried to shut the door. The man's foot was in the gap and he hit the thick wooden door hard with his shoulder. I staggered back and he threw himself after me, his shoulder hitting me amidships. I crashed backwards down the hall, the momentum taking me nearly into the living room. Before I could recover my wits or my balance, the mountain of a man landed on top of me and knocked what remained of the breath out of my body. With one of his knees in my stomach he pinned me down. He was heavy and I could barely move. His powerful hands went round my throat and his thumbs pressed savagely into my neck.

He was going to kill me and I knew why. I knew who he was.

I couldn't get a grip on his clothing. My hands slithered off the leather and found no purchase. I rolled to my left, located the edge of the door and slammed it into his shoulder. He grunted and then snarled at me and increased the pressure. My eyes were losing their focus. 'You slag,' he said through clenched teeth. 'I told you I'd do for you. Where's your whore?

Isn't she here to protect you? You put the filth on to us, didn't you? SO6. You thought you could fuck me up, you bastard.'

The pressure eased on my neck as Reynolds shifted his position. The brief moment of relief gave me a chance to heave my knee upwards but I merely caught him in the thigh, not the crutch.

'Naughty,' he said grimly. He hauled me upright and hit me over the right eye. Christ, he was strong. I tried to scramble to my feet – never, never stay down on the floor if you can help it. His heavy boot caught me once, twice in the ribs. I decided to stay down on the floor after all.

Nothing happened for a moment and then I heard the crash of glass as Reynolds stove in a cabinet. Through my half-closed eyes I saw him put a boot through the television screen. I was stunned by the blow to my face and still dizzy from being half strangled. What the hell was he doing? I knew I couldn't escape and I knew I couldn't take him on and win. Weapons? Nothing within reach that I could use.

Now he was in the kitchen and, judging by the racket of falling crockery, he wasn't admiring my recipe books.

I was lying partly on my right side and suddenly became aware of my keys and my change digging into my hip. The least of my worries, I thought grimly. I heard Reynolds coming back into the room from the kitchen. Then I remembered. The keyring and the silver toothpick that was attached to it. Maybe . . .

I'd got my right hand into my pocket when the bowl of cold water hit me in the face. I shuddered but found the end of the toothpick that was attached to the main keyring and began to turn it between the thumb and forefinger. I felt the sharp end of the toothpick begin to extend.

'We'll take our time, slag,' Reynolds said, as he loomed

over me. 'By the time I've finished, your whore won't recognize you. Your own mother won't recognize you.' He took off his helmet, placed it carefully on a chair and then casually kicked me in the leg.

I knew I'd only get one chance at Reynolds and if I failed . . . I hooked my thumb into the keyring and clasped the toothpick, now fully extended, in my curled forefinger.

'So I ruined your plans, did I, Reynolds? I suppose you and Stacey were ready to do your disappearing act, were you?' I saw Reynolds' face go rigid with rage. Here he comes. 'Cheap crooks like you never quite get it right, do they?' I finished.

Reynolds lashed out furiously with his right boot. The water he'd thrown over me and the short respite gave me enough energy to roll slightly and take the blow in the back of the leg. For a moment Reynolds, enjoying his revenge, stood back to take stock of me. It was my chance. I ripped my hand from my trouser pocket, rolled towards him and thrust the toothpick upwards towards his groin. He tried to turn away but the metal spike went straight through his leather trousers and into the tender flesh on the inside of his thigh. Reynolds screamed as I pushed hard and twisted the toothpick savagely. Instinctively, I ripped the pick clear as his hand came down to the injured spot. Somehow, with all my damaged muscles screaming in protest, I scrambled to my feet, grabbed Reynolds by the hair and stabbed him with the toothpick, once under the chin and once in the side of his neck. That evened the score for the kicking he'd given me.

He reeled backwards, hands now at his own throat and I put all my remaining force into a straight-arm smash to his face. I felt the bone of his nose crack and the cartilage give way. That made it even over the trashing of my car. He crashed into a table and slid on to his knees; his hands were scrabbling at his face and neck and blood was dripping through his fingers.

I collapsed into a chair and probably blacked out for a moment because the next thing I remembered was hearing the shocked voice of Mrs Bradshaw: 'Chris, what on earth's happened?' She was in the doorway and I became aware that Reynolds was on his feet. I gathered myself for another phase of the battle, rose from the chair with difficulty and looked around desperately for a weapon. There was a heavy pewter jug on a nearby table and I picked it up. Reynolds was lumbering towards the door, thank God, and I shouted out to my neighbour, who looked as if she was thinking of grappling with him, to let him pass.

Mrs Bradshaw moved back from the door and Reynolds went through it, apparently oblivious of her presence.

'I heard all the noise and the screaming,' she said, advancing on me. 'I thought you were being murdered.'

'I was.' I started to tell Mrs Bradshaw who he was and why he had paid me a call, but didn't get beyond telling her that he was Paul Stacey's partner.

'I'm going to call the police,' she said firmly, as she looked at the swelling over my left eye. 'That man should be locked up.'

'He probably soon will be.' I explained that the fraud squad were investigating him and Stacey. 'He won't be back and he hasn't done me any real harm.'

Mrs Bradshaw protested that Reynolds might report *me* to the police for causing grievous bodily harm, but I convinced her that, when he went for some treatment, he'd swear that he'd been attacked by 'a person or persons unknown'.

I don't think she was convinced but she conceded my point and questioned me about my injuries. I began to shake a bit at this stage and Mrs Bradshaw insisted on calling a doctor.

'Meanwhile,' she said, 'you'd better have a soak in the bath. It usually helps the bruising.'

The doctor on weekend call at my local surgery arrived within an hour and pronounced that there was nothing broken. He asked me what had happened and made no comment when I told him I'd been attacked in my own flat. He gave me some pain-killers and recommended that I have a precautionary X-ray. Mrs Bradshaw had already made a start at clearing up the mess which Reynolds had caused and she advised me to get some rest. Off she went, telling me that she'd look in again later.

The telephone woke me from a deep sleep. The bedside clock told me that it was after seven o'clock; I'd been out for the count for several hours. No surprise in that. As I reached for the receiver the pain in my ribs made me gasp.

The voice of Toby's private detective, distorted by static, told me that Tilden had left Welbeck's house by taxi, had kept it waiting outside his flat for a few minutes and then taken it back to Welbeck's place. He had been carrying an overnight bag and was, presumably, staying there until tomorrow. I told him to keep watching and then telephoned Toby.

'I'd guess they'll be going early tomorrow to the Swan Hotel near Sandwich,' Toby said, 'to make sure everything's set up for the auction.'

'Let's hope that Tilden comes back to London because it'll complicate things if we have to snatch him from his hotel.'

'Maybe it's for the best,' Toby said. 'The later the better so that he can't warn anybody about us.'

Laura arrived soon afterwards and was suitably aghast at what had happened to me. She insisted on spending the night in the other bedroom so that she didn't make any inadvertent contact with my bruises.

We spent a frustrating Sunday waiting for confirmation of Tilden's movements. Toby had predicted them well. Tilden and Welbeck drove to the Swan and stayed there for most of the day.

Several hot baths and some gentle stretching helped to soothe me. The bathroom mirror told me that my bruises were already beginning to show their colours; my left eye had a technicolor bump over it and was half closed.

Late in the afternoon, Mr Bostock, the private investigator, informed us that Tilden was on the move back to London. Nearly three hours later he told us that Tilden had dropped Welbeck off and had just got home. I called Toby and asked him to get over to Holland Park.

Laura and I took a taxi and we got out at the end of Tilden's road and walked cautiously towards his flat.

Toby's investigator had told us to look for a green Nissan saloon but we were unprepared for its battered appearance. A middle-aged man with sandy hair was sitting in the driving seat. He had a styrofoam cup in a holder on the top of the dashboard. I tapped on his window and he invited us to sit in the back of the car. We moved a briefcase and several files out of the way and Bostock apologized for having half his office in his car.

'Your man entered his flat at about seven-thirty,' he said. 'He's alone. That is, unless someone was already inside. Nobody has gone near his door since.'

We sat in silence for several minutes. I suggested to Bostock that sitting around in cars for hours on end must be the common currency of a private investigator's work. He confirmed my theory and added that there wasn't much call for heroics in his job; he then asked me how I got my black eye.

'Rugby training,' I said vaguely.

'Christ, what are the matches like then?' he asked cheerfully.

A tap on Bostock's window signalled the arrival of Toby. I got slowly and painfully out of the car.

'What the hell have you been up to?' Toby asked, without much hint of sympathy. 'Hit by a truck? A visit from the VAT man?'

Bostock started his car and, with a wave, headed into the traffic. Briefly, I told Toby about my contretemps with Reynolds.

'You won't be much good if we have to get physical with Tilden, will you?' he said, as though I'd done it deliberately.

'We won't have to,' I replied. 'He isn't the combative type. Anyway, Laura's photos will be more than enough to make him talk.'

# Chapter 36

Tilden answered the door clad in faded blue jeans, open-toed sandals and a crimson shirt which was open almost to his navel. His welcoming smile faded abruptly when he saw us. I told him that we needed to talk to him.

'What about?' He looked down his nose at us. 'I'm rather busy. In case you've forgotten we have a very important auction tomorrow at midday.'

'That's what we want to talk about,' said Toby.

'I've told you all I want to tell you on that particular subject.' Tilden spoke up strongly but his knuckles were white where he was grasping the edge of the door. 'Anyway, I'm expecting a visitor.'

'We won't keep you long,' I said and brushed past Tilden, with Laura in my wake. 'It's just a few questions.'

'Look, I didn't invite you in here and I don't have time to answer questions about anything.'

We were standing in a sizeable hall with a tiled floor. There was a dining area straight ahead and a corridor. The furniture was mostly high-tech modern and an array of prints and paintings adorned the walls. I could glimpse a kitchen to my left; on the right must be the bedroom on which Laura's camera had been focused. I went to the door and peered inside. Yes, it was the bedroom.

'Look here,' Tilden began, 'keep out of my . . .'

I walked towards him and lashed him across the face with my right hand. He cried out and cowered away from me. I followed him, grabbed him by the shirt and thrust my battered face close to his.

'We're here to talk about three murders and a kidnapping, Jamie. You're an accessory to all the crimes. Now is confession time and I'm prepared to knock the truth out of you if I have to. In fact, it'd be a pleasure,' I stared into Tilden's eyes which were dilated with fear. I supposed he'd never been hit in his life.

'Why don't we do this in a civilized way, Jamie?' suggested Laura. So, we were playing nice guy and nasty guy. She'd offer him a cigarette in a moment.

Roughly, I turned Tilden around and pushed him towards the corridor. He turned right into a large room; french windows led to a patio that was packed with flowers and shrubs. The furniture was traditional in here and more paintings crowded the walls.

With a show of defiance, Tilden stood in the centre of the room and began to speak.

He didn't get far because I hurled him backwards into a chair and said, 'Start answering questions, you shit. Where is Amy Kincaid?'

Tilden tried to do up some of the buttons on his shirt. His hands were shaking like a junkie in need of a fix. His chest was tanned and smooth; I wondered if he shaved it. Toby sank into a sofa and Laura perched on its arm.

I stood over Tilden, my fist clenched. He flinched. 'Where is she?'

'Tell us, Jamie,' Toby said quietly. 'I wouldn't maintain any silly loyalties to your friends. They'll go to the wall, whatever happens. But you can do yourself some good.'

As Toby finished his sentence, the doorbell rang. Tilden tried to rise but I shoved him back into his seat. 'Stay put,' I said harshly. 'If you make a sound, I'll spoil your looks.' The bell sounded again. 'Laura, would you go and answer that, please? Say you're a friend of Jamie's parents and you're staying with him for a night or two. He won't linger.'

Ready to clamp my hand over his mouth, I stood next to Tilden. Within a minute Laura was back. 'Jason says he'll be in touch, Jamie,' she said. 'Not really your type, is he?'

'He's just a friend,' Tilden muttered.

'Talking of friends,' Laura said. She reached into her shoulder-bag and brought out an envelope. She handed me a small stack of glossy black-and-white pictures. Tilden stared at them as if he already knew what they depicted.

'A few candid shots of you and another of your friends, Jonathan Wright. Excellent quality, Laura. I congratulate you.'

Laura grimaced at me. Tilden took the photographs but only looked at two or three. He was now even whiter in the face, the sweat breaking out unheeded on the surface of his skin.

'I wonder what the gossip columnists could do with those,' Laura said.

'You can find a home for them, can't you, Toby?' I said.

'I don't suppose your family would be too pleased, eh, Jamie?' Laura added. She was much better at this than me, I thought. In fact she was a nasty piece of work. 'Your mother would be . . .'

'No, you wouldn't . . . my mother . . .' His voice trailed off and he put his head in his hands. For a moment I thought he was going to burst into tears. He held out the photographs and Laura took them from him.

'Is Amy Kincaid dead?' I asked quietly. I put my arm on his

shoulder. The gentle touch seemed to work best – but I wasn't about to kiss him better.

'No. Wright's hidden her away to keep Julius Kincaid quiet.'

'Where?'

'On the coast. Ted Merton's place.'

I exchanged a look with Toby. 'OK, Jamie, let's have the full story. Tell us about Ito. You and Welbeck set him up, didn't you? Why? And you had Goodison killed because he was suspicious about the stuff Welbeck has put in tomorrow's auction, didn't you?'

'It wasn't me,' Tilden moaned. Again he hid his face in his hands. 'It wasn't me, it was Jonathan. He's the one behind all this.' His voice was muffled and I pulled his hands away from his face and made him sit upright.

'Jonathan Wright?' He nodded miserably.

I wasn't surprised to hear that Wright was the moving spirit behind all the mayhem. When I'd first seen them together I'd been perturbed by the influence Wright exerted over Harry Goodison. Although Harry had explained that Wright, as Welbeck's protégé, was in a powerful position, I'd felt there was more to it than that – that there was a ruthless quality to him which was alarming.

'Wright set it all up, including the robberies,' said Tilden.

'What? At Royal Dorset and the other two clubs?' Toby asked.

'Yes. All timed to perfection. Sir Nicholas knew exactly what was worth taking and Jonathan organized some experts to break into the clubs. He went with them to finger the stuff they wanted.'

'And he killed the steward?' I asked.

'I don't know. I wasn't there.'

'And all the goodies went to Ito?'

Tilden nodded. 'They were out of the country within hours and, yes, on their way to Charlie Ito. He had buyers lined up who were willing to pay way over the odds. Several million pounds were at stake. A fifty/fifty split between Ito and the rest of us.'

'So what went wrong?'

'Ito wouldn't pay up. He only offered a quarter of a million and said take it or leave it. Of course, Sir Nicholas was willing to negotiate but Jonathan wasn't. He went alone to Ito's flat and killed him.'

'But that didn't solve the problem,' Toby said. 'He still didn't get his money, did he?'

'No, but . . . it wasn't a matter of logic for Jonathan. By then he wanted his revenge.'

'So where's the money?' I asked.

'In one of Ito's accounts in Switzerland or the British Virgin Islands. God knows where.'

Once he'd started Tilden seemed relieved to be able to tell us what he knew and the words coursed from his lips without much prompting from us. Welbeck had always been an inveterate and unsuccessful gambler; not merely on horses but on the futures markets and other financial ventures. He had seen the golf antiques market as relatively easy to exploit and had foisted dozens of forgeries on to collectors in Japan and the Far East, Australia and in the USA. The robberies organized by Wright had merely been a variation on an established theme.

'And the Matisse? Is it a forgery?' Laura asked. Tilden nodded.

'I hope nobody tells the Queen.' Toby was enjoying himself. 'She wouldn't be amused. What about the Jones diaries?' he added.

'Nothing to do with me,' Tilden claimed. 'Sir Nicholas dealt with all that himself.'

'So, who actually stole Welbeck's pictures?' I asked.

'Jonathan arranged it. It was done properly so that Sir Nicholas could claim the insurance without any problem.'

'But the Van der Neer was a copy,' I said. 'The original's already in Japan, isn't it?'

Tilden nodded. 'Yes, Sir Nicholas sold it years ago. He also sold a copy to someone else there. The latest copy, the one stolen recently, is in Hong Kong.'

'Don't these collectors ever talk to each other?' Toby asked wonderingly.

'No,' Tilden replied. 'Because they're in competition with each other. And if they've come by a work illicitly, they have to keep quiet about it. That's Sir Nicholas's strength.'

'Not any longer,' Toby muttered.

Finally we pressed Tilden about Goodison's death. Miserably he confirmed what we had already deduced – that the auctioneer had been murdered by Wright when he had threatened to expose Welbeck's treasure trove of clubs as fakes.

Toby, agitated, got out of his seat and stood in front of Tilden. 'You mean that a good man was killed just so that a bunch of cheap crooks like you made sure of their money?' Tilden said nothing and I thought that Toby was going to strike him. 'Is that what you mean, you miserable heap of shit?' Toby shouted.

'It's all right for you,' Tilden muttered. 'You don't know what Jonathan's like. Harry Goodison panicked and told him he was going to the police. So Jonathan had to stop him. It was nothing to do with me. I hate violence. Christ, I wish I'd never gone anywhere near him or Sir Nicholas.'

'That's easy to say,' Toby replied. 'But you liked the money and the good life that their activities brought you, didn't you?'

Tilden bowed his head.

I ushered Toby out of the room so that he could calm down; I also wanted to discuss our next move. We now knew the whole story and where to find Amy Kincaid. We had to trust that her husband would turn up at the auction in time to help us expose Welbeck and Wright in as public a way as possible. As we were uncomfortably aware, the auction began at noon on the following day. We could intervene but we needed Kincaid – he was the heavy-hitter in golfing antique circles.

# Chapter 37

Within half an hour we were all back in my apartment. Tilden hadn't even tried to argue against my stipulation that he must spend the night locked up in my spare bedroom. I think he felt safer with us – he was obviously scared stiff by the possibility of a confrontation with Wright.

I told him that our quarries were Welbeck and Wright, not him. But that he would have to seek his own salvation when the police got their teeth into the case. Bluntly, Toby advised him to tell them everything he knew.

We agreed that we should get Tilden to the auction just before it began. His absence during the morning would provoke Wright's suspicions but, by the time he arrived, it would be too late for him to do anything.

I called Kincaid's hotel to establish whether he had arrived. He hadn't but the receptionist told me that his usual suite was reserved from that evening onwards. I felt relieved that he would be at the Swan Hotel for the auction and prayed that we would find Amy where Tilden had said she would be, otherwise I couldn't see Julius uttering a word against Welbeck.

Laura went back to her own flat, with a promise also to be at the auction, her camera at the ready. She said she wouldn't miss it for all the Matisses in the Queen's collection.

Although I didn't think that Tilden would try to make a

295

break for freedom I made sure that all the windows in the spare bedroom were locked. Then I locked us both inside and, to put my mind completely at rest, I slept on the floor by the doorway. This avoided an argument with Toby as to which of us would enjoy the comfort of my bed.

At just after five o'clock on the following morning the alarm buzzed. Although I'd slept on a few cushions from the sofa my body creaked from the ill-treatment it had received – it was only thirty-six hours since the beating Reynolds had given me.

At well before six we were heading for the south coast, Toby in the passenger seat and Tilden crammed into the Porsche's rear seat.

The sun had risen some time before we set off and a gentle breeze shifted a few insubstantial clouds across the glistening blue sky. 'What a day for golf,' Toby said longingly. 'A few holes and then a nice long lunch.' That was the *News*'s golf correspondent's idea of proper golf.

I grinned at the thought and then suddenly remembered. 'Oh, bloody hell,' I muttered. Toby looked questioningly at me. 'Jake. He said he'd have today's practice round in the afternoon to suit me and I haven't confirmed it.'

'You can call him when we get down to the coast. We'll have time to sort Welbeck out and then you can resume your duties as Jake's caddie.'

'Yeah, all in a day's work,' I said sarcastically and reminded Toby that we didn't have the freedom to expose Welbeck unless Amy was safe.

Even in the pure light of a summer morning the Camber Sands Workers' Co-operative looked no more prepossessing than when Toby and I had first seen it; to my eyes it was even more run-down. There were no signs of life. But it was only half past seven.

Ted Merton's workshop looked exactly as before, its sturdy door padlocked and the windows barred. I'd come prepared this time. I opened the boot of the car and got out some heavy duty bolt-cutters. They made short work of the padlock and in we went, Tilden between us to ensure that he didn't try to make a run for it – not that he showed any inclination to do so.

The room was neat and tidy; all Merton's wood-working tools were still in place above his bench. There were dozens of clubs in various stages of repair and construction, and most of them were nineteenth-century in shape. Toby picked up a long-nosed driver and waggled it. For a moment he seemed to have forgotten why we were there.

There was a desk in one corner and a small partitioned room to one side. The lavatory, I assumed. Toby pushed open the door and said, 'Look at this, Chris.'

For one moment, I thought he'd found Amy. Please God, not dead. Toby saw the look on my face as I strode towards him. 'It's OK,' he said, 'but someone's been here.'

The room did indeed contain Merton's lavatory, through a rackety door at the far end, but the rest of the space was occupied by a mattress. A duvet was folded neatly on top of it. Propped against one wall there was a plastic bin bag. I looked inside and saw several empty bags, some sandwich packets and plastic cups. A paperback novel by Jackie Collins had been left open on top of the duvet.

Toby picked it up. 'Page eighty-three. An heroic effort in the circumstances.'

'Amy's been here,' I said. 'Everything's clean and tidy.' I pointed at the washing basin, which had a towel neatly folded on its rim. 'Look, clean as a whistle.'

'We've got to find Ted Merton.'

We drove towards the nearby village, Tilden once again squeezed into the back seat. He had recovered his spirits sufficiently to complain and suggest that he and Toby changed places for a while. Toby didn't even bother to acknowledge his plea.

A general store-cum-newsagent seemed to be the best source of information about Merton's whereabouts. We received a chorus of advice from the owner and two customers who directed us to a side road a few hundred yards down the street. I left the car parked on the main road and got a crowbar out of the boot. I wasn't going to take any chances – my body had already suffered enough.

Merton's house was a pretty flat-fronted Victorian cottage with a small garden. The beds around the tiny patch of lawn were larded with roses, sweet peas, chrysanthemums and a host of summer colour.

'What a pretty garden,' Toby said appreciatively, as though about to call on the vicar for tea.

The curtains of both the downstairs and upstairs windows were closed. I stopped Toby from ringing the bell and looked at the lock on the door. An ordinary Yale. Easy. A credit card would have opened it. I handed the crowbar to Toby, produced my silver toothpick, stepped up close and eased the lock's mechanism open. The door opened a few inches and then stuck. I guessed that there was some mail behind it and gave it a shove. The bottom of the door trapped a letter and I heard it scraping on the tiled floor as I made enough room to get inside.

Toby needed a wider space and I kicked the mail inside to free the door.

'Who the fuck are you?' The voice came from above me. I looked up the stairs and saw a slender man with a shock of black hair which hung down to his shoulders. He was wearing red boxer shorts with little yellow figures on them. His body was tanned and well-muscled. He started down but, half-naked, must have felt at a disadvantage. I had to seize the initiative. I hurled myself up the stairs and hit him hard in the midriff with my shoulder. Winded, he went down beneath me. I grabbed him around the neck and then hauled one of his arms behind his back.

There was an awful moment when I wondered whether we'd got the right address. So I tightened my grip on the man's throat and said, 'You Ted Merton?'

Not the toughest opening line but he gasped, 'What's it to you?'

'Where's Amy?' I countered, twisting his arm more.

'In the attic.'

I became aware that there was a muffled banging from above.

'Toby,' I said, 'hold on to that crowbar and knock this bastard senseless if he tries anything.'

I didn't wait but ran up the rest of the stairs towards the source of the racket. Amy was alive and kicking – boy, was she kicking. She'd obviously heard our noise downstairs and decided to add to the clamour herself. I found a ladder against a wall, went up a few steps and released the catch on the trapdoor. I pushed it up and then felt the weight taken. Amy loomed above me, her face undecided whether to smile or cry.

'Hello, Chris,' she said tremulously. 'I wondered when you'd show up. Where's Julius?'

'You'll see him as soon as we get you out of here.'

I guided her feet on to the ladder steps and down she came.

'What happened, Amy? Did that bastard Merton . . .?'

'I'm OK, Chris. No harm done, so don't get heavy with

Ted. He's kinda sweet, actually.' I wondered for a moment just
how sweet. 'Is Julius OK?'

'He's been worried sick. We all have.'

'So've I. They warned me not to try anything. If I did, Julius
would be the one to suffer, they said.'

'They?'

'Wright.'

'He kidnapped you?'

'Yes. And chloroformed me and I woke up locked in Ted's
workshop. Then he moved me in here.'

'Come on. I want to have words with friend Merton.'

Amy spotted a telephone in the hall and asked if we could
try to find Julius for her. He was not in his London hotel nor
had he arrived at the Swan. 'He's obviously between London
and Sandwich,' I said. 'You'll see him in person in an hour or
so.' She nodded and smiled, though she was close to tears again.

The rumble of Toby's voice was discernible in the hall and
we followed it to the rear of the little house. The three men
were seated around a wooden table. Toby rose at once and sat
Amy, who had started to tremble a little, at his side where he
hugged her reassuringly. Tilden, probably feeling cleansed by
confession, had lost his terrible pallor and was looking as though
he might live after all.

A big white pot of tea sat in the middle of the table and each
of the other men had a mug in front of him. Ted had donned a
sweater.

'Ted, you're in big trouble,' I said. 'I want some answers
from you and I don't have much time.'

He gestured at the teapot and said disarmingly, 'But you've
got time for a cup of tea, eh?' I nodded. I was dying for a cup.

When we had all settled at the table again, Amy with a mug
of coffee, I asked Merton whether he realized how deep in the

mire he was. 'You could do seven years' porridge for this.'

'I'd no option, mate,' he said. 'Wright's got me by the short and curlies. I'm an accessory to fraud on a large scale, as he never tires of reminding me.'

'The fake clubs and balls?'

'Replicas. They're replicas and I never intended them as anything else.'

'Come off it, Ted,' Toby said.

'So Wright blackmailed you,' I cut in. 'He told you to keep Amy under lock and key or else.'

'Said he'd kill me and then her if I didn't. And I believe him. You don't know him – he'll do the necessary, whatever it is. I'm shit scared he's going to put in an appearance now.'

'He's too busy with the auction now. Did he intend releasing Amy safe and sound?' asked Toby.

'If I kept her quiet till afterwards, everything'd be fine and I'd get a bit of a bonus.' But even as Ted Merton said it, we could see the sudden uncertainty in his mind.

'He said he'd give me ten grand.' We let Ted's doubt about his own safety – and Amy's – hang in the air for a moment.

'OK,' I said, 'tell us about the fakes. You've been churning them out for years, I suppose.'

'Replicas,' Merton insisted. 'I've never tried to con anybody. What other people do with 'em, that's not down to me.'

'But you've done some *special* jobs for Welbeck, haven't you, Ted?'

'Well . . . I've refurbished some of his stuff. He's been a bloody good customer to me. He's sent me some lovely clubs in his time. A pleasure to work on them.'

'Did you renovate that eighteenth-century square-toed iron for Welbeck?' I asked sharply.

'Well . . .'

301

'Come on, Ted,' Toby said sharply. 'We don't have time to mess about. Tell us the truth. Then, if Amy agrees, we might have a loss of memory about your aiding and abetting a kidnapping.'

'It's Wright and Welbeck we want, not you,' I added. 'So tell us about that iron. The one with the alder shaft.'

'I put it together for Welbeck, yes. He had the head made from some old piece of iron and I cannibalized another club – it wasn't worth much – for the alder shaft. Then I made the club up for him.'

'And you made the featheries?'

'Yeah and a bloody horrible job that is. But I learned how to do it and how to put the right names on. They're as good as anything those old Scottish buggers ever made,' he ended defiantly.

'Genuine fakes,' Toby said.

'You could say that.' Merton got up. 'Let me show you something. A couple of things I put by for a rainy day.' He went to the front of the house and we heard a door open and shut. 'Here you are. Two featheries, one by Allan Robertson and one by John Gourlay. And here's a driver by Hugh Philp and a spoon made by Thomas Dunn.'

'Except they're not, are they?' Toby said. They were beautiful pieces of work, whoever had made them.

'All my own work,' Merton said proudly.

'Ostensibly there's up to fifty grand's worth of antiques there,' I said.

'That's it,' Merton replied. 'Part of my pension plan.'

'Two things, Ted,' I said. 'I'll have to borrow the clubs and the balls.' Ted began to object but I reminded him that he was a party both to fraud and to a kidnapping. I promised to return the replicas and he agreed, albeit unwillingly. Then I asked to use his telephone again and contacted Jake, who let me off my caddying duties for the day.

'But be there tomorrow, Chris,' he said trenchantly. 'I need your undivided attention.'

I looked forward to providing it. But first there was the little matter of dealing with Welbeck and his partner in crime, Jonathan Wright. I called Laura's flat but the line was engaged and we decided to make a start for the Swan Hotel.

# Chapter 38

It wasn't easy to squeeze four adults into my car and the only solution was to put Amy on Toby's lap in the front seat. For once he didn't protest about the discomfort; and to Amy, now that she was safe and knew her husband to be unharmed, the whole business seemed more like an adventure.

The journey from just east of Rye to the outskirts of Sandwich looked relatively simple on the map, but a huge traffic jam in Folkestone added nearly an hour to our trip.

It was after midday when we got to the Swan Hotel. I knew the auction would have begun dead on time. The hotel car park was blocked with vehicles and we had to leave the Porsche at the roadside some way from the hotel. I left my passengers stretching themselves and rubbing parts of their bodies which had suffered from the long and confined journey, while I raced ahead to the auction.

The big conference room, on the hotel's first floor, was crowded. Every seat was occupied and dozens of people, standing, were crammed into the back of the room. I eased my way amongst them and saw that Wright was presiding over the auction. He was wearing a dark suit and a conservative tie and he was clearly intent on rattling through the early items in the auction. I looked at a catalogue over someone's shoulder and saw that there were less than 300 items, a relatively small number. Wright was already selling lot number 20: six iron-headed putters which were quickly knocked down for £100.

I was anxious above all to find Kincaid but, as I stood on tiptoe to see over the press of people, my eyes alighted on Welbeck. He was sitting on the end of the front row – his mane of silver hair, every strand in place, was unmistakable. To my surprise I spotted Chief Inspector Rattray sitting two rows behind him. People around me muttered irritably as I shifted my stance and craned my neck over the surrounding heads. At last I saw Kincaid. He was against a wall near the back of the room and was looking anxiously towards the doors. Laura was at his side. With more apologies I scrambled my way back towards the exit and waved vigorously in his direction. He saw me and waved back. How do you convey to an anxious husband in dumb show that you've rescued his beloved wife from her kidnappers? I gave a wide smile and even from that distance could see the tension leave him.

A minute later the three of us had gathered outside the auction room. 'Amy's downstairs, waiting for you,' I said, as Laura threw her arms around me and clung on tight. Behind her, Kincaid was grinning broadly. I disentangled myself, partly because one of her cameras was sticking into my bruised ribs.

Kincaid patted me on the shoulder. 'I'm real grateful, Chris, you've done a helluva job. Laura said you'd find her and, by God, you did.' He removed his glasses to wipe his eyes which were moist with emotion.

I led him down the stairs and found Amy and Toby in the reception area. Amy saw her husband coming and skipped joyfully across the floor and into his arms. I closed my ears to their endearments and asked Toby what had happened to Tilden.

'He's gone into the coffee shop. He said he was hungry.'

'Don't you think we should keep an eye on him?' Laura suggested.

Toby shrugged. 'If he does a flit, the police will soon find him.'

'He's a key witness,' I said. 'Laura, would you mind interrupting his lunch and bringing him upstairs?'

'Not at all. I'll drag the bugger out by his ears if necessary.'

The Kincaids were sitting on a sofa, arms entwined like lovelorn teenagers. I winked at Toby and we walked over to them.

'So, you found what you were looking for in Japan?' I asked.

'Sure did, my boy. It's waiting in the manager's office. I visited a few old friends and they came up with the goods. How about you, Chris?'

I told him about Ted Merton and the work he'd done for Welbeck and all about Patrick Moloney's part in the various frauds that had been perpetrated.

Kincaid nodded. 'Laura's told me that Tilden's spilled his guts about Wright. He's in the frame as the murderer of Ito and Harry Goodison and the steward at Royal Dorset.'

'Let me get those fake clubs and balls,' I said. 'You get your stuff from the manager's office, Julius, and then we'll decide what to do.'

By the time that Toby and I, Amy and Julius Kincaid, Laura and Tilden had made our way upstairs and into the auction room, Wright was selling lot number 88: a play club made by Tom Morris. In no time at all he sold it for £1100. I told Amy to stay out of sight but close to Tilden and to scream blue murder if he tried to leave. To be fair to the man, he showed no signs of wishing to make his escape and seemed resigned to his fate, whatever it might be.

307

We had to move fast because Kincaid had already warned us that all Welbeck's treasures were grouped together, from lot 100 onwards. Amid ill-concealed murmurs of protest, Toby, Kincaid, Laura and I pushed our way through the crowd at the back of the room and along a narrow corridor between the wall and the rows of chairs, until we were alongside Rattray. Wright had registered our presence and there was a slight hesitation as he introduced lot 94: a cleek made by Willie Park. Kincaid was carrying a large holdall made from soft leather and I had Merton's clubs and the two golf balls half hidden in a plastic bag.

I leaned over Rattray, enveloped as always in his aura of stale tobacco, and said quietly, 'I'm glad you're here, Inspector. Mr Kincaid and I have a couple of surprises in store for Wright and Welbeck. Do you promise not to interfere? And Jamie Tilden is at the back of the room. He's got lots to tell you.'

Rattray looked at me quickly and nodded. 'OK. Been in the wars, have you?'

'Er, yes. I slipped in the shower and bumped my head.' I don't think he believed me.

The audience was hushed and expectant as lot 100 was declared by Wright. 'Ladies and gentlemen, we now come to the items you have no doubt been eagerly awaiting. The next forty lots are offered for sale by an art and antiques expert and collector of international renown – Sir Nicholas Welbeck.' There was a murmur of excitement and a scatter of applause. I watched Welbeck turn and look at the audience. A hint of a smile hovered on his lips. Just you wait, you supercilious bastard, I thought. He seemed to be on the brink of rising to his feet to acknowledge the audience: an audience he was trying to con. I guessed that he was already computing the money his fakes would generate.

Wright raised his arms to quell the interruption. 'Thank you, ladies and gentlemen, thank you.' He waited until the room was silent again. 'We will begin with this long-nosed wood used by Willie Park when he won the first Open Championship in eighteen-sixty. We have a document which verifies the provenance of the club.' Wright held up the club and a yellowed piece of paper. 'Shall we begin at fifteen thousand pounds?'

My heart thudding, I was about to step forward and prevent Wright continuing. But Kincaid gripped my arm and said, 'Let it roll, Chris, just for a while. So that Welbeck thinks he's struck gold. Then we'll move in for the kill.'

The bidding for the first four items was vigorous. The serious collectors on the floor were eager to participate, although I noticed that one or two of them cast anxious looks in Kincaid's direction – they were wondering why he wasn't bidding. Above all, the contest for Welbeck's clubs was fuelled by the telephone bids which were coming in from Japan and the United States. Seven people manned the telephones and passed the bids to the auctioneer.

To the surprise of most of the people in the room, and to Welbeck's evident satisfaction, the four clubs made just under £200,000.

'Now we have three of the most beautiful wooden clubs ever made,' Wright said, holding them up. 'They were made by that Stradivarius of the golf-club maker's art, Hugh Philp, and he presented them to William the Fourth when he became King in eighteen-thirty. Although the King wasn't an active golfer he had important connections with the game, not least as the Duke of St Andrews.' Wright held up yet another yellow piece of paper. 'Here is Philp's letter to His Majesty in which he humbly begs him to accept the gift. This is a magnificent collection of woods and it has, of course, a unique place in history. Shall we begin the bidding at one hundred thousand pounds?'

There was an exhalation of breath from the audience and then a short burst of conversation. Within a couple of minutes the bidding had progressed to £150,000. On it went, until the clubs were knocked down to a Japanese buyer for over £250,000.

The square-toed iron, ostensibly made in the eighteenth century but actually cobbled up by Ted Merton, was next on the stand. The same Japanese buyer coughed up nearly £110,000 for it. So far, the auction had realized over half a million pounds and there were plenty of goodies to come.

'And now the Horace Rawlins niblick,' Wright said. 'He was the winner of the first United States Open Championship.'

Kincaid dug me in the ribs. 'Off you go, Chris. I'll be right behind you.'

I walked straight to the front of the room and pulled Merton's two clubs out of the plastic bag. Then I reached into it and found the two feathery balls. I stood beside Wright's lectern but out of his range. He could do a lot of damage with a niblick and for all I knew he had a gun or a knife in his pocket which he might be mad enough to use.

'This is a Hugh Philp driver,' I shouted, 'and here is a Thomas Dunn spoon. They were made this year by an associate of Sir Nicholas Welbeck's. They're fakes just like all the other trash he and this crooked auctioneer have foisted on you today.'

Out of the corner of my eye I saw two security men, summoned no doubt by Wright, advancing on me. The room was suddenly in an uproar. Most of the people in the audience seemed to be on their feet and yelling questions at each other, at Wright, and at me.

Wright tried to shout everybody down. 'This man is

310

deranged,' he bellowed into his microphone. 'His aim is to discredit Sir Nicholas. It's an absurd vendetta, ladies and gentlemen. Please settle down and we'll proceed with the auction.'

The security men had me by the arms and began dragging me towards a door in the corner of the room. Wright leaned over his lectern as I went past and said, 'I'll see you in hell for this, you bastard.'

Suddenly Rattray appeared in front of me. He brandished his warrant card at the security men and ordered them to release me and to stand aside. It was about time the cavalry arrived. I saw that Laura was busy with her camera.

The large presence of Julius Kincaid next took centre stage. Calmly, he reached over the lectern, detached the microphone and addressed everyone. 'Please listen to me,' he boomed. 'My name is Julius Kincaid and some of you will know that I'm a collector of golfing art and artefacts. My friend here,' and he gestured in my direction, 'is absolutely right. All these clubs sold here today are fakes, just like most of the stuff Sir Nicholas Welbeck has churned out over the last couple of decades.'

Welbeck was also on his feet, his eyes bright with rage and his face flushed a shade of red too dangerous for a man of his years. 'This is absolutely disgraceful,' he shouted. 'My reputation . . .'

'Yes, it *is* disgraceful,' Kincaid said loudly. 'It's disgraceful that you've conned collectors out of millions of pounds.' He reached into his holdall and produced three canvases. Kincaid balanced two of them against the legs of the lectern and held up the third.

'This is a famous painting of a golfing scene by Van der Neer,' he said. The room was suddenly quiet and Kincaid didn't have to shout. 'It was stolen from Sir Nicholas's house earlier this year. That's correct, isn't it, Sir Nicholas?' Welbeck said nothing. 'Except that it wasn't. Sir Nicholas sold it to a Japanese collector five years ago for three hundred thousand pounds.'

Kincaid put the painting down and held up a second version of it. 'This is the copy folks – I repeat, the *copy* that was stolen from Welbeck's house. Though stolen is the wrong word because Sir Nicholas arranged for its removal himself – and made an insurance claim for half a million pounds. An associate of his sold it to a collector in Hong Kong who, you might've guessed, wishes to remain anonymous.'

There was some strained laughter then the room was silent again when Kincaid brandished the third version of the painting. 'Another copy of the illustrious Van der Neer, ladies and gentlemen. Sold for nearly four hundred thousand pounds to a Japanese enthusiast two years ago. He was sworn to silence about the transaction, of course. Fortunately, I know him quite well.'

Laura had moved in close to us and was still snapping plenty of pictures: of me and Kincaid, Wright and Rattray, and also of Welbeck who was slumped in a chair, his chin on his chest. Toby was scribbling hectically in his notebook. There were two other journalists from national newspapers present to cover the auction; their editors were going to be tickled pink at the way it had turned out. But Toby had the inside story and his editor was going to be ecstatic.

I had been keeping a vigilant eye on Wright who had been standing, his body rigid and his face white, behind the podium while Kincaid and I addressed the milling throng before us. I knew Wright was strong but the violence of his reaction still surprised me. He leaped down from the heavy oak plinth, tilted it and shoved it hard in my direction. I jumped back, taking a security guard with me and the floor shuddered as the podium thudded onto it. Splinters and dust flew from the old piece of furniture.

Then Wright was off towards the door, his legs and arms pumping. There was no one to bar his way, except a middle-aged security man who diplomatically stepped aside.

I jumped over the fallen podium and scampered after him through the door. He was halfway down a flight of stairs by the time I reached the top. I realized that I still had one of Merton's wooden clubs in my hand and, in despair, I hurled it at Wright's retreating form. I got lucky. Somehow the club bounced in the right place on the stairs and became entangled with Wright's legs. I heard the shaft crack apart and saw Wright stumble and clutch at the banister. Then down he went, tumbling towards the floor below.

I raced down the stairs three at a time. I must have been six steps from the bottom when Wright got to his feet and turned towards me, his mouth snarling and his eyes livid with anger. Feet first, I jumped and landed on him just above knee level. He screamed as he went backwards and my momentum caused my knees to thud into his chest. I got my hands around his throat and my thumbs on the pressure points, just as Max had shown me. I ignored Wright's flailing arms and his struggles quickly subsided.

The next thing I remembered was Rattray's arms around *my* throat, as he hauled me backwards off Wright. 'For Christ's sake,' he said, 'three murders are enough. Let the bugger go.'

The incident was headline news the next day and Toby ended up with a spectacular scoop; Laura sold her pictures all over the place and made a lot of money, some of which I'm happy to report she spent on me; and I was a hero for a few hours. The tabloids turned on their own in a feeding frenzy when the activities of Nick Adams came to light; and the world of golf antiques promised an 'agonizing reappraisal', especially when Welbeck confessed the full extent of his fraudulent activities. Ironically, Julius Kincaid replaced Welbeck as the authority on golf antiques and memorabilia.

For me it was back to normal life on the following day as Jake and I tried to plot our way around the great championship links of Royal St George's – and what a relief it was. I gloried in my familiar role as a caddie to a professional golfer.

Jake's game looked in very good order and I even risked a tenner with the bookies that he'd be the top Briton when the Open reached its climax on the Sunday evening.